Men of the State

Men of the State

Written by B. A Liberatore

Last Gen Publishing

www.lastgenpublishing.com

This book is dedicated to the unrecognized men and women who commit their lives to the service of others, every day.

Preface

B.A Liberatore

The starting point of every man's journey is defined by his own individual experiences. Manhood, and what it means to be a man, has been built up, torn apart, recreated, and destroyed again and again –and now emasculation is the norm. There are all types of books that tackle the question, "how to be a man".

And in this era of mass social influence, the definition of manhood continues to be ever evolving. Is that because the definition of femininity has evolved over time? Has man redefined "manhood" subconsciously to maintain his ability to procreate?

Has society blurred the lines so much that we are now willing to erase definitions and live by the essence of our own individual being, as true natural spirits?

I'm not sure.

And those are big questions.

This book follows the journey of a flawed man who grapples with the existential, metaphysical, emotional, and real life components that manifest masculinity.

This is the story of a man who is defined by his own experiences – shaped by his experiences and determined to overcome at all costs.

Men of the State is the story of one man's epic journey through life, trauma, self-healing, and his rise to manhood and fatherhood. Manhood is first defined within the confines of a juvenile correctional facility, where masculinity is defined by violence and in its abuse masculinity is acted out in the worst fashions. Despite the context, this book is not just about one man, because countless numbers of men have felt what Anthony has gone through.

You will travel back in time and see how his life unfolds through the process of self redefinition. Anthony's story is one of trial by fire — a fight to be better than his absent dad; to be better than the other men in his life who have also failed him; to be better for the friends, colleagues, and children who rely on him; to be better than his past selves. The unraveling of Anthony's relationships provides insight into the psychology of men and its intersection with fatherhood, professional development, and relational commitment.

His mind and thoughts will change, as will the writing to reflect the juxtaposition of his thoughts and actions, and their eventual collision.

Men of the State is just the beginning of the rise, fall, and rebirth of a man. The vision is for men to see hope through their own desperation no matter what life throws at them.

So, no more "man up!" or "be a man!"

Our stories are unique unto ourselves – with ups and downs, good and bad, and mental, emotional, physical, and spiritual struggles. Find inspiration in Anthony's story, and let it give you insight into the psyche of a man.

To the women – mothers, daughters, partners, sisters, and wives – know that men are trying to understand, and do better, but as you will soon experience ... life has a way of testing you, to see if you really are who you say you are.

Chapter 1

The Beginning of the End

The cell door slammed shut. I locked it, and wiped the blood off of my knuckles. It wasn't mine. I felt the intense throbbing from my heart pulsating directly into my palms.

"I want to call my mom!" I could hear him gurgle from the blood in his mouth.

"Shut up! You had your chance. You're done!" I was furious.

"Come back in here, and I'ma kill you!" his voice bellowing in the distance with his increased anger, and most likely the deep fear of his realization. I was already walking away because I held his freedom in the palm of my hand. And then he swung.

But before he could my training kicked in and I pushed him in the chest and he skittered back into the corner of his cell. I seethed. Face tight. Eyes red. Heart pounding. I looked directly into his eyes. I spoke with the finality of a god.

"You're done."

Three steps backwards, not daring to take my eyes off him, and I was out of the cell. I locked it again and looked at Jenkins.

Jenkins was a former professional heavyweight boxer and was still built like one. He looked at me with a concerned, almost sympathetic look, and softly said, "You good Ace?"

I ignored him. "*Shut up Jenkins! Do your damn job!*" is what I wanted to say. I didn't. Instead I marched to the bubble and made the call to the Central Services Unit (CSU).

"Get a packet ready, I'm not staying late for this shit tonight.", I ordered Zimmerman over the phone.

"Sir, are you ok?" she responded through the walkie talkie.

"AOD to CSU, that's not appropriate radio talk!" with the harsh tone of a drill sergeant.

"CSU to AOD, copy that."

This was all on me, no witnesses, no one else needed to sign off or provide statements for the mandated documentation required when physical force is used in a state juvenile correctional facility. I checked the necessary boxes, wrote my statements, wrote "refused" medical attention, "refused" phone calls, and "refused" to sign documentation, where I was obligated to provide such opportunities. No care was given to him. No concerns were left for him, I was done.

I submitted the paperwork for the director to review the next morning, placed my walkie talkie on its charger, took off my cuffs, placed them in my secure locker, grabbed my car keys and proceeded to my car. It was negative fifteen degrees outside that night. The ground was solid. It wasn't just frozen, it was as if everything had turned into rock ice. Hard, sharp, and dangerous, like ice and rock. And deadly.

The men and I laughed about the black ice on the road all winter. Exchanging disses on driving ability and attacking each other's manhood for using their brakes. Encouraging each other to not care, bragging about the rear end of a front wheel drive car swinging out and how overcorrecting one way and to the next to straighten the car out, all while maintaining the consistent speed not designated by the road sign, was a badge of honor. It displayed our control, our willingness to live on the edge, our willingness to knowingly participate in an act that could ultimately take our lives, and our unsaid agreement that these things made us men.

Like every other night, we exchanged highlights from the shift in the parking lot. I didn't have anything to say that night. The men all seemed determined to talk about anything else but what I had done. "Ace, grab a beer bro!" Cash said with enthusiasm. Cash was a young former college football player, at 25 he still had the physical attributes of a young black man who had dedicated his life to athletics. I considered him one of my closest assets on our shift.

"Not tonight my man. I need to get home, see my kid and kiss my wife."

"No doubt!" he replied, and in unison he and the men said "Get home safe."

I was still an emotional wreck inside, but my exterior bravado would not allow me to show it. I drove home faster than usual, even while acknowledging the black ice and mentally laughing at the stories the men and I shared about our driving exploits. I knew the road, felt as if I could travel it in my sleep. In all honesty, I often did. The 2-10 shift was taking its toll on me. I often found myself falling asleep going home, not remembering how I even got home sometimes. I was on autopilot. The road was always solitary in the night. I never passed a car, it was too mountainous for deer to hop out at you, but I wound through those mountains as I always did, half asleep, half processing the events from the shift. Up hills and down, sharp horseshoe turns that reminded the driver of the road's age, I drove.

They say when you are close to death you will know. I always promised myself that if I looked death in the eye, they would know it's me, because I will smile back at the darkness. The rear end of my car lifted, I felt it float off the ground. I counter steered confidently, overcorrecting and back, in the same manner described as a "professional" to my men. But I wasn't a professional race car driver, or an expert on anything closely related. I was a man of the state. And when I knew control was lost, I held on to the steering wheel as tight as I could, and smiled.

Chapter 2

Two Years Earlier

My goal, and life plan, had nothing to do with being a man of the state. I had always seen myself as a soldier for justice and equality. Growing up poor and experiencing so many acts of injustice, feelings of disenfranchisement, lack of validity, and the acceptance that so many thought I wouldn't make much of myself. But these false insecurities were diminished as I accomplished so many of my life goals.

I had become a teacher, started a family, and was doing the work I felt I was always born to do. When my partner told me she was pregnant with our first child I felt as if I was about to embark on, what I thought, my life goal was. I was being recruited by an organization out of Boston to gain a fellowship. Building Better Schools (BBS) had just invited me to their last interview for the possibility of creating my own school in the Boston metropolitan area. I was also a final contestant in a fellowship to Harvard's Kennedy School of Education. I felt like everything was a lock for me to achieve not only my life goals, but the ultimate revenge on those who doubted me my entire life. There is no better "get back" than becoming so much more than those who look down on you could fathom.

At the time my girlfriend, Alyson, and I were living in Miami. I could not wait to move back to the northeast, go to Harvard, start my own school and become part of the systemic revolution in education that would change the world. Your dreams and aspirations are so innocent and concrete before real life hits you. It's not that I haven't experienced the blows of "real life" before. But this was different. I had worked hard, stood out, gained access and opportunities that were never meant for me to have. Yet, there I was on the cusp of being able to have a seat at the table in discussion with those I looked up to. Cornel West, Howard Zinn, Noam Chomsky, Thomas Sowell, and others would all have to deal with me once those plaques were framed and my school was up and running.

Life often reminds you that it's not your life to control. Especially if you have purpose. Life is for you to serve your purpose and that purpose is usually for the sake of others.

Others.

When Alyson told me she was pregnant, I remember feeling angry. Angry because I knew that that was my purpose. I was angry because I knew I wasn't going to Harvard. Angry because I knew I wasn't going to have my own school. Instead, I would have to "work" in a school. Instead I would have to be an "employee" not an "employer". Angry because my life would now be revolving around her, my child, and not my own personal aspirations of greatness and influence. Angry because I wasn't in love with the woman who was having my child.

It wasn't like I didn't love her at all. Maybe I just wasn't completely "in love" with her. I did know that it wasn't until she was pregnant that our differences came more in the form of obstacles rather than symbiosis. I guess I should have seen it coming. I seemed more intune with the pregnancy from the very beginning. There were these two mornings that I will never forget. I decided that I wasn't going to drink coffee anymore. Alyson and I were enjoying the abundance and array of South American cuisine and the irresistible southern fried anything. But I had woken up and told Alyson, "I'm going to stop drinking coffee."

She chuckled and had to ask, "How come?"

"I feel like..." and I paused before I answered. We both understood nutrition and health very well. "It just makes my body too hot, and I feel bloated and inflamed."

I knew she would understand. When we first met she was training to play softball on an elite level. My brother, Zeek, was being recruited to play football by Penn State and a few other Division 1 schools. So I was training him on the side to keep him prepared for the college training camps he had registered for. We both loved athletics and competition, and we found ourselves competing humorously over the simplest things. I think it was her competitive nature that won me over. She was never the prettiest, she wasn't super fashionable, but her simplistic sporty attire; little tight sporty skort, fitting tank top and sneakers, and the way her blond hair would lay across her blue eyes. And her eyes told me from the beginning that she would be mine forever if I wanted her to be.

She never had a real relationship, and wasn't jaded from a broken heart. In the intimate conversations that create relationships, she only shared one sexual experience with me. She described it as her first. It was rushed, unloving, but served its purpose for her. She was different from any other girl I met, previous to that time. She had finished college and had a goal, was working towards it, and we both thought that we were going to have one great summer together and that that would be it. A year and a half later, she followed me to Florida. Six months later I decided to not drink coffee one morning.

"Good luck!" she said with another laugh. "Take it easy on the kids."

I smiled back. We embraced, I kissed her and left for work.

It was the drive to work that hit me. This uncontrollable urge to vomit. I was on the I-95 express way into Miami. A massive ten lane highway that has all kinds of off ramps, and dividing ramps that are built like hills to go over neighborhoods and other highway ramps. It is dizzying at times, so I wasn't too put off by the feeling. I mean, I did try to go without coffee for the first time ever. The rest of the day was fine, and I paid no mind to it.

But when it happened on the second day, I took heed. I remember thinking, *am I having morning sickness? I remember that time I thought I may have not pulled out quick enough when we were having sex? Oh no! No, that's not it.*

I rushed into our apartment.

"Hey!" Alyson greeted me with a smile.

"Hey!" I gave her a quick kiss. "Let me see your boobs!"

"Uh What!?!" she responded, rather put off by my unwarranted , and rather odd demand.

"Yo, seriously, let me see your tits." and I started laughing.

"Ace what the fuck is going on?" Alyson laughed, but she had sharpened her tone.

"How do you feel?" I asked her.

"Ace….what are you doing?" she said slowly and sternly.

"I think you should get a pregnancy test. Something is telling me that."

We just stood in our kitchen together and stared at each other.

"Okay" she said softly.

The next day I found out I was going to be a father.

Alyson wanted to move back to our small Hudson Valley New York town. Her family was there, mine was there, and we were both deeply rooted there. For me that was every reason not to move back. Our tone shifted from humorously competitive to aggravation. We began to argue about our future. Where would we live? What would we do? What would our money look like, and again, and more and more, we talked about money. She desired to be a stay at home mother. I honestly honored her for that because I knew what that meant. She was willing to sacrifice her own goals and aspirations to ensure the betterment of our child. How could I attest that? She was a damn good ball player and would surely have made it to the elite levels she was working towards.

However, I still battled with the entire premise. I thought about the potential future earnings I was throwing away. No Harvard and no prestiges PhD. No one would listen to me the way I wanted them to without any serious accolades. Hence a PhD from Harvard was my guarantee of my desire to be heard and my desperate need to be a part of a change that was larger than myself.

We fought.

She cried.

I became distant.

We fought, she would cry, and I would pretend that I wanted to do what's best for our unborn child. But inside, I wanted to still reach for greatness. For myself, but most of all, for those who may have thought that I had just become some mediocre school teacher. To say that that was hard to accept was an understatement. In the end I agreed to move back to the Hudson Valley and search for employment as a teacher. She wanted that. I thought by honoring her choice it would better serve our child, and that it would ultimately keep us together.

We moved into Alyson's mothers house. This alone was a complete 180 degree turn from a notion Alyson held strongly to. She hated her mothers house. She hated the smell of damp dirt, old sour cat urine, the musty basement, the dust, and the complete lack of home care that she felt had such a negative impact on her own being. Her father wasn't spoken about much, just that he and her mother split and he moved to the city for business. She did say that her parents would always argue about how messy the house was, and that her mother didn't care too much about his opinions on that. Nevertheless, we moved in and I immediately started renovating and cleaning to ensure my own sanity.

When a woman is carrying a baby, I am told by many women that it is the greatest feeling in the world. Scary, yet knowing that there is life inside you, growing, needing you, completely codependent on the mother for their own health and well being. They say that that is what makes mothers, mothers. From the very onset of pregnancy they are the nurturer. For men, I believe it is different. I felt many of those same emotions. Scared, proud, life giving, all of that. But I also felt pressure. Pressure to secure a job, and to provide. Pressure to be a better man, especially a better man than my father. Pressure to be a good dad, especially better than my own dad. The eternal care that the father and mother will develop for her child both starts internally. For the mother it is in her physical body, for the father it is in his mind. The mother naturally seeks the care of the child. While the father naturally seeks the care of the family. At least, that is what I believed.

In my search to provide for my new family I had secured two interviews in school districts that I thought would be absolutely locked in. I knew people in the districts, they had vouched for me and provided strong references as well. I kept that Harvard chip on my shoulder during the interviews, and believed that they were insane if they didn't hire me. Perhaps I was the insane one, because I wasn't offered either one of the positions.

My feelings of inadequacy began to deepen. I lost my greatest opportunity to be the person I always saw myself as, a Harvard professor, enlightening the minds of our nation's next generation of leaders and great thinkers. I wasn't going to have my own school to develop and implement social reform and social justice as an educational foundation to inspire the next, next, generation of leaders and great thinkers. I wasn't even going to be a teacher. I lost myself in meaningless chores and remodeling of Alyson's mothers house. Hating and despising every second of my existence there.

I had to do something.

As part of my daily routine, one morning I was looking at the job postings on my computer. The Office of Children and Family Services (OCFS) was hiring teachers. OCFS in New York oversees all child care facilities, daycares, rehabs, anything that has to do with children, if it is state funded, OCFS is watching . They also oversaw all juvenile correctional facilities. I was familiar with the state and the position that they had. My first teaching job was at a maximum secure facility for OCFS. I remember thinking how am I going to put into practice all of the pedagogical applications that I've just learned and spent so much money on for my undergrad degree? I worked so hard to not display my own "street" behaviors and bad habits. I worried that everything I tried to step away from would ultimately catch up.

However, they didn't. The students there respected me. They saw me as someone who had made it through the same area, the same streets as them, and they appreciated the "Independent Life Skills" I was teaching and sharing with them. As great of an experience as this was for my first teaching job, it was short lived. I was called to Miami to join Teach for America.

That's why leaving Florida and coming back full circle hurt so bad. I had given up the opportunities that I worked so hard to ascertain. The very opportunities I stressed my students to work hard for and to make sure they take full advantage of, I had left behind. Not only did I leave them behind, but I was back desperately looking for a job, about to be a dad, with a woman I didn't truly love, who stepped away from her own dreams, to live in her mothers house, and me, I didn't feel like a man. In fact I didn't feel much like anything. I wasn't a teacher, a man, a dad, or even an employee. I was just a guy.....not even a guy. Some boy, searching for hope.

I thought, *Maybe this is what I need.* I reminded myself that this could have deeper meaning. They say the universe works in mysterious ways. Maybe the universe was trying to tell me something. Another part of me said, *"If you don't get this job, you mine as well chalk it up, start selling drugs again, shoot, you may want to see what the crew is doing, you're going to have to get money somehow! Step up! Be a man! Get it done!"*

Your mind can cause its own destruction sometimes. Thoughts are hard to control. They weigh heavy on our complete being. They can torment, tear apart, and ruin most people if they are left to frolic in the ether of their existence long enough. Thoughts can become reality, even if they aren't real. That false reality created by our pervasive negative thinking has the ability to create what we call a mental health "crisis". Yet, very few people have the full mental capacity to say to themselves - "Crap! I'm about to have a mental health crisis. I've been reacting to my own negative thoughts and emotions and now I am about to be out of control ." - No. People don't do that. They just become out of control. And then, it's too late.

I felt myself getting out of control. I felt the little love I had for Alyson slowly oozing through my pores. It was being replaced with resentment, contempt.....hate. I hated Alyson. I hated my present existence. I hated that I was becoming a dad, I hated that I had to clean her entire life up, literally, to ensure I had a clean place to live and raise my family, which I now didn't want. I needed this job. I needed to be a man. I needed to at least love myself again.

So I pressed "Apply" for the job to submit my application.

It seemed like forever after that minuit life action was taken. My son was born. Thanksgiving came. Then Christmas came. I had very little to offer, very little desire, and felt- very little overall. New Years came and there was no resolution. I had nothing to aspire to be better at. I wasn't doing anything that I needed to address and improve, because I literally wasn't doing anything with my life.

Alyson's experience seemed much better, despite the burden of carrying a baby. She was constantly checked on. And every and any request, no matter how obscured, was carried out in the exact manner and detail described, or hell was to be paid. But again, maybe that's just another difference between men and women.

Then, 2 days after New Years day, I received a phone call.

A phone call from OCFS.

I had gotten the job.

I remember the feeling of relief, joy, and a piece of my manhood falling back into place. I wasn't full and complete, but I had a job. I had health benefits, from the state, the best that I could possibly have. I had a job to do. I was going to be able to provide.

I was able to provide.

I had to walk into this new role, this OCFS facility, as a man. Not the teacher "guy" who was just happy to have a job. I recharged myself, revisited old experiences, and re-read some books about the school to prison pipeline. I wanted to maintain my armor of justice that I had worn for so long which now had collected dust in the backspace of my mind. I took out all of my "teacher" clothes. I washed them, ironed them, and re-set myself as a new man, a dad, a husband, a teacher. And something that I could truly be proud of, a way to freedom.

The facility was almost two hours away. It was January, so the true beast that a northeast winter can be had shown its gruesome face. The first morning's drive was bitterly cold. At least two feet of snow was on the ground and the entire ride I had to ask and re-ask myself, "Where the hell am I?"

The facility was an old military boot camp correctional facility. The employees were all former military men. They were military retired, retired veterans, national guard, and many had recently returned from active duty in Iraq and Afghanistan. They had transitioned from the military code of conduct for the facility, to the new legal codes written for all OCFS facilities. These new codes mandated less use of force, and required all to understand and utilize de-escalation techniques, and to take a healthier mental health approach when handling the youth in these facilities.

I delved into these new policies like it was a Harvard class. I felt rejuvenated and back to my scholarly self, seeking knowledge to share, eager to spread the light of truth I felt they needed. Not only that, the position paid $63k a year. A salary a man who is single handedly providing for his family should start at. I was going to teach English, which was even better. I would be able to share books, and use books as insight to a life they may have never imagined or dream of without a book. I was going to give them an education. I thought of my first position in OCFS and how they loved me, and how proud I was of them.

However, reality always provides the last laugh, and I felt it laughing at me the first seconds my tires slowed down in front of the Sergeant Henry Johnson Youth Leadership Academy, known as the YLA.

Chapter 3

The Teacher "Man"

Poised to actually be teaching again, regardless of where it was, I had given myself motivational speeches, empowering the empty audience that filled my car, and the road it didn't share. I was sure. I was ready to use my skills. Skills I yearned for. I was ready, or so I thought.

It was dark when I left my home. Alyson was sound asleep. My two and a half week old son reached for his warmth as it left him. Yet, the sun was just peaking over the northern tip of the Catskill mountains when I arrived at the YLA that first morning. I had not been to that side of the mountain before. It was all new to me. The brisk cold air wasn't moist and slightly soft to the nose as it was down in the valley. No. The air was hard. The wind cut. And the cold was felt in your core. I had been there for my interview, but somehow it was different. I looked at it *not* with hopes and aspirations, but with reality.

It's as if I didn't notice the thirty foot tall steel fence, the razor wire wound on top, encircling the entire facility, and the gate that held a small metal box with a button. I pressed the button, and it buzzed back.

"You have to let go of the button!" a voice statically answered through the gray, steel, box.

"Uh, sorry about that", I responded. "I'm Anthony Cortes, the new teacher. Today is my first day."

I felt them laughing at me through the camera above. I felt the camera zoom in on me, scour my appearance, my nervousness, all to pre judiciously inform the men in CSU of its analysis. The Central Services Unit (CSU) is the main control center for the prison. There, a main CSU controller operated the opening and closing of every single door and gate on grounds. They channeled all calls. And most of all, controlled all of the cameras.

I felt the cameras. I felt the men behind it. I felt the sadness. The loss, and the pain. I saw broken dreams shattered all over the ground. Lost in the dirty snow, lost in the frozen mud. The dreams of the youth now just blew in the bitter cold wind that cut my face. I stood, staring at the tall military obstacle of a tower that looked down on the facility. The ropes were bent from the ice and screamed that they were not in use, nor have been.

I had to flex my hand, and reflex it again and again because the cold was freezing the sweat in my palms. It was in the single digits in temperature, yet I was sweating. I felt wet, cold, damp, I felt small, again. The motivational speeches left my head and left steam in my ears. I knew what I thought I was going to do, how I thought I was going to teach, but the man I thought I was going to be was not what was needed here. At that moment I yearned to hold my newborn son. I wanted to smell him. I smelled my hands in hopes that I could pull a memory from the turmoil of hot and cold swirling in my hands. I smelled nothing. I thought of Alyson. How I left, not saying goodbye, and the dark drive I took alone into the light of my new life.

"What the fuck did I do?!" I asked myself.

BUZZZZZZZ!!!!!! The gate sounded. The cold steel unlocked with strength and exuded the sound of a freight train coming to a hard stop. The gate parted, but not like a majestic experience expressed with Moses parting the Red Sea. This was like Satan himself opening the doors to hell, and laughing because you yourself chose to enter. I took a deep breath, crossed the threshold of the gate and proceeded to CSU.

It's only 37 steps from the main gate into CSU. Everystep felt like a marker in my life. With each step an experience rushed through my mind. My first teacher who believed in me. My street life. My adventures in the underworld. My college life and professors who believed in me. My family, who doubted me. The young people I had already been a savior to. These memories didn't help me, they haunted me. If I teared up, no one noticed because they froze. That was good, because I did.

At the 36th step, the CSU door buzzed and unlocked and I walked in. Instantly I left the emotions in the cold. I channeled the cold. I gave a cold stare at Bruce, the last name of the man who operated CSU. I gave a cold stare to Riggins, the last name of the man who was the OP 2 for the day. They both nodded in a manner only understood in the silent modes of communication between men. A nod as if to say, "Respect is given, but you ain't shit until we see what you can do."

I knew that that was their expression and feelings behind their nods. I saw their "Are you shitting me eyes" as they looked at my Italian leather shoes, now wet from the snow and slush, my freshly ironed khakis, blue shirt and Express tie that was perfectly put together in a double windsor knot. I had a blazer underneath my wool black trench coat. I was a teacher, a man who educated the youth, and I wanted them to see me as that.

Expectations are like wispy clouds on a hot and humid summer day. They're there. But there isn't much substance to them. As pressure systems move the weather, the clouds will dissipate, break up, move on, or connect to another cloud forming a new form of visual spectacle. Expectations move in the exact same manner. They take form depending on the weather and they change instantly with the current of time. They can turn into new goals and form new ideas, and spur on a variety of more ideals. But just like the clouds, there isn't much to expectations. They are just that, expectations. They are not to be met or to be held dear. They are not even to become reality. They are momentary and change with the everlasting flow of your existence. Clouds may manifest into a storm when interacting with the atmosphere creating something new. Rain, snow, sleet, hail, or even breaking apart to let the sun shine in. Expectations do the same. They collide with reality, forcing you to interact with your own atmosphere to create something new. A new vision, a new goal, a new reality, all crushing all notions imagined. Because most expectations are grounded in false perceptions of the reality one is experiencing at one particular time.

They saw me as what I wanted them to see, a teacher. But in a world where manipulation and physical domination are mandatory skill sets, they weren't impressed.

Chapter 4

Taking it to The Streets

When men meet other men they immediately size them up. It's a primal instinct that is an internal function for survival. As most men function on a primal level, the initial perception of another man is extremely important. We gauge their looks to our own, and compare ourselves as mates. Does he dress better than me? Is he better looking than me? We decide whether or not he makes more money than us, or has the ability to do so. And most of all we ask ourselves, "Can I take him?" This is the ultimate question. Do I have the ability to take his life if I needed to? That is a "man" question. We need to ask ourselves these questions to understand where we are in the competition for a mate. These questions guide our actions and interactions with women and other men.

The later question determines everything.

I knew they thought they could "take me". I knew that they perceived a small and weak man, an educated man. A man who took his time to strengthen his mind and not his body. A man who was concerned about his appearance, but not his appearance as a strong man. But none of this was new to me.

The same applications are just as poignant in the streets as they are anywhere else. Being physically imposing is an asset. One can get away with many criminal acts just by physically imposing their will on someone else. Extortion, bribing, racketeering, dealing drugs, and keeping an illegal operation functioning, all takes some sort of forced, and enforced, will upon another.

As a man who could never physically impose their will upon someone else, my experiences forced me to be more creative. I knew that my "one up" on the average street player was my mental strength and toughness. I knew I had made money not by forcing people to work with me, but by displaying the benefits and growth that can be had if proper decisions were made to cooperate. If one looked like they had money or presented themselves as someone who could be a potential large earner, that gained respect. If you were a potential large earner in the streets, eventually you would have to impose your will on someone if you were to maintain any financial growth.

Those who have to out-wit their adversaries with hard calculated decision making, are even more dangerous than someone who is willing to inflict physical harm. One can prepare for a fight, find ways to defend themselves, recruit support, or simply hide. Yet, the mentally strong, wait, use their patience, wait until their opponent is at their weakest, carefully maneuver to strike in a manner that is hard, fast, has lasting effects, and most importantly, they ensure they leave their rival with the empty feeling of, "who done it?"

That was me.

I never lost.

I made money.

I never backed down.

They couldn't break me.

It was 5:20 am when I left my house. It was now 6:52am. My first class was at 7:35. I checked in my personal belongings, was given my classroom key, and Riggins sternly said, "Follow me Teach!"

"*Teach?*" I thought to myself. "*Teach!*", who and what did they see in me to only provide me with the title of "Teach". Was this a dig at my attire? Were they mocking my proper English and presentation? Who and what did they think I was? Did they think I was soft?

"Fuck it!"

I wasn't there for them. I was there to help my people. I was there to teach young people how to gain freedom in a system that had their entire communities ensnared.

"Right behind you." I replied, ensuring my voice matched his depth.

He marched with a cadence expected. This was a former military run facility. He marched as lock step as I ever have seen, hands perfectly pinned to his side, only moving with the appropriate leg, he had them in half fist, thumbs tight. His broad shoulders informed me he was a formidable man, with physical assets. He said nothing as we walked through the industrial light blue and white hallway. We passed several steel doors with the same industrial light blue paint. Only the doors were scratched and scraped leaving evidence of struggle. The pain filled the air of the corridor. We made it to the last door, this door was not marked up with fights and emotions of terror, and he simply stated, "Teachers have their morning meeting here at 7:10." I looked at my watch and it was 7:02.

The first minutes seemed like a lifetime. Add the almost two hour drive, and I felt as if I had already completed an entire day. I was exhausted. I missed my baby boy at home. I wondered what Alyson and he were doing. I wondered if they missed me the way I missed them at that moment in time.

"You goin' in?" Riggins asked somewhat jokingly, not wanting to give off any impression of kindness or real humanity.

"No doubt! Wasn't sure if my key unlocked the door or not." I replied, trying to provide a valid excuse for the momentary mental processing, ensuring he couldn't detect any emotions that were racing through my entire body.

Riggins provided the necessary instructions, "Your key will unlock all the classrooms, but that's all you have access to." Those were my instructions.

"Got it." I responded and tried to give off an energy as if to say,"Alright, I got it from here, beat it!"

"Have a good day man, good luck!" he said with an aboutface. He marched away, shoulders tight, legs wide, fist clenched. I slid my key into the door, turned it left, then right, it unlocked and I entered the office.

Sitting at the long rectangular table were three other teachers. A short, mouth breathing, blonde haired woman named Martha Downing sat one side. Downing had terrible hygiene that was not only evident from her teeth, as they could be seen from her open mouth inhalation of air, being stained dark brown, black on her top gum, and a smile that looked like broken glass, but she was terribly overweight and smelled of wood chips and country body dirt. That must have been the reason the only seat available was next to her.

Across from me was Betsy Dorland. Besty was a grandmotherly woman, with glasses, short grayish hair that still showed her dirty blonde original color. Betsy had her teacher's journal open on her desk. However, it was covered in connecting doodle mazes and dark shaded areas that she spent several mindless minutes coloring perfectly. Next to her was Trent Bears. Trent was a short man, and one could tell even as he sat down, with a stern square jaw, small head with a military cut. But, the Bears was very well built. His arms were the size of my thighs, his back prevented his arms from laying naturally to his side. His legs forced him to walk like he rode a horse, as he prevented his well trained thighs from getting in the way of each other.

As I was just completing my own mental perceptions of these new entities and creating my own diagnostic assessment of the situation, the back door opened and two more people came out. One was Sharon Lazzarro, the Education Director who I interviewed with. She was a kind woman. Yet, her own life wore on her face. The disappointment of life decisions weighed her wrinkles down. You could tell she was forced to be someone she truly wasn't. You could tell that she was once kind, thoughtful, maybe even pretty. But now, she was clearly hardened and was far removed from her days as a teacher.

The second was Todd Olivier. Todd was having his own "Oh shit" moment as a new employee for the state. A former medical salesman, who had lost his job due to the recession, traveled from Utica to be the special education teacher.

"*Utica?!*" I thought to myself.

"I thought I had a rough drive this morning." I said, trying to make a joke. It fell on deaf ears.

Todd said, "Yeah, it's the first time I've been away from my wife in a really long time." And he proceeded to tell me how he needed this job because he had lost his job in the medical field. He hadn't taught a class in over fifteen years. "It's a good thing I have my Masters in Ed. I knew it would come in handy."

I had to check myself.

I wanted to say,"...you knew it would come in handy because....?"

But, I didn't. I also made sure I changed the expression on my face. I wondered what he meant. Was he here out of default? Did he even want to teach? No one else paid him any attention. They all sat with long, soulless looks in their eyes, and waited to go into the slaughter of their classrooms.

I introduced myself. Provided my experiences. Told them that I was very happy to be there and to have an opportunity to improve the lives of the residents of the facility. Bears looked at me with an eye. "You sure, you came to work in the right place." he scoffed. The rest chuckled.

"Oh, Trent, leave'em alone." Betsy said the way a grandmother would. "We're glad you're here Anthony. Please let us know if you need anything."

I asked for her name again, and was grateful for her kindness. I made sure I showed my gratitude, to which Downing responded, "Yea, I'm in room 2."

"Ok. That sounds good. I appreciate you, thank you." again with another kind response.

Sharon started the morning briefing and covered the pertinent information for the day. She escorted me to my classroom and entered with me. What happened next I will never forget.

She softly put her hand on my shoulder and very sweetly said,"We are glad you're here Anthony. I know you worked at Goshen, but it's different here. I know that you're a great teacher, and I know you have the passion for education. Hold on to that, you need it, we need it, and so do the kids. They're going to need YOU, Anthony!"

I felt what she was saying hit me. Again, I tried not to tear up. I wondered if she was testing me for softness. Was she pumping my head up because she could tell I was wondering why I took the job and that I was already doubting my desire to be there. I questioned all the angles I thought she was coming from. Just like a street survivor assessing his enemies agenda to plot. Every angle was calculated with the risk assessment that came with it.

"*Who does this lady think I am?*", I thought. I looked into her eyes with the depth of my own darkness. I saw she was being genuine, kind, and that for her, there was no angel. She just knew what I was about to find out.

"Good luck! I know you're going to be great!" She placed her key into the lock, turned it, and exited the room. Before she was completely out of the door, she said, "They're done with breakfast Anthony, they will be here in a couple of minutes."

"Thanks Sharon!" I responded with a deep strong voice to signal that I was ready.

As in all important aspects of life, there is little preparation for certain situations. You have to adapt and overcome challenges faced. Sometimes it's on the fly. Sometimes you can prepare. But more often than not, something happens in life and there is nothing to do, but allow life to change you.

I didn't see this position as life changing. I didn't think that I would change. So maybe I had to tap into an old part of my life to be successful in this environment, but I wasn't going to change. I was going to teach. Then I heard…..

"YO! Get the fuck off me!" in the hallway.

"Thomas, off the wall!" a grown man's voice boomed down the hall.

"Bitch ass! Hats up hoe!" a young man's voice shouted back.

Static over the walkie-talkie, then - "Code Yellow in the hallway."

I stood next to my door. All I could see through the fogged out, bullet proof, wire enforced, four by six inch window on my door, was red blurs and black blurs of body shapes, that were my students and the men who were assigned to duty that morning.

"Back up!" an order was given.

"Don't fucking touch me! YO…..YO……. YOOOOO….."

Static on the walkie talkie again. Then, "Code White hallway", a voice said with no emotion.

"Back Up!" The same voice yelled out again in a reinforced tone.

"Get off of me!" a youth pleaded.

Footsteps marched heavily down the hallway from the opposite direction.

"You gonna calm down?" A man questioned.

"Fuck you bitch!" was shouted back in anger.

You heard the sound of several youths laugh and mock the man, who seemed to be in charge.

"Pussy ass faggot!" They yelled at him.

"What? You next?" the man responded.

A new voice rang out over all of them. It was a woman's voice. With the strength of a general she ordered, "Send them back to the unit! Get control of these boysSmith!"

"Yes ma'am! All right!!! Ya'll ma'fuckers need to turn ya' asses back around and go back to the unit."

The youth all laughed. The sounds of "Aight, good!" and "Word! No school", echoed loudly. The young man was still in the hallway. One man held the kids' arms behind his back. Another man was lying on his legs. Another man stood above him and asked in a monotone voice,"Are you ok Joseph?"

"Yeah, I'm fine. Can you let me go now?" the kid asked.

"Slowly now, and don't pull no shit!" the man barked back.

About ten minutes later Sharon came into my room. She informed me that a resident had to be restrained in the hallway.

I laughed,"Oh, is that what happened?" I continued, "I get it, I know how it goes. This is not my first rodeo." I tried to assure her that I was fine. That the violence didn't phase me.

"Yeah, I know. You'll be fine." she replied. "It's just that if they have a restraint early, they will cancel the school program. They might resume later if they can get them off the unit."

"They're going to try this again?" I was a bit surprised.

"Probably not. They know there are 2 new teachers starting today." She added the final tid bit.

"I guess, I can decorate my classroom then." I said confidently.

"There ya go!" Sharon encouraged me.

But I didn't decorate my room. I sat at my desk. Eyes wide open in disbelief. I didn't teach that day. I didn't plan. I just wanted to get home to my son. It seemed like forever before 2:10pm came and I was released to go home. I walked to my car, making sure I didn't look up to make any unwanted eye contact that would lead to a conversation on how my first day went. I started my car and didn't even wait for it to warm up in the hard midday cold. I just drove.

I always wanted to be a person for the people. A teacher for the people. I wanted to share my experience and help young people get out of the streets. Instead, I knew what I had to do. I had to take it to the streets. I had to survive. I had to be a strong man, not a teacher man.

Chapter 5

Miami Flashbacks

The ride home took forever. When I left it was dark, and when I arrived home, it was dark. My day was dark. The light I held so tightly for it to shine bright, became dark. I pulled into the dimly lit driveway of Alyson's mother's house. Turned off the car and took a deep breath. I stepped out of the car and walked slowly to the house, even though I was eager to see my son. I got to the front door and opened it.

Every man has fantasies of coming home from work to a wife that has dinner prepared for them, the kids run up and hug you with joy and fulfillment. The wife comes over and kisses you and asks you how your day was, with sincerity, and you tell her, and she listens. She comforts you and brings you a hot meal. You bless the food and smile. You provided for your family, they're happy, kept, and well. That's a man's fantasy. And it's just that, a fantasy.

I had flashbacks of Miami on my way home. The sea salted air, warm breeze, sunshine and warmth. I saw myself at "Shuckers", a famous fried seafood hole in the wall of a restaurant. Eating freshly shucked fried clams, lime in my drink and joking about even if we asked for lemons in Miami, we'd still get limes. Alyson and I recognized that even though it was different, the tropical food consumption and lifestyle was much better than New York.

We would ride my motorcycle in a straight line towards the sun set. No turns. And after you got past the fake developments they called towns, after the rows and rows of shopping centers and the entire beautification called capitalism, after that, there was nothing.

We would race the moon back to the beach to drink, play pool, and go home to our pleasure.

I smoked cigarettes then. I would sit on the balcony of my 3rd floor apartment. The complex had more than I had ever paid for in New York, and was much cheaper. I would smoke and watch the iguanas battle for supremacy in the lake that nestled in the back side of the complex. It was clearly man made, with a fountain in the middle. But if you have ever been on vacation to Florida, all of the apartment complexes have the timeshare like amenities, equipped with a large pool, work out room, walking paths, etc. With all of that I found myself spending the majority of my time on that balcony, smoking cigarettes. And watching iguanas.

The iguanas came in all sizes. The tiny ones would congregate under the bushes and would scamper around chasing insects. They usually hung out in clusters. They were brown and iridescent colored. I called them the chipmunks of Florida. They served the same purpose, which to me meant that there really was no purpose for them. They were just there in hopes that they survived. Like all bottom feeders, their pure existence was a numbers game.

Then there were the adolescents. Which came in a range of sizes due to age. And these were indicated by their colors turning green, have already turned green, or are transitioning into stripes. Depending on the size at this age, some would actually be able to run on water. I remember being drunk and confused when I first saw this happen. But I was able to witness on numerous accounts, these adolescent iguanas engage in a violent battle, and one would try to run away, and would only have the water to turn to. They would run so fast, that they would actually take 3 to 4 steps, sometimes more depending on their speed, on top of the water before diving in and swimming away.

I have always been in love with nature and fascinated by its wonders. It is moments like that where I had to stop and appreciate the blessings of life. Especially when I would witness the adults go to war.

Often in a tree. For a prime sun location. They would fight, jabbing tremendous jolts at each other's necks, gripping and wrestling. Until one, or both of them, fell flailing in the air into the water below.

I often thought of those iguanas, and watched them, during deep times of thought. I often felt like their struggles were exemplified in my own life. The struggle for survival and the battling of the elements. I mean iguanas would get cold, be taken for dead, thrown away, only to wake back up once their bodies have reached homeostasis, crawl out of the garbage, and carry on with their day like nothing happened. It was like I was an iguana, I would laugh to myself. But I wasn't in the cluster of babies scrambling for bugs. But, I wasn't quite the top notch looking down from the thirty foot, Spanish moss covered tree either.

I thought of myself as the iguana that could run on water if I had to. I was able to do absolutely anything to survive, for good or bad. I also saw that age of the reptile as the most quintessential stage in their development. That is where they learned their true nature and understand and utilize their full capabilities. That is when, if they survived, they too would endure the battle for that great tree.

Your environment is everything. To those lizards that giant tree was the Mecca of all. But it was just a tree. In context I put this lens on the world. Our environment dictates how and what we become. Those that survive adapted and overcame better than those around them. Those who could do it best, gained a better position. However, there is always room for violence. The iguana on the top didn't get there from being a role model to the other lizards. Quite the contrary. He earned that position by defeating his adversary, by hurling him back to his place in the order, off of a tree, into the darkness of the water.

Men do the same thing.

"*Shit!*" I thought to myself on the backroads of nowhere. If I'm going to do this, I'm going to have to walk on water. I can't be the one who reigns with violence and fear. Survival is a skill, no matter if it's by defeating an opponent, or simply not engaging with an opponent. One can't lose, if they refuse to play the game.

I knew the drive was too much. I knew the pressure I was feeling was becoming overwhelming. So overwhelmed that I ended up at the front door of the house, still caught in my iguana analogy.

Deep breath.

I made my way to the front door of the house.

I found myself itching for a cigarette again. My mind played in rewind a mental rolodex of the rocky ride that had landed us back here. I remembered how my stomach dropped into my feet when she told me that she was pregnant. Maybe my eyes gave it away. Or perhaps it was because all I could say was, "So, what do you want to do?"

Her pupils enlarged as she responded, "I mean…I don't know. You have so much going on and I mean, like, I'm not ready for that, like, I feel, like, I don't know. We never talked about this Ace….I don't know."

That frantic nervousness was followed with an immediate sense of relief when she agreed with me saying, "Well, maybe we shouldn't, ya know. I agree with you. I mean, you're right, this isn't something we talked about, or are ready for. But, we kinda have to decide soon."

And we did.

She went to the doctors office the next day, confirmed that she was about three and a half weeks pregnant. We got a date for the termination of the baby on the last day of the sixth week. The very last week that the procedure was legally allowed, and we were set. And we felt as good as we could about our decision through the few weeks until that date.

Then I got news that a close uncle of mine had a stroke. My uncle "G", as I called him, lived in Cleveland. The man was one of the few older male figures in my life who I actually spent quality time with. At times it was not so quality, but that didn't matter knowing he was possibly on his deathbed. I booked a flight from Ft. Lauderdale to Cleveland with ease, and then I realized what day it was. I was going to be away while Alyson had the abortion.

"No, you should go," she said.

"Yeah, but you can't go alone, and I.....wait, how bout Carlos?"

Carlos was a very close friend of ours, who we trusted, and was like a younger brother to us.

"Ok. I'd go with Carlos." she said assuredly.

And, of course, in Carlos fashion, he came through, and I hopped on that flight to Ohio.

"The Heart of it All '', was Ohio's state license plate slogan, and when I landed into Cleveland's Hopkins International, the warm welcoming of my family, whom I haven't seen in years, felt just like that.

But it was my conversation with G that changed the course of my life.

"You look good kid," he said in a faint voice. "But you look like you're carrying a lot of stress."

I laughed, "Well, c'mon bro, look where we are." Trying to deflect what he could read on me.

"Yeah" he said longly. "But you're carrying something heavy, kid....." he took a deep breath. "Talk to me, what's up?"

I told him what was happening, and where I would be the next day if I hadn't flown to see him. He looked at me tenderly, concerned, and said.

"Oh Papi, the one thing in life I regret the most is not having my own children. You're my boy, but you're not MY son...." he took another pause and a deep breath. "As a man you have opportunities that only come once so often. God doesn't always provide you another chance ya' know…." and he smiled and looked at me.

I held his hand, and brushed his hair back with my other hand. He slowly closed his eyes. He got well and lived, but I called Alyson that night. Her and I both cried together as we decided that we would keep the baby, and that we would do our best to raise it better than we were.

And my feet had brought me to the doorway.

My hands turned and pushed. I heard and saw nothing. I listened. Still nothing.

I walked into the kitchen which was separated from the front doorway area by a small hallway that housed a bathroom. Within a few steps I was in the kitchen and saw Alyson's mother holding my son, smiling, as he was wrapped in his perfectly quilted light blue baby blanket, and she said, "Isn't he precious". And turned and walked away from me, the baby still rocking in her arms.

"Where's Al?" I asked.

"Sleeping." she said softly so as to not wake the baby.

I didn't hold my son until I went to bed that night, a few hours later. There was no dinner. I ate leftover spaghetti from two nights before. Alyson didn't ask me how my first day was. She told me how hard it was for her to breastfeed, and that her nipples hurt. I consoled her. Listened to her. I held my son.

I didn't talk. Perhaps because I was already changing. Maybe I just needed to be a man, and not worry about how stressed I was about my first day. It was just that, my first day. "*You'll get used to it,*" I told myself.

I didn't know that there was more to come. I was going to walk on water.

Chapter 6

Hard Winter Hard Decisions

It only takes two weeks to develop a new habit. Two weeks. A lot can happen in two weeks. It only took me that long to recognize the new patterns of behavior that I was creating at home. That was also plenty of time to have the YLA figured out as well.

At home, that was rather simple. The trend continued. Her mother cared for my child in my absence, while Alyson fell apart both physically and mentally. Struggling to breast feed she felt inadequate as a mother. She would have long fits of crying at night about how tired she was, her lack of desire to return phone calls from friends and family, and how she just wished her body would work the way she wanted it to.

As complicated as this may all seem, for men it is different. There were no problems to fix in any of the ills Alyson provided me. There was no purpose or conflict for me to utilize my strengths in. I couldn't offer her a resolution. I couldn't make her feel better. In fact, it became clearer that her pain and discontent was somehow my fault. After all, she was fine prior to being pregnant. And I got her pregnant. There wasn't a problem for me to solve because I was the problem.

I had to do something different. Her mother was driving me crazy as she monopolized the time with my son. Alyson just slept. The dark drive. Downing's mouth. I was alone with silent conversations that couldn't be resolved in the solitary confinement of the mind.

I thought - *I get it now. I see why men leave and mothers are left behind with the children. Men come into a situation with certain*

expectations. Once these expectations are met, it creates a perception of that situation as "satisfactory", as it meets our mental image of what and how that should feel and look like... And if that fits the reality we want, we then accept that as reality for ourselves. As time goes by, the reality becomes ever more comfortable. Expectations have long been met, and no new expectations have been formed. - Enter complacency. - The perception is still intact, due to the patterns of behavior that are formed over time in the shared reality of the relationship. Yet, while this is all happening, the satisfaction levels decrease, and the dissatisfaction sets in, and often burns like wildfire in the minds of the dissatisfied. That fire has only so much to burn before it is out of control and nothing but unharnessed rage and destruction are left in its wake. There is nothing left for men to do, but to leave. They become violent. They have to leave. They'll drink, they'll have to leave. They become absent, the woman will leave. The reason is never the problem. Only the effects of the reasons are weighed, measured, and tried. So, men know that they lose no matter what. And they leave........
My dad did.

Solution found.

I got us a small apartment in an old farmhouse, in the middle of nowhere, that I passed on my way to work, everyday. It was terribly small. Outdated. Meaning 1970's linoleum outdated, and everything else matched the decade. We had more house plants than the space allowed, but we didn't give up on them. We lived in that small jungle, farm house apartment that entire winter. It brought us closer. It wasn't our luxury apartment in south Florida. I mean the entire apartment would have fit in the living room at our complex. But, we would exchange memories and comparisons laughing together in silence while snuggling the baby.

Alyson seemed happier. She was breastfeeding with ease now and from all perceptions satisfied with her reality. It was different for me. Inside every josh given about Miami, Florida, the school system, Boston - Yes! Boston - would open a wound, and I would bleed deeply, never showing my pain or discomfort. I took it. I acted like a man. I made the move in order to save my family. In order to not be like my dad. To create something different for my son.

Instead, everything about that apartment made me feel like a failure. It's size. The "country poor" smell of the stairwell. The solitude of the area, and emptiness of our now suffocating jungle farmhouse apartment. I started to hate it. And then, I would get,"....at least we're here together.", from Alyson in a manner that gave me Miami flashbacks of when she said those very same words, and I believed her. I no longer did.

We had our moments. Like the time we went snowshoeing, baby and all. Except, the snow shoes we had were my grandparents. They were three feet long, made out of lackard wood, with leather straps. We were so eager to relieve our cabin feverish daze locked away in the Catskill mountains that we attempted to traverse the farm's old terrain that hadn't been used in decades. Marching between trees that split the fields. I had my son inside my jacket in a carrier. We stopped and collapsed into the deep snow laughing about how he was looking at me like '*what the hell are you doing daddy!*'

The wind blew hard on my face and my cheeks tingled. I looked at him. "*What the hell am I doing?*" I thought to myself.

"We should go back." I said, and took a deep breath and exhaled a deep cloud of steam.

"Really? Ok." Alyson replied with disappointment.

But she knew. She knew we were desperate too. Desperate to make sure that this really wasn't becoming our reality.

But it was.

That's where it gets complex.

After two weeks at the YLA, I had seen and heard all I needed to in order to make a full assessment of the expectations, perceptions, and reality.

Expectation - I was going to make $63k a year. Perception - that is enough to provide for my family. Reality - they informed me that because I didn't have a Master's degree, the yearly salary was $37k a year.

How can I expect to provide for my family on that salary alone? What kind of perception do I give off not being able to provide for my family? What can I do about that to make sure that this is not my reality?

Expectation - I was going to teach. I was going to provide these young men with a quality education. Perception - This man thinks he can walk on water. Reality - I better.

School kept getting canceled because of early morning "disruptions" to the program. I started going to the unit by myself and I encouraged the other teachers to do so as well. They were reluctant at first. But I told them that once the kids see that they will have school either way, they'll start coming to the educational buildings just to get off the unit. If not, so be it. We need to provide a certain amount of education time, required by state and federal law, and that's how we'll get them.

Bears laughed about how he'll have to be in more restraints, and how he was tired of their "crap". Betsy, in her grandmotherly way, was incorrigible, and wanted to do the right thing, " You know, by the book." Downing "didn't care either way". Olivier had concerns about "their ability to stay focused", and "are we then truly providing them with an education?"

I was getting sick of Todd . I felt that every altruistic comment he said made him more and more of a cartoon character. I saw Todd as Ned Flanders from the Simpsons television show. Yet, Ned Flanders, if you know, truly wanted to help people in all of his most absolute sincere corniness. Ned was truly a loving and God fearing man. Todd was not. He was a cartoon character to me, because he was just that, a caricature of someone who actually is a god fearing, love all, be all, good man. I mean he was crying over missing his wife on day one, for god's sake.

He once said, "Utica was once a great little city. Until they built the prison. Then all the 'prison people' ended up moving up there to be closer to their families, Ya' know, inside the prison. And now....I mean there's areas I just won't go to. It's just a shame."

You could smell the distaste on his breath as he said it in his Ned Flanders voice.

I held my growing hate for Todd inside and would often walk away, or just ignore him all together when he would start talking. "Can't lose if you refuse to play", I would remind myself. His input was meaningless, and Sharon agreed, and ignoring him is what we did.

But I kept that story in my mind, and all the stories and realities I was absorbing from the YLA. Tales of youths running away from their counselors on court trips. One kid was M.I.A for 5 hours in the Forest Hill projects of Staten Island, before they found him in his cousin's apartment. Another raped, and attempted to rape, 10 woman on his first day out in Harlem. Another was released to an aunt and uncle, only to be thrown out 2 days later, where he shot and killed another teenager. There were countless kids who were sent home with unproficient skills for grade level school work. Many of them were 2 years behind. We knew this, sent them home anyway, and would wait to hear about what happened to them after they got home.

We heard about Malcolm X's great nephew being so institutionalized that when he was released from the facility, he threw a fire extinguisher through a shop window and waited for the police to come. From what I gathered, much of that is true. I heard a lot, and a lot of it was all true.

I saw the young men being wrenched by grown men. I saw the hate the men had for the youth, and the hate that was reciprocated. The residents once planned a riot on the unit. A few of the "top notch" kids refused to go to school. Considering they were the toughest, strongest, and gave the least fucks. The staff didn't want to risk a larger early morning "disturbance". So they let them stay in the unit and one man stayed behind to supervise the four youths. The rest were taken to breakfast and then to school.

In hindsight, I was surprised they didn't see what was coming. The rest of the kids from that unit went to breakfast and school, and so did Unit 2. Now all the residents and staff were in the education building. To ensure the full safety of the education program, Op2 (short for operator 2 - really as "Option 2") and the AOD (Administrator on Duty - He is the Option, the 1 in charge) were all in the building because "too much shit is going down in the morning preventing school from happening and it can't keep going on like this". So, they got stricter with their enforcement of the rules. More imposing. More violent. They were able to corral the "babies," who, just like the baby iguanas, wanted their basic needs met.

But the "adolescence" were learning their power, and true capability, and were just waiting for the right time.

That came after breakfast.

The students were divided into their educational groups. This is the only time of day that the units interact with each other. The YDA's (Youth Division Aide - really youth correctional officers) were divided up to their assigned groups for the day. After all were settled in and the program commenced, Op2 was to go to the kitchen and bring the residents who were back on the unit their breakfast. Those youths were still in their cells. Op2 made the cold walk from the main facility, surrounded by the 30 foot fence, and guarded by the mammoth steel gate, through the gate side door, with trays steaming in hand.

He arrived at the unit and radioed,"Op2 - CSU, open D1 Unit 1" - that being door 1 to unit 1. No one has keys in and out of the unit except for the rank of A.O.D or higher. All other's have to radio in for all doors to be unlocked. Essentially locking in all who are on the unit, and many other rooms in the facility. The door opened and he entered the corridor and radioed, "Op2 - CSU, open D2 Unit 1", and it unlocked.

Usually Riggins was Op2. He had been there 15 years and he had long earned the position for being reliable and, for his size, his short stout self, proved me correct. However, Burch was Op2 that day. Burch was an alcoholic, and although he and Riggins were similar in height, their stature were completely opposite. Burch was built like a drunk. He was thin and frail. He always had the energy of still being drunk, and constantly smelled of USA Gold cigarettes. Which he thought he could cover up. Riggins proved to have a good demeanor. He laughed often and you could tell he was once a good soldier.

Burch, in attitude and being, was an angry little man. A defiant and begrudging "Yes man". Burch walked on to the unit with the hot trays and sat them down. Graham was the lone YDA on the unit. Graham was a large 6 '3, 275 pound, "black" man from bumfuck upstate New York, where only "white" people lived, making him one giant country Uncle Tom. At least from the perspective of the youths in the facility.

For me, he was a kind, gentle giant. He started at the facility when he was 20 years old. He was about to turn 50. He had put in a full 30 years and was going to retire with a rather large state pension. His body displayed the thirty years of OCFS life though. His knees were shot, and he often missed work after being in a restraint due to a "knee injury". His shoulders were out of whack from holding angry, violent, teeneagers in a restraint, pulling, tugging, kicking, spitting, bitting, pinching, headbutting, and that's just what they do with their bodies. He was broken. But he would often tell me how thankful he was that I was there. That he learned so much in my class even if the kids were being assholes.

We bonded. I trusted him. The residents saw him as the target. The "big Uncle Tom nigga" who if, they thought, they took out first, the rest of YDA's would be scared and panic, and they would be able to get them too. Divide and conquer. Take out the big man first, destroy the little ones, and show them who's really in control. Without letting them know where or when. A classic maneuver.

Burch radioed to exit the unit, and was cleared. Graham proceeded to let the young men out of their cells to eat breakfast, and watch Sportscenter. They sat down, started to eat breakfast, and waited.

Radio static - "Op2 to CSU, Gate 2" - radio static - "CSU to Op2, copy that."- radio static.

And as if the Sportscenter theme song was the "Go signal" - they attacked. Sitting all together at one table, the first of the 4 youths bashed Graham in the face with his food tray, not only leaving Graham stunned, but also with a face full of hot breakfast. The second, had a broken leg from a sleigh riding adventure the YDA's took the residents on. Yes, the kid broke his leg, full knee high cast, and worst of all, crutches. He whacked Graham in the back with one of them and then gave him another blow on the top of his shoulder. The other two residents went for his radio.

Static on the radio - "CSU to AOD- Code White on the unit."

I heard the exchange sound from the YDA's radio, who was sitting in my room. We looked at each other with the same deep concern.

"Ah shit, them niggas. Gettin' lit in there!" a resident in my class laughed out loud.

They all responded with their own expressions of joy and excitement in the vulgar manner only appreciated by a few.

"Op2 CSU, en route" we heard Burch's voice

"AOD CSU, en route" we heard Wright's voice

Wright was the AOD for that shift, and split the day shifts with Smith. They had two different approaches, but both usually ended up violently. Wright usually got right to business and put kids' faces in the ground. At 6'4 and holding the weight of a country man to match, he clearly had little concern for the youth the facility housed. He didn't mind sharing his discontent with "those kids" in between spits of tobacco into his Stewarts paper coffee cup.

Burch and Wright weren't even at the gate yet. Graham was fending for himself, which for him must have felt like hours, during those tumultuous minutes. During that time he managed to get to his feet by grabbing the one crutch from the resident and used it to fend off the other attackers.

"AOD - CSU - GATE 2" a calm Wright radioed in.

I sat wondering what was happening. Time seemed to have stood still. Each second hand tick could have been a day. I continued to teach. We were reading "This Boy's Life", and they were into the story of a young kid who was left to the whims of his mothers decisions as she desperately searched for a quality father figure for her son. Only to end up losing herself and leaving the boy to his violent step fathers will. Those boys understood the mother and why she lived her life the way she did. They understood the effects that it had on the kid in the story. They understood the violence of the step dad. The violence on the mother, and the violence on the boy. They felt that impact too. The young men knew the ramifications of the actions taking place as they read the book. They hated the step dad. Battled over emotions for the mother. Saw themselves in the boy, even when they thought he was soft for not standing up to that " bitch ass" step father of his. They felt. They thought. They were uncomfortable. But they went to that vulnerable place with me.

The seconds ticked by and even though I was holding their attention with a discussion, all I was thinking was, *I can't let this be the reality for them. I can't let this be a reality for myself.*

Wright led Burch on to the unit. They had already calculated their actions. Once in the door Burch grabbed the other crutch from the youth, grabbed him by his shirt and threw him to the ground. His leg was broken and since he couldn't stop himself from falling, he fell on his cast and cracked it. He crawled off to the side, and balled up in the short edge of the cell doorway. Wright was already there. He unlocked the cell door, opened it, picked the resident up and threw the boy into the cell, broken leg and all. He closed the door and locked it.

In that time Burch and Graham quickly attempted to restrain two of the three remaining residents. Burch grabbed one up and as they struggled, they fell. This allowed Burch to get a position on top of the youth and he pinned him down and immediately put handcuffs on him. He held him down and watched Graham restrain another, only he had him in a standing restraint. - the youths arms behind his back, straight down, Graham's arms holding each arm in between his own bicep flex, his hands flat in between the residents shoulder blades, and holding him slightly off the air. It's almost a crucifixion but hanging from the shoulders. And the more the large, gentle giant Graham , squeezed, the more the arms and shoulders of the resident stretch, in ways that no natural movement would allow. Wright looked at the last resident and marched him to his cell. He was the smallest of them all, and once the big boys were subdued, he was harmless.

There was a knock at my door. Sharon was there to tell me to keep the residents in my room until further notice. That they were canceling school again. A few minutes later, the YDA instructed the youths that they were going back to the unit. No one seemed to mind. I know I didn't

At the time I didn't know what had happened, but I felt it. I also felt this burning guilt inside me. *If I just sit here and accept this, then I am part of the problem.* And there was no way in hell I could participate in *this* part of the problem. I wasn't getting paid enough to suffer with my family. I wasn't getting paid enough to watch my people get brutalized in the prison system. I wasn't getting paid enough, period.

I made a decision right then and there, by myself, no discussion, no reference, just me in my industrial light blue classroom, posters now ripped and drawn on. The desks were in disarray, and I decided that I would become the AOD.

Chapter 7

What the Fuck is an AOD?

Winter was wearing Alyson and I down. I had quit smoking cigarettes around month two of Alyson's pregnancy, but now found myself sneaking an e-cig smoke in the closet of a bathroom we had. It was weeks since I filled out the paperwork for the Youth Counselor 1, pay grade 18, position. The very same day those boys tried to take down the men who guarded their freedom. That was the state employee job title, YC 1, but in the facility it allowed you to be the AOD. That pay grade 18 was the stepping stone to a very long and steady trajectory of salary growth. New York State employee health benefits are known as one of the best employee health care systems in the entire country. Matched with a base salary of $55k, plus salary steps starting at $1,200, and only increasing from there, every year, plus paid vacation, and everything else I needed to provide for my family.

With all that, I still hadn't told Alyson that I applied for the job. It's difficult to explain why I didn't tell her. Perhaps it was the fake silence we shared pretending not to see the color slowly fading in our once beautifully lit shared reality. Or maybe it was just beautifully lit because Miami always had a way of making the light of life more vibrant, ultra three dimensional, as it fully illuminated one's senses. And here, in the Catskills of upstate New York, it was just gray. White. Small. I knew she would ask me if it was worth it. And I wasn't prepared to answer that question.

"Shit Ant! You already sleep on the couch away from us so you can rest." She'd say.

And I would respond with,"You don't understand I need my sleep to stay on point at this place. Like, I really *need* the rest. To ensure I come home safe."

That was it, right there. - To ensure I get home safe.

For a man, that kind of job is something you can be proud of. To say that you put your life on the line everyday really is something to be truly proud of. But, I wasn't doing that. My life wasn't on the line. But my sanity was. Telling her the truth would only start an unwanted argument. Because for a woman, they need to know that they will be safe. If their man, their main protector, is at risk everyday, that implies that her provider could be taken away from her every time he walks out of the door. Some women aren't built for that.

We would often go back down to the Hudson Valley on the weekends. Alyson would catch up with her mother and rest. I would go to my old friend's house, Rick. Rick and I went way back. We came up together on the streets and as young black educators. He was solid and we always stayed real with each other, no matter what. So I told him my plan.

"Bro! What the Fuck is an AOD?!" Rick questioned laughingly, but was serious.

"Well, they basically run the entire shift. Like their the fucking guy they call when shits about to go down." I replied excitedly.

"Why the fuck would you want to be that guy?" he passed a spliff and coughed.

I hit it. "Because they control the violence." I said clearly, and hit the spliff again.

He looked at me more seriously and with more attention.

"Look." I continued. "Everytime some shit goes down they call a Code, right…"

"Right…" Rick followed.

"So I need to be in a position to be able to identify situations before they pop off and a code is called. Or at least, respond before a restraint is necessary." I paused and looked at Rick.

We exchanged the spliff.

"Bro, all we know is how to get what we want through violence. If we give them no other option, I'm doing them no good. They need to be taught how to communicate, how to advocate for themselves, how to get themselves help. That's how we reach our people. If we're trying to do that for these kids in these white public schools, why won't we do it for our young brotha's locked up?! I've been all over bro, all over this country trying to help my people not go into these types of institutions. Here's my chance to help those already in there." I continued my declaration to my one man audience."It starts with this pay grade 18 shit! Once I pass this test, that's it. I can apply for any other state job at that pay grade or higher. New York State Department of Education, shit, I'll run OCFS. But it starts all at that paygrade." I toned down, and passed the spliff that had gone out from my rant.

"Ok, I feel that." Rick responded, giving me a firm man shake of a dap, ensuring he understood the confidence in which I spoke.

"I could at least make my facility a better place, a safer place. Some of those kids are from right here in the Valley. I mean, that's home, you know…." I knew he would feel that. I was hoping he would. I needed some sort of reassurance.

Rick was a solid man. Even though he became a teacher, he stayed connected to the streets. He had his first child at 16, but now was happily married with two little ones. He owned a house, with a pool, in a great school district, and taught in an even more affluent one. He provided. He stayed true to himself. He gave back. To me, he was a man. And that was my man, so his input always held tremendous weight.

"Word!" He said after pondering off. "You know" he continued,"think of all of our boys, right. The ones who got locked up early; Franky, Josh, Erin, Vance, I mean those kids never stood a chance once they got out, and you wonder why they do what they do. Shit, maybe if someone would've put them on earlier, maybe shit would be different. But then again, shit man……it's like you're a cop bro." and he laughed, tossing the end of the spliff to the ground.

That hit me too. But I wasn't going to be like a cop. That's what I told myself, not Rick.

I left his house feeling confident enough to tell her. Even in the haze my mind was in from smoking that spliff. I hadn't smoked in a long time and the high messed with my mind, as I thought deeper on my conversation with my closest friend. I was trying to justify why I would want to take this job. With all of my social justice reform language and ideology, I tried to justify my decision. *Why would I take orders from men who I know want to inflict harm on my young people? Why did I think I could change that? I couldn't convince myself. How could I convince Alyson?*

On the way home that Sunday evening, we shared that dark lonely drive. I told her how I hated the apartment we lived in. How the smell made me feel young and poor. That I needed to make more money. How WE needed me, to make more money. And that this was the way.

She held my hand, and softly said,"Ok."

We drove the rest of the way home in silence. Together we shared the road with no one. The road twisted and turned through the backside of the Catskills. The dirty slush, forced us to take our time. The cell phone service imposed a silence that could not be remedied. In relationships many nights, days, and conversations become lost in the annals of time. We often forget the importance of one car ride. We often will lump all of our judgments into one statement and say something to the effects of, " You *always* -insert action here -". And continue to show how those actions hurt the relationship. But we seldom say, "Remember that one night…….yeah, that one night was the night we lost it all."

Chapter 8

A New Season

In nature, in what we call the wild, all living things live to maximize their output in life. All living organisms do this. A tree will plunge its roots deep into the ground. They then stretch, and reach for the sun, sprout full leaves, and continue this cycle until its death, sometimes hundreds or thousands of years later. The tree will never say, "You know, I'm a bit tired today, I'm not going to sprout my leaves." The tree will never say,"Yeah, ya know, I'm tall enough." Why? Because if the tree stops living, and growing, and going through the processes that make it living, it will die.

I assumed ———----- One doesn' need to be a scientist to know this fact of life. *All* living things do this. They strive to maximize their living output, or they cease to exist. That is, all living things, except humans. Humans seem to strive for comfort. They will maximize themselves long enough to gain a certain level of satisfaction, and once they feel secure, and comfortable, they no longer strive for optimum output. Humans do not continue to grow and develop, and this is done on a conscious level. They choose to be complacent.

It's as if we already have a predetermined stage in life, that we have accepted for our own reality, that we need to reach, in order to feel "successful". It may be a monetary goal, a career goal, or a simple family life goal. It doesn't matter. But once that goal is reached, we no longer grow.

What happens after you become a millionaire? Yes, you may acquire more money and assets. But does the individual continue to grow, as a human? Has their knowledge multiplied in the same manner in which their money has in their bank accounts? As is if all we are to do in life is to accumulate wealth. Isn't a long and fruitful life, full of growth and expansion, that develops longevity and posterity, what we all truly want?

My mind was lost in the death and seclusion that winter creates. I was grateful as it started losing its grip on me and the landscape. The spring thaw was expanding its reach. I had planted my seeds. I had taken my exam, and passed it with a top score. I agreed to start as an AOD after they found my replacement as a teacher. The YLA was also hiring a score of new young men to be YDA's. There were many of us now who were entering this "facility life", together. All of us were eager to grow and maximize our own potential. Their energy was like the warming sun on a tundra. We were going to soften the hardened frozen ground and allow new growth to form to cover the landscape.

Alyson and I also found new ground. We were still in the same dank, farm house, only we had moved into a larger apartment. I felt a little better about the space, but I still yearned for more. I wasn't receiving my new salary yet, and money still remained extremely tight. Yet, as the sun warmed the ground, it also softened my own sense of being. I was satisfied with being able to earn a larger salary. Satisfied with my role of authority, and sense of power, I wasn't about to allow myself to get complacent.

Before the opportunity to be complacent could manifest itself, we were all sent to the OCFS Training Academy. It was here where we received our crisis management skills and standard operating procedures (SOPs). We also learned how and when to utilize restraints, and how to effectively manage critical and dangerous situations. The training was held at the Red Hook facility. Red Hook was an OCFS destination for drug abusers and sex offenders. They were sent to this facility because these offenders were less prone to violence, and were deemed more in need of mental health services than punitive style "correction". I found this a little odd. From what I had witnessed, they all needed mental health services, they all needed digression from punitive and physical correction. But, I wasn't there to analyze the system and its malfunctions. I was there to learn how to do my job. For me, I was there to learn about those malfunctions, correct them, and create a better and more just OCFS.

It helped that some of the new YDA's and I were sent to the Academy together. We had talked about the facility objectively prior to arriving on campus. We all identified the same inconsistencies in the facilities SOP's, and the misapplication of policy and procedures. We all agreed that there were way too many restraints. The month prior to our attendance at Academy, our restraint number was 69. Sixty-nine restraints in one month. We never had more than 22 residents in our facility at one time. As we did the math we were all saddened that that meant, numerically, that every single one of our residents would have been restrained 3 times, or more, a month. Or even worse, a select few, maybe 4 or 5, were getting restrained 10 or more times a month. When we broke that down, we realized that some residents were getting restrained 4 or 5 times a week. I, and my newly formed crew, could not accept that.

These young men were not all war veterans, and they were not prejudiced men. They were men just looking for a job, a way to take care of themselves and their wives or girlfriends, and they understood the benefits of state employment. The average age of these guys was 25. They never had a real paycheck, full benefits, and skills training like we received. We had already started creating our bond before we left the YLA together. We arrived at Red Hook and we were the only facility that moved as one before, during, and after our Academy experience. The four of us were the foundation of what we were going to build once we returned to YLA.

There was Darien Cash, 25, the former college football player. Trent Bears did nothing but praise and describe his "beast" like abilities in the weight room. He was a local kid, and all who worked and lived in the area went to the same personal access gym to work told stories of his impressive workouts. I believed Bears and his stories about Cash.

His squatting of 600lbs was very reasonable considering the size of Cashs' legs and calves. His back was broad and muscular, and his physique made the ladies of our facility stare in adornment, and the men nodded with respect as they recognized his imposing build.

Nick Icheman, another local kid, age 24, was as upstate and country as they come. A large man standing at 6 '3, weighing 350 lbs, he had a shaved head, and long red beard. He drove a truck that had the picture of an American flag on the tailgate. The truck had large mud tires and a gun rack filled with fishing tackle. His family was a founding family of the area, meaning that they were one of the first families to settle in the region. Their name was well known , and he seemed to know everyone west of Albany. His tattoos of flames and skulls displayed his true self, a side his super polite, kind, and religious based demeanor did so well to hide. He would become my best friend.

Then there was Tyrel Johnson. With a name like his we all assumed he was black, but he wasn't. Johnson was another upstate country boy, and at age 27 had done a tour in Iraq in the Army reserves, had a daughter, and was genuinely an extremely good man. He was tall as well, around 6'2, with a lean athletic build. His tour left him hardened, but his true softness as a man was always shown when he talked about his daughter. He never shared any stories with us about his tour in Iraq, just that he continued to frequent Fort Drum for training as he was still enlisted in the Army reserve.

Icheman and Cash were buddies from high school. They cracked jokes and dissed each other like they were at the lunch table in their high school cafeteria. Their youthful humor and naivete allowed them to be optimistic. They believed in what I was telling them when I said, "Look, we are going into this together. Let's lock in how we're going to move now. So when we get back to the YLA, we can straight lock it down!"

They saw that I wanted to do what was right with the power that I was inheriting. They wanted to be the defenders of that belief. Johnson was more careful. Perhaps because of what he witnessed in Iraq. He would often provide logical humor to our discussions that used brash language to describe the mess we called our job. We respected him for that and he stood firm as a very pragmatic man.

All the facilities had sent new staff to this training Academy for this particular session. Trion, Brookwood, Goshen, Industry, Red Hook, Highland, Finger Lakes, McCormick, Taberg, and us, little ole YLA. The four of us stood tall, together, and as brothers, while we watched while the other facilities members co-mingled, ate, and roomed separately, and seemed eager to work with other people from other facilities. We didn't feel that way. Not that we were anti-social, or anti other facilities or their members. We were developing something different. We were forming a bond that only men who have no other option, but, to protect and defend each other, can form.

They knew me as a teacher. They knew what I stood for, and they would listen to me like students when they needed to. In return, I listened to them, made myself available to listen and provide support in navigating their personal relationships, and their own path to manhood. They were my little brothers. I was their big brother who they would put their life on the line for.

In every session we moved together. We never deviated from each other. We would switch up partners, but only between the four of us. We exchanged notes as we listened and learned the "OCFS way". We shared how the YLA wasn't doing what we were instructed to do, and we shared that in unison. The other new employees from the other facilities were silent and more eager to get it all over with than to fully understand their role within the system. My men weren't that at all. They pushed back on the trainer. They would provide the scenarios that they witnessed during their "floor training" before the Academy. They identified where their senior staff missed directives, failed to follow SOPs, and violated the rights of the residents. They were mad, disgusted, and they started to do exactly what I prayed they would do.

They said, "Ace, we're going back and we're going to do this shit right!". I remember my eyes watering. I remember them seeing that. I remember them appreciating that I cared. I remember how we all man-hugged each other and vowed to have each other's back from that day forward.

We continued to build and learn. We looked forward to the rest of the training and most of all, the day we went for full restraint training. Out of the thirty plus new state employees present for this Academy session, I was the smallest. Smallest by size and attitude. But my three guys were three of the largest there, in both. My attitude was quiet. Deep down inside I was missing Alyson and my son. I wanted to be home with them. I felt guilty that I was bonding with these strangers, forming an alliance with them, and not doing the same for her. But at least she was home with our son and her mother, and I reminded myself of what I was protecting.

Then the day came for restraint training. We were all up earlier than others. We felt like we were preparing for a real battle. The guys and I knew that this was the day that we would learn how to monopolize the violence.

It was Max Weber, the German philosopher who once said, "The state is a community that successfully claims a monopoly over violence , which requires it to have legitimate and legal authority." I shared that statement with the men. I made them understand that as agents of the state that we were going to monopolize the violence. That we would set the trend on what the environment will be. That if we are successful at that endeavor, we will all go home safely, and we will do that often.

So this was the day that we became legitimate, and our authority was valid, in every way, as outlined by the "state". We ate the generic breakfast of instant eggs, hard french toast sticks, sour juice, and week old fruit. We proceeded to the training room and awaited instructions, and again, we were the first ones there.

The trainers for that day came in. There were five of them. They were all clearly OCFS veterans. Hardened faces, solidly built frames, knee and elbow braces, and athletic gear that gave us the message that today was going to get physical. They greeted us with man nods, and hand shakes.

"Morning fellas." The lead trainer acknowledged us.

"Good morning, Sir." We replied as one.

The lead trainer was the shortest man out of the 5. Yet his experience showed in his eyes. They pierced right into you. There was no reflection of light in his pupils, just dark. I felt comforted that he was the smallest, but clearly their leader. I tried to envision myself as he, and made mental notes of his behavior and the manner in which he addressed the staff, and those he led. He displayed concern and care. He exemplified strength and courage, and order and structure. I wanted to lead like him. With certainty and confidence, and experience that made him feel indestructible in the face of carnage.

He led us through the motions of restraints. He took care in instructing every particular application for each type of restraint and when and how to apply them effectively. We covered the supine, standing supine, sitting supine, double supine, securing the legs as the "second" in the restraint, and most importantly when these were all legally applicable.

As an AOD in training, I was most interested in the correct way to handle every situation. I paid close attention to when, and if, de escalation was unsuccessful, and when to order a restraint, or when to have my men stand down. I realized that my role was to never be involved in a restraint, as it was my job to ensure the safety of all involved. Who will monitor what is happening if the AOD is stuck holding down a resident?

It all made sense to me.

I was proud watching my boys perform all of the restraints with careful precision. They were intent and calculated. They asked all the right questions and made all the right moves. I knew that I was going to have to be a damn good AOD with the way they progressed through the sessions. Then the time came for live action. The trainers asked us to split ourselves up in order to work with others and to gain our own understanding of a dangerous situation. My men and I didn' do that. We clustered together in a hudl, and prepared ourselves.

I think the trainers saw that because they let us go last.

"OKAY YLA!" one of the trainers said loudly with a stamp of approval for our defiant act to stick together. "I see you! Y'all better watch out for that YLA, them boys ready!" He continued to praise us.

We were ready.

The live simulation consisted of the five trainers providing a real life scenario of what it would be like in a "large group disturbance". That being defined as 4 or more residents moving in coordination to disrupt or enact violence during the daily active program. They did all they could do to not call it a "riot". They provided us with the proper terms in order to protect ourselves. How we described the situation on the paperwork after a restraint was more important than what actually happened in any documented event.

Correct paperwork could prevent us from being sued, held liable, or even from being fired. One can be held liable for an injury with no repercussion. They just had more paperwork that stated they were at fault. But, we could be sued by the family if we omit actions, or do not follow through with the correct follow up procedures when a youth is restrained. Yet, none of those things would make one lose their job though. However, if your words were not accurate, if you stated you did something that you did not do, did something you did not state, or if you did not outline all of the procedures that needed to be followed prior to physical action, and then you signed that paperwork, one could lose their job if they didn't have "permanent" status as a state employee. Ironically, that "permanent" status was on delay. There were guys who had been working for several years who hadn't received their "permanent" status yet. And they all were fucking up, and we knew that that was why they were hiring all these new people.

We were all disposable at the slightest incorrect action, and we knew that.

"Ok, YLA here we go!" The large loud trainer who gave us props before, now looked at us like lunch.

They switched up the scenarios in each simulation. So we didn't really know what was going to happen. And then it did.

The lead instructor flipped over the couch and yelled "Fuck that! Y'all want it!?" At the same time the larger man, who was eyeing and pumping us up, yelled "Let's get it!" and came after Icheman.

Cash responded to that immediately, and he and Nick quickly put him in a standing double supine. Both with an arm and wrist in lock behind the man's back. He rocked and jolted to get free, but my guys didn't budge. I had to snap out of my state of feeling impressed and proud, and do my part as lead in the situation. I ordered Johnson to put one of the men in his cell, and Johnson did it with the conciseness of a soldier trained for the moment. I ordered the other to go to his cell, and he refused. At the same time the lead trainer looked right at me, and with all the disrespect he could muster, said,"You don't want it bitch!"

Honestly, I didn't know what to do. There were two of them, one of me, they were both larger than I, and I had given orders that created that situation for myself. It was only a split second before my street senses kicked in. I stepped to the man, the man who called me a bitch, toe to toe, looked him directly in his eye, and said,"My man, you don't need this." and in the same breath I pointed at the other trainer who refused my directive, and gave Johnson the order,"Put him down

Johnson!" And Tyrel immediately wrapped up the last trainer, and put him in a seated restraint. The struggle was meaningless, he had him.

It was now the lead trainer and I. Starring each other down. Him breathing hard, trying to characterize the emotion I would later witness in real life. I looked deeper into his eyes. And with a clear, calm, confident voice said,"My man, you don't need this. You need to go home. I can help you do that, but not if this is what you're going to do. C'mon man. It's over. Let's just chill." The man's eyes softened. He kept locked contact with me, but you could tell that that was just for effect. He seethed a deep breath a few more times for the show. Then he stopped, shook his head, and provided me with something that was so precious, so sincere and intimate, especially amongst men. He said to me, and the entire group,"That's what an AOD does right there! Good fucking job gentlemen!"

When men give other men compliments it's rather unconventional. Women will promote each other and inflate compliments to each other in order to make them feel good. Men usually use a disrespectful comment and expect the other man to understand the sarcastic nature of the comment, and to take it as a compliment. That's just part of the unspoken understanding of men.

Yet, this man. This hardened veteran of OCFS. A man who had made it to the otherside of the chaos, verbalized his compliment and stated it directly. All present saw me, heard him, saw my men, and recognized us as "those guys". Icheman, Johnson, and Cash looked at their leader with pride. I was the smallest man there. Yet, I was the one who maintained control, maintained my discipline, maintained communication and eye contact with my men. He later told me, when we had a moment alone, to never forget what I am capable of, and that if you do that, those boys will climb a tree to the moon if you tell them to, and "Trust me." he said, "You will need them to."

Chapter 9

Training Day

They say,"Find something you love to do and you will never work a day in your life." I found this to be true as a teacher. I started working with kids at age eighteen and found myself, and the love, in working with children and their families. I felt like I had never really worked because I loved every minute of every day. I took pride in using my experience of trial by fire, and surviving and thriving, to inspire and help others to do the same.

Life will do that to us, it will give us trial by fire in order to see if we are what we claim to be. This is especially true after we make hard life decisions. It's as if life says to us, "You think that this was a good decision, well here take this and let's see what you do. Because you never know what I'm going to throw at you next."

Then life throws its curve ball and tests you in ways that are most uncomfortable. Life will measure your resolve and resilience. It will bend and twist you to see if you will break. Life will target your weakest points of existence and put pressure on you in order for you to understand your own breaking points. And we all have breaking points.

I had completed my mandated 5 days and 4 nights at the Training Academy. Cash, Johnson, and Icheman stayed for their continued training that lasted another two and a half weeks. I was surprised by this scheduling. The men and I laughed when we were still at Red Hook, highlighting how that all made sense since the AODs back at the YLA were doing such an inadequate job. They clearly needed the entire training as well, if anything, they needed more training considering their role in the facility. I left them with some words of motivation. Reminding them,"....that you guys will be the ones who will bring about the change back home. I'll go and set the stage, but I need you guys ready to make it happen."

They replied with a staggered,"Yes, sir!"

Those words echoed in my mind the entire ride back upstate. They continued to sound off in my head when I returned to the YLA. "Yes, sir", I kept hearing. Only men with authority are called "sir" in this environment. This was a level of leadership I had never felt before. Although I still had two more weeks remaining as a teacher it was time to transition into my new role, as AOD. As a leader of MY men, and as a man who would be in charge, and a man in control.

The last two weeks as a teacher were difficult for me. I was already mentally not there as an educator. I was already personifying myself as the AOD I wanted to be. My students saw this happening as well. The residents cycle through just as fast as new employees. We had an entirely new cohort of residents, and many were clueless as to how the facility was run just a few months prior to their arrival. They didn't know the reputation established by the military prowess of the YLA. This round of youths appreciated the education program, and although there were still disruptions that would lead to the cancellation of school, the sentiment was largely, "Don't stick up the program because staying on the unit is bullshit."

You could see the street hierarchy develop within the units. There was always an unspoken, unit leader amongst the youths. At this particular time, a 15 year old from Freeport Long Island, named Morales ran unit 1. And a 16 year old Dominican kid from Queens, ran unit 2. Morales was half Italian and Puerto Rican. He was a smart kid, and was set on doing his time, going home, and forgetting about this short period of time in his life. I respected the kid for having such a mature outlook on his situation.

I would often allow him to come to my classroom to listen to music and talk about life. On one of my last days as a teacher, he said to me,"Yo Ace, you my man, but don't turn all Hollywood on us when you come to the unit."

He stopped, checked his emotions. I could tell he was trying to tell me something, but he had to maintain his own sense of protection of his own emotions, as a man. He looked back at me and continued,"It's like here....we know that you're helping us. Those ma'fuckas out there don't give a shit about us. Why do you think I keep telling these stupid fucks to come to school. Bro! You're here! Yeah we read and shit, but we really just come here to chop it up with you. You gonna still do that, right?"

The look in his eyes gave me no choice but to.

"I got you son." I responded. He dapped me up, and we ended our music session and I walked him back to his unit, alone.

He made me think, and think hard. I walked over to unit 2. I sought out Perez who was playing spades with three other residents. Perez was different from Morales. He was street hardened at a young age. His trauma was displayed in violent acts that usually consisted of a tossed chair or desk, followed by an immediate assault on whoever was his target. Morales didn't fight. He moved how I did when I was a street kid at his age. He used his smarts and personality to gain respect and credibility. Perez was your classic intimidator. He was visibly strong, both in physique and expression. He would simply say,"Naw, it's a stick up" in the most calm and respectful tone. Yet, the entire unit would follow his words and refuse to move.

The YDAs were beginning to fall back on the restraints. Word from the main office in Albany was that they were going to investigate allegations of abuse and excessive force. When those who are charged to enforce any laws or rules, are stripped of, or have to give up their authority, only chaos can reign. When the violence is no longer monopolized, when force is no longer the agent of control, you leave the violent acts to be perpetrated by the agents of chaos, and not by the agents of control.

The YDAs were becoming reluctant to enforce rules. They were scared of losing their jobs, their retirement, everything they put their bodies on the line for. They were no longer willing to do that part of the job. The residents were running the program now and I couldn't wait for my men to get back from the Academy.

In the meantime I had to finalize my role as a teacher and establish a new form of authority as I was managing not only the youths of the facility, but also the adults. One of my final acts as a teacher was to put Todd Olivier in his place. He continued to spout all sorts of classist, racist, prejudice, regional bias and all of the toxic social ills I wanted to squash and stamp out like a cigarette that had been smoked to the filter. I wanted nothing left of his cancerous spreading of fear based hate, and the sheer audacity and self entitlement he used to verbalize his poison so freely.

There were many times Olivier was saved by a YDA for saying something he shouldn't have. I personally had to tackle a kid who was trying to go after him on the unit. He had told a resident that the kid stole his pen. Whether or not that's true, was never even attempted to be clarified. He told the kid to give the pen back. The kid said,"Why don't you take it back bitch!?"

Todd looked at the YDA next to him. A female former navy aircraft carrier technician named Parker. Parker was loved on the unit, one because she was a female, not because she was good looking, but simply because she was a woman and their pubescence provided little self control. The other reason was that Parker was hard as nails. She put up with zero bullshit, and would not hesitate to put a kid down, and was very clear about that. She imposed her will, monopolized the violence, and the residents would do anything for her. So when Todd looked at Parker and said,"Are you going to let him talk to me like that?" and she responded with,"Um NO! I think the question is are you going to let him talk to YOU like that?"

"OOOOH SHIT! That's right bitch, whatchya gonna do now?!" the resident immediately shouted for the entire unit to hear. "Get your pen bitch!" He told Todd again.

Olivier did something we all couldn't believe. He told Parker right then and there to restrain the kid.

"Fuck you! You want to do that go'head, be my fucking guest!" Parker commanded back to Olivier.

The kid got up, and two more who were close by and heard the interaction also started making their way over to us. Todd was befuddled. He stuttered and looked at me for solace, I gave him none. Speechless, scared and seeing that he wasn't going to gain any support from us, he made his way to the door. But the three residents weren't planning on letting him go. Perez was one of them. He liked Barker and needed her harsh motherly love. Todd was able to out pace the other two residents to the door, but Perez was waiting. Todd radioed to CSU to unlock the unit door. Perez sought to turn him off and would have done so with the blind sided right cross he was going to throw. I wrapped him up in a bear hug, held him, told him "Naw, Junior (that was his real name and I only used it when I had to), he ain't worth kid, 2 more weeks and you're gone. He'll still be here. Be easy baby." He softened in my arms, and gave a sucking of his teeth as he watched Todd power walk back to the education building.

But that wasn't it. My last straw with Todd was when we were in a meeting discussing the education programs. We were talking about our ability to meet the needs of students while instructing them on the unit. We shared our positives and negatives, and ideas that we could implement to increase learning and preparedness. Todd , in his smug fake Ned Flanders way said,"Well I know that I get distracted when they are doing each other's hair. I mean, it's like their monkeys grooming each other."

That was it. I snapped

"Who the fuck do you think you are Todd !?" I said angrily."Monkeys, fucking monkeys! I've sat here and listened to you say some really outlandish shit over the past few months, but that's enough!" I imposed, and gave him the darkness of my stare. Sharon calmed me down and called us both into her office. Before she could say anything, I switched up my tone, reset myself as a professional, and geared up to set Todd straight.

"Todd ," I started. "You are the special education teacher here. The IEP's you write are living breathing documents that these kids will be relying on when they leave here to better themselves. How can we expect you to create these lasting programs, that these kids will need, if you use such bias in your lens. How dare you compare them to monkeys and expect anyone to appreciate your educational point of view." I stopped.

He replied,"That is not what I meant, Anthony. I apologize if I offended you."

I stopped him."No Todd , that is what you meant, and all you do is offend. You have done nothing but spew prejudice, racist and complete bullshit since you started here."

He repeated, "I didn't mean to offend you Anthony."

"You're right Todd , you meant to offend the kids on the unit, because they aren't here to hear you. That's why no one saved your ass on the unit."

"Listen." I tried to settle down and give him some knowledge. "This country was built on the backs of slaves, their ancestors, my ancestors, were forced into enslavement, and now look where so many are housed. You need to understand your role and what you represent to those young men, and you need to do that now, Todd ."

Todd 's response sealed his fate at the YLA. He said, "This country was built on the backs of immigrants like my family. And I had no part of their peoples' enslavement. All they do is call me a redneck, hillbilly, and a hick. I mean they're the ones who live in one place their entire lives and do nothing else, who's the real hick here?"

I looked at Sharon, she looked at me. She said softly,"Todd , I think that's a very skewed point of view."

I looked at Sharon, and with my eyes and posture, asked if I could leave. She acknowledged my silent request and approved. I exited her office and went directly to Sue Conklin's office. She was the current acting director of the facility. I went to report to her, as an AOD should, about Todd , what I had been witnessing and my suggestion for his termination. This was a bold move on my part. I wasn't really an AOD yet, but the relationship I had developed with Sue made me confident in my actions.

Sue was only the temporary director, and her real position was the Director of Mental Health. She was an Army retired veteran, and a long time social worker, both privately and for the state. Taller than I and built tough, her hands were larger than mine. And if it wasn't for her age, bad knee and shoulder, she would clearly have an advantage over many of the youths she encountered. She was a kind woman who had turned to steel without choice. Yet, she would show that softer side of herself when she talked with me. A side that still believed, still had hope, and looked for light in the cracks of the darkness.

When I brought Todd 's comment and behavior to her attention, and provided my solution, surprisingly she agreed. A week later Todd was fired. I didn't see him off. There were no last words or looks to exchange. I was later told that he said that the YLA deserved everything that had happened there and that "this place is hell personified."

Perhaps it was.

Conklin had informed me that my teacher replacement was ready to start in a few days and that I would need to take some shifts as AOD for "field training."

"Your first shift is going to be an overnight shift. I'm doing this so you can train with McIntyre. He can go over the SOPs, show you the security rounds you'll have to make around the facility, and all the other daily tasks you're going to have to fulfill on your own shift. The overnight is tough, but I feel it's the best way to ease you into the position."

"Thank you ma'am." I responded and gave a slight smile on one side of my face. The other side I tried to keep as steel as hers. She smiled back and said,"Cortes, it's different on this side. But stay true to yourself. Those kids need what you bring and I am really glad you decided to do this. We all support you in this."

If only that was true.

That was a Wednesday, and on Friday I was assigned my overnight shift. I explained all of this to Alyson. She was upset because we were supposed to go down to the valley and see her mother. I couldn't lie, I wanted to see Rick, get high and vent about what had transpired over the last few weeks. I was going to start to get my pay grade 18 salary, the pay would increase, but this was just the start. I tried to explain that my role was different now and that there may be circumstances that would call me to be there, and stay there, even when I was needed at home. I tried to explain that that was the job. She would always provide body language and responses that inferred her saying "that's why I didn't want you to take this job" stance on the situation. There was nothing I could do. This was "the way", I reminded her, and myself.

Friday came. The overnight shift was from 10pm to 6am. Alyson decided that she would go to her mothers alone and stay the weekend. She softened it with "You'll need to rest, and catch up on your sleep, and we'll come back Sunday early afternoon."

This was easy to agree to as I didn't get much time to myself. I also wanted to be alone to shift my mentality. I was preparing myself for a regressive change in mind, body, and soul. I was going back to my street grind mentality. I wasn't going to be "Hollywood", but I was going to let them know that I meant business.

Time to get to business.

I only had, what I considered, teacher clothes. I was still wearing a button up shirt and tie, khaki pants, and nice shoes. I always felt like that distinguished me from other teachers and showed that I took my profession seriously. I wasn't going to wear any of that.

It was spring, so the weather had the confusion that spring air provides. Warm in the day, yet still cold at night, and the wind still held on to the threads of winter. I put on hiking boots, jeans, and a black fleece under an all gray Columbia ski jacket. Black and gray, right, I assured myself. The farm apartment was a short 12 minute drive, a right turn out of the driveway, turn left and you're there, type short. I wanted the drive to last forever. It seemed like thirty seconds, and I was there.

I arrived at 9:30pm. I wanted to check in with McIntrye before the shift briefing. I wasn't really sure why I wanted to do that though. I sat in the parking lot, thinking , *"Dam, still a half hour before the shift starts."* And I didn't really like McIntyre. He was a tall 6 '4 slim, strong built, former Army veteran, whose hair and classic eighties mustache were as red as he was red-neck. He was a sergeant in the army so his position as AOD was of significance to him. He believed in rank and file. And was honest about all the new people being hired. Their lack of experience, and how the "new hug a thug" policies were putting everybody in danger.

For clarification, there were sweeping new policies enforced by the agency that removed certain restraints. Many of which were used in the prison system and by local and state law enforcement. These styles of restraints were deemed unfit and harmful to the youth. There were new Crisis Behavioral Management Interventions introduced. These prompted the use of de-escalation techniques and safe ways to restrain a youth without bodily harm. It also enforced the implementation of more mental health services and programs. Those were the "hug a thug" policies.

"What are they going to do when one of these kids are trying to hit you with a desk, or better yet, they gang up on you, then what. There's no management at that point. No, you take them down?" He would say, trying to prove his point.

"*Shit*", I thought to myself. "*I really fucking hate McIntrye already!*"

I stepped out of my car into what had turned into a rather chilly evening. I made my way from the parking lot, following the glowing yellow lit pathway up to the front of the facility. I had to walk in between the units to make the fifty yard straight line to the main gate. It was that yellow that only shines at night, that shines warm, but provides no sense of security, kind of lighting. As I came around the bend to walk that straight away, I heard hell.

The echoes of grown men yelling, and the wild yelps of young men in response.

My heart started pounding. I raced up to the unit and could see inside three of the cell windows. One had the door open and I could only make out heads moving fast back and forth in the unit. In the next window, a resident was pacing and peering out of his cell door window. The last one was standing on his desk and was banging the plastic out of the fluorescent light above him. I watched him break a piece about 7 inches long, perfectly into a sharp point, and then he caught eyes with me.

He stared at me. Smiled and nodded. He jumped down from the desk and started kicking his cell door.

"*What the fuck?*"

I didn't know what to do. I ran to the front of the unit. They had installed new door switches, so one just had to press the button on the door, it notified CSU, and then they unlocked the door. That happened with timely precision, as they were watching me and what was happening on the unit simultaneously.

The second door opened.

I walked on to the unit floor. The lights were turned out. Only the low limited glow that emergency wall mounted lights provided were on. The couches were all flipped, papers and garbage everywhere. The YDAs were still trying to get one resident into his room. One final shove and the cell door was closed and locked. Another resident came walking out of his cell, no shirt on, walking around like he owned the world, and before he got close to me he bent over and flipped a couch. It was already turned over, but his message was being sent.

I heard a YDA yell,"C'mon Mills!"

And then, with his back turned, I restrained him. Arms locked, perfectly, and I felt my palms straighten him out when they reached the soft spot in between his shoulder blades. I marched him straight forward and let him go in his room. It was my first real restraint, but it wasn't really. It was the first time I had to put a kid in his cell, and by far the easiest. The unit was in complete disarray. Already men were picking up the garbage and rearranging the furniture. They adjusted the unit back to its original condition and cleared it all with CSU.

And then the AOD that night, a former Marine named Mike Thompson, proudly exclaimed,"Alright boys, let's get this paper work done!"

Chapter 10

The Dark Side

The ease in which the men shifted from chaos and violence, to calmly rearranging the furniture and picking up the debris on the unit, displayed a sad accepted order of operations that I didn't know existed as a teacher in the facility. We were often told to check the write up log in CSU prior to coming in for the morning meeting. But there were never any details provided. Only the time a code is called, the resident and staff involved, and if they went to medical or not. That is all that is required for the log book. The book that is designated to legally document all happenings in the facility. That simple log book can make or break an employee, an AOD, and can determine the outcomes of many more.

Although the log book is designed to keep track of all events in the facility, the paperwork is king. When Mike Thompson said to everyone, "....Let's get this paper work done." I realized then and there that the "paperwork", the documentation of events, were not just simple forms for answering questions, checking boxes, and placing initials and signatures. They were legal documents created by the Division of Juvenile Justice for Youth (DJJOY) for all employees to fill out after physical force or intervention is performed on a youth. Typically it will work like this, a YDA will call a code, and attempt to correct the resident, he then fills out paperwork that states a code was called, the correction attempted, and the manner in which it was remediated.

For example, let's say a resident refuses to leave the unit to go to breakfast. This is a disruption to the program. The YDA is to utilize a series of ways to encourage the residents to follow the program. If they continue to refuse the YDA is to call a Code Yellow. This indicates that there is a resident who is refusing to follow a given directive - Code Yellow means there is someone who is "sticking it up". These can usually be de-escalated rather easily, a positive conversation, reminder of release dates, reminders of past successes, can usually get a kid going and getting with the "program". However, if a youth is set on not following the program, and becomes a danger to himself or others, a Code White is called. A Code White indicates that a restraint is about to happen, or is in progress.

The catch is, Code Whites are rather subjective. The YDA present is the one who can call the code. A weaker YDA, will call a code in order to have someone else come and handle the situation for them. A stronger YDA, will call a code when they are just about to take a kid down. One of the responsibilities as an AOD is to review the restraint, document the event and to identify if the correct procedures were followed. Considering that, when reviewing the incidents , the AOD's have no audio sound from the security cameras to utilize, they use the documentation to follow the order of events. This is where people get caught up.

If they did not document something that happened prior to, during, or after a restraint, we - the AOD's then, have to follow up with documentation that identifies the inconsistency and recommendations for correction and remediation. This correction and remediation usually comes in the form of a training "refresher". The refresher training only covers what the employee did incorrectly. So they may have to perform the restraint properly on the trainer, or explain what and why they performed the action incorrectly, how to do it better next time, and sign official documentation that the refresher was completed. The staff were not concerned about the corrective efforts of the state. Nor were they concerned about any repercussions from the facility. Even though in training, we were informed of how important all of the SOP's were for the protection of all involved, including staff and residents.

I wondered how so many actions, that led to residents receiving injuries, both hidden and observable, all the "large disturbances" that seemed to go unacknowledged, the violations and offenses reported by residents against staff, and the mishandling of so many horrendous actions, could go unnoticed and unchecked?

When Mike Thompson gathered everyone up to do the "paperwork", I understood what he was doing. As a former Marine, and a veteran of two tours in Iraq, Thompsons Military Operation (MO) was the lead command of an armed courier. Their job was to ensure that all transport of supplies and equipment reached their destination. In this role, as the ranking man of the transport unit, he was used to telling other officers who out ranked him, how/what/where/why and when the orders were given and to conduct the movement. He wasn't much bigger than I was, however his Marine bravado gave him an air that I did not have. He was a veteran, witnessed war, lost partial hearing in an attack, and the men somewhat honored him for this.

He sat everyone down together to fill out the paperwork in a coordinated effort to ensure all was covered. The YDA's that evening were Burch, and he was in his usual "Fuck them all" drunk mentality. Paris, a large man, Army retired, but no combat experience, who never said a single word, nor shared an expression. He still had his military style buzz cut, with a small strip of hair down the middle, which indicated to me his longing to still be an enlisted man. The man followed orders as if he were still trying to earn stripes on his arm.

The third staff member on the unit was Samantha Easten. A young woman in her mid twenties, blonde, with a country girl shape that made all the men swear she was God's gift to the YLA. She was pretty considering how isolated we were, but she was more respected for her physical abilities which she never shied away from. Easten wanted to be a police officer. She talked and walked like she was a law enforcement agent. She was waiting to take her State Troopers exam, she had no issue flexing authority on the young men she hoped to arrest one day, and lock them up for good.

And Michael Walker was the Op2. Walker was a former Airman, and was proud that his boys joined the Airforce as well. Although Walker was the usual Op2 for the overnight, he was steadily getting overtime and was always the driver for transfers and court appointments. It was estimated that he made over $120k in salary with all of his overtime included. That night he was working a double shift, again.

Those three were running that unit, on the 2-10 shift, on my first night.

When completing the "packets", what we called the paperwork, Thompson gave directives on who did what, when it happened, and the actions that were taken. He coordinated every one of their statements to match concisely with each other. This ensured that they were all covered, in classic CYA (cover your ass) form. The last resident who was put in his room suffered an injury. Thompson made sure that they all worded the "injury" as an "ailment that was acknowledged prior to the restraint", in order to not be held accountable for the resident's sprained wrist during the event. Although residents were throwing garbage cans, and flipping couches, actions that wouldn't really hurt anyone, they were described as "resident threatened to throw unit furniture at staff. When the resident refused redirection, and was unable to be redirected, the resident was placed in a single standing restraint." That was the summary.

They carefully outlined the CBM techniques used in each phase, provided approximate times, which YDA said what, the resident's supposed response, and how they continued to use every single option in their arsenal before applying physical force. They, in limited state detail, provided what took place.....together.

9:00 pm - Resident White refused to lock in. Resident was told to lock into his   cell at residents designated Level 2, lock in - 9pm. Resident was provided hurdle help, one on one attention, and focus redirection. Resident White said, "Fuck that shit my nigger! I'm not locking in. This is a stick up!"

9:02 pm - Code Yellow called on resident White -YDA Burch

Resident was provided space. Resident threatened YDA Burch. Resident was directed to lock in again.

9:04 pm - Op2 arrives on Unit 2

9:07 pm - Code Yellow called on resident Smith - YDA Easten

Resident Smith sexually harassed YDA Easten and threatened her, stating "Suck my dick bitch!" This a stick, hats up!"

9:09 pm - A.O.D Thompson arrives on unit 2

A.O.D Thompson gave a directive for all other residents to lock into their cells. Resident Perez said "No, Fuck that. I'm not locking in for shit. You can suck a dick!"

9:10 pm - Code Yellow resident Perez - YDA Burch

Resident Perez refused to follow the directive endangering the safety of others.

9:12 pm - Code White resident Dartent - YDA Paris

Resident Dartent flipped over the couch and yelled "This is a stick up!"

After the initial Code White is called, it's all up to interpretation of what was written and what is seen on the video camera. What was seen on the video camera was described by the men as;

Resident Dartent flipped over the unit couch and yelled "This is a stick up!" Resident Perez then grabbed the garbage can and threw it at YDA Easten. Resident Smith then grabbed the other garbage can and threw it at YDA Burch. AOD Thompson and YDA Walker secured uninvolved residents into their cells. Resident Smith was placed in single standing restraint by YDA Burch and was placed in his cell. Resident Dartent attacked YDA Paris by punching him in the face. YDA Paris was unable to secure resident Dartent in standing single restraint, and YDA Easten assisted in a seated double restraint. Dartent continued to not follow directives provided during protocol and continued to resist by kicking and spitting. YDA Easten and Paris then attempted a double standing restraint. Dartent was told to go to his cell. He refused the directive, and was placed in his cell. Resident Perez and resident White attempted to punch AOD Thompson during the restraint with resident Dartent. AOD Thompson and YDA Burch placed resident Perez in a double standing restraint and the resident was placed in his cell. Resident White continued to run around the unit. He kicked the garbage can at YDA Paris. He attempted to punch YDA Burch. YDA Walker and AOD Thompson place resident White in a team standing and place resident in his cell.

I didn't need to see the video to know that that was not how it went down. But there is a code amongst those in law enforcement, and it's a brotherly code. It's a code I recognized well as I found picking up patterns as a skill in life. It allowed me to maneuver through the street world and, for lack of a better word, the legit world too. Interestingly enough I found that both worlds were very similar. In fact they were one in the same, just in completely two juxtaposed contexts.

Most who have to deal with the dangers of street life don't always choose that life, and they certainly don't choose any decisions that the lifestyle manufactures. Most usually don't have much of a choice, many options, or support. They create their own family. A family that produces longevity and wealth, just like "legit" families desire and do. Those they build with, know the dirt they participated in and what they're fully capable of. They would never turn on their family. One, because they also did dirt with the family. And two, they know what the family is capable of and understand the consequences. So a "ride or die" mentality is created in order to protect the order of the family.

Powerful families of every ethnicity practice this "ride or die" mentality in some form or fashion. Whether it's cloaked in trigger words like bias, prejudice, or non inclusive, the meaning is the same. It's one side keeping their best interest in mind to protect the posterity of their "wealth". On the streets and in law enforcement that wealth is life. To simply be able to live another day.

I saw those men do exactly what I had done with my crew years back. Orchestrate exactly what went down, state it as such, and let it ride. I also knew that I wasn't part of their crew, and I damn sure wasn't family.

But there were those on the dark side who would become like family. The two overnight YDA's who teamed up with Walker were Kevin Smith and Ryan Ericson. These two were "work" best friends and had developed a deep bond and trust with each other. Ericson was 6 feet tall, 360 lbs, and never had an issue putting a kid down. Yet, he rarely had to. He would often talk with the residents and knew things about them most didn't. He had been there for 8 years and reminisced of the old days of the military camp with fondness. He would often manage to empathize with the residents and would explain policies to other staff members in simple language. Those debates usually ended in them agreeing with him. He also was a big stoner, and so was Kevin Smith. So we often enjoyed that commonality.

K. Smith had a slim frame and stood 6 '1, he had a security gig on the side, and prided himself with the newest equipment for his personal defense. He always talked straight. His wife was Puerto Rican, and he felt there was no room for "racist bullshit". His "a good man is a good man" attitude and his always sincere honesty made him impossible for me to not gravitate towards.

There were also my men who would be making their way back from the Academy. In the meantime, I still had a job to do. I had to have a better understanding of who was who and how it all went down. It didn't take long as I just looked for patterns.

There were three shifts; 10-6, 6-2, & 2-10. The 6am to 2pm shift is where those old clowns who were supposed to get the residents to school and run the day program. They had three YDAs for each unit. They were all senior guys as this was the prized shift. Stanley and Bruce would switch between CSU and being on the floor with the residents. Bruce was a country block head, Army grunt. He walked with no arm movement and no matter the event, he talked with a monotone matter of fact voice. Stanley was an old rough shaved man with glasses. He was originally from Brooklyn and still held his original accent, although he transplanted 35 years prior. He always smelled of cigarettes and coffee. He and I would reminisce about New York, the food, event venues, and how much things changed. They both were worthless on the floor. Bruce would just move to secure other residents, and Stanley would always somehow not be around.

There was Klien, a PTSD-ridden Navy man. He would often stare without blinking, at anything, randomly. To be honest, it was weird and the residents would often tell him to stop looking at them, and thought he was gay. I recognized the stare he would get lost in. My mother's first husband was a Vietnam Vet, and I would watch him get stuck in the most mundane actions, like putting on his socks. He would get stuck, starring, lost in a memory he was hoping to never revisit. I saw that in Klien. He was kind, but too physically strong of a man to let the kids push him around. Klien often was the first to be attacked. He rarely took a day off from an injury, or from anything for that matter. Graham also worked the day shift and was still counting down the days until retirement. Burch, Easten, and Paris would round off the 6-2 shift.

The overnight, 10pm - 6am, was locked with Walker, Smith and Ericson, and whoever else filled in the other two spots. That left the 2pm to 10pm shift. They filled this shift with new employees and balanced it out with the much desired, but widely abused overtime for the senior staff. There were new employees who had completed the Academy and were working full time now. However, the few new staff who actually stayed, and were actually beneficial to the facility, were minimal. Only one from the several months of new employee cohorts stayed. His name was Levy Simms. He was a young black man from

Brooklyn, who had recently graduated from Binghamton University. He was the closest thing I had to an old street friend. He also navigated both worlds as I did. The kids loved him, and I saw him as one of my biggest assets.

There were other YDAs, but they were all scattered between different shifts as needed. And if you haven't realized by now, they were terribly understaffed. That put a lot of pressure on the AODs and Counselors. The two counselors, assigned to each unit, were Pearson and Holland. Both men were built like bears, but only one of them possessed the willingness to use their monstrous demeanor. That was Holland. He was born and raised in Central New York, an avid fisherman, and proud American, even though he never served in the armed forces. He had a bachelor's in science, and was a constant provider of negativity. Unless he was talking about his daughter the world was shit, and there was nothing any of us could do about it. He was best friends with Mike Thompson.

Pearson was another gentle giant. He was a light skinned black man, who played football, and went to college for criminal justice. He would joke and say how he wanted to be a court officer and would highlight that they have their pay grade 18 and don't do a fraction of what we did. Although he had to stick with the "family", he appreciated me as a teacher, and he and I would often talk about better ways to run programs and to ensure the residents were successful after their release.

The Counselor was the resident's "paperwork" ticket out of the facility. The Counselors primary responsibility was to ensure that the residents on their caseload followed the program. They aligned services such as school, housing, and community after care (aka probation) for the residents. If those three were not all properly in tune with each other, the resident would not get a release date assigned. If a Counselor slacked on the paperwork we all paid for it.

Depending on the shift, and who was available, one of the counselors could also be the AOD for the shift. The other AODs, and whose primary responsibility and role was strictly AOD, were Smith, Wright, Sporacco, McIntyre, and Mike Thompson. Vernon Smith was the YLAs version of a Navy hardened Samuel L. Jackson. He spoke exactly like him, had the exact same swagger, and truly "didn't give a fuck." He was an interesting man. He was a rank in file man as well, and would always complain about how racist everyone was. He always managed to ruffle someone's feathers, push a staff member the wrong way and call someone out on their bullshit. He would yell at residents, and punk them out. Yet, everybody loved V Smith. He silently ran the entire place. I saw that, and wanted to impress him.

Wright was leaving, and I was his replacement. Sporacco was retiring and that was a good thing, He was an old Vietnam helicopter pilot. If you know anything about the history of Vietnam, you know that the helicopter was the life line to the soldiers on the ground. Known for their insane bravery and unwavering loyalty to the men they served with, the pilots were the exact type of men you wanted to come thundering in from the sky to save you in a time of hellish despair. That was Sporacco. He walked around with packets in the pockets of his all blue military fatigues. He never gave a fuck, and he had no problem with any and everyone knowing how little fucks he had to give. Since he was retiring he had taken Thompson under his wing. Thompson spent his first year under Sporacco's tutelage. And that year, Rocco, as we called him, could only train the YLA's next version of himself. A hardened soldier who just had a job to do.

The complex dynamic these men and I shared consumed my thoughts. I never knew who I was working with, who my staff would be, when I was working, and had no set schedule for about a month. I embraced the dark side of the facility. I knew how it worked. They were giving me all the shit to see what I was made of. They wanted me to quit. I had already pushed back on many of them during my time as a teacher. I never faltered on my belief in a quality education for all, and my determination to provide such a service.

They all thought I was out of mind when I suggested that the teachers come to the unit. Besides that one incident with Olivier, there never was an issue. They recognized that as well. They saw that I wasn't afraid to have multiple residents alone, and could teach the most "unteachable" combination of students. They knew that they could rely on my classroom to run smoothly no matter what. But, they didn't think that my philosophy would transition over to their side of the game.

It is true, men fear what they don't understand and hate what they can't conquer. When a man is having difficulty measuring another man up, he usually falls back, plays standoffish, and waits to gather more intel. If they come to an understanding of inferiority, they will seek to destroy you, in some shape or form. Men do this. They will fear you in a way that is not necessarily a feeling of being scared, but they watch to see if you are an actual threat. And if they feel that you are, and that threat is something they can't match up against, they will hate you. Hate and fear run the dark side.

Chapter 11

Life on The Homefront

I continued to keep the challenges faced at work to myself. Trauma is dealt with differently from person to person. For men, I believe there is some universal behavior. Men often will not, and feel that they cannot, show weakness. This directly impacts how we deal with trauma. My dad was also in Vietnam, and never shared his trauma from the war. He never shared how he earned his purple heart and how he managed coming home wounded, both physically and mentally. It wasn't until we watched *Saving Private Ryan* that I realized how bad it was. Sure I had seen my mothers husband zone out. I had witnessed dozens of his staring at nothing moments, always wondering where he was inside his head.

For my dad, I didn't see those moments. But at the end of the movie, when Matt Damon's character asked his wife if he was a "good man", I saw him get lost. He asked his wife, Janet, the very same question. Her response was ,"Is this a trick question?" I still have no idea why that was her response. Maybe she wanted to say no, maybe she really thought that he was going somewhere else with that question, maybe she really had something to say that was going to impact him positively. Instead, she said what she said, and my dad did what he did.

He grabbed her by her neck and picked her up off of the ground.

"Everything I've done for you, and that's all you have for me?"

My dad did everything he thought he was supposed to do for Janet. He moved into a large house that she wanted, that fit her perception of a successful reality. Her and my dad moved from Ohio to Florida for his health. He battled cancer for years prior to the move. The warm weather was supposed to comfort his lungs. The veterans hospital was supposed to take better care of him, and he was supposed to heal. He didn't. Maybe that's why he snapped. Perhaps he knew that he had limited time here on this plane of reality with his loved ones and he just wanted reassurance that he had done things the right way, for all of us. Then again, maybe he was just so traumatized that he couldn't recognize that he was a good man, that he did do the right thing, and that he was loved.

I do know that it took every ounce of strength in my body and mind to convince him to let go of her neck.

"Dad! What the fuck are you doing? Let her go…." He didn't.

I saw the red in his eyes. "I'll kill this bitch!" he responded.

"Dad, I know. Please. Dad, it's Anthony, your son. Look at me, let her go." I pleaded in a calm collective voice.

He looked at me, eyes bulging, teeth clenched. I had seen my dad in this mode before. I watched him manhandle my uncle, his younger brother, after he abused his step son and wife. My dad also broke my mother's nose causing the division and strife in my own life. Seeing him step up and support his sister-in-law gave me hope that he had moved on and healed himself from the demons of his past.

But as I pleaded with him to not hurt his wife, while my brother and sisters were in the other room, gave me the truth of his reality. He wasn't healed. His trauma was too much. Even as he tried to heal his physical self, his psyche was still that of a PTSD plagued war veteran. He let her go and looked at me.

"I just needed to know that I was a good man….." he said, and he started to cry.

I told Janet to leave the room.

"Ant…." she whimpered.

"Janet. Please." I softly commanded.

She sniffled and bustled away. I heard the cushioned steps of my brother and sisters hastily returning to their rooms. I looked at my dad, eyes still bulging and breathing hard.

"Dad what happened?"

He proceeded to tell me how the movie affected him. And how he just needed to "know".

"Know what?" I was confused.

"To know I'm a good man" his voice was pleading to me. Like he was begging for verification that he could die a "good man".

My dad's cancer had come back with vengeance. He was given a time period to live, and as he put it, he was "short", a term he referenced to from his days in Nam. The fact of the matter was he only had a few months to live and he was preparing to die. I knew why he stayed away from watching war movies. I knew why we never went to watch the fireworks on July 4th. I knew why he cried at the Vietnam Memorial and why he so painstakingly painted his "paint by number" painting of the memorial at home. The care he took in the soldiers of the painting. The uniforms and badges of rank. As his son, I knew what he couldn't tell me.

I certainly watched *all* of the Vietnam War movies of the 1980's. I played *Platoon* by myself in my back woods as a kid. I had a "War" themed birthday party where everyone dressed up for war, and we played with toy guns and ran through the woods all day, pretending to kill each other. Cursing and ordering commands at each other. Taking prisoners and pretending we had P.O.W camps. It was as if, even though he wasn't around when I was a child, I knew somehow that this was a theme to life, my life, and the lives of my bloodline.

Even when we were back in each other's lives, he never spoke of any of that. He didn't even show me his purple heart. That honorable piece of history was only found after he died. Tucked away, in a box in the garage. Men never speak on what truly hurts them. I continued that same practice with Alyson and my family.

I felt trauma. I was educated on how to identify and treat trauma. I was reliving many traumatizing events in my life, and the YLA was just bringing everything back to the forefront. I never told Alyson about my first day. By the time she returned home, late Sunday evening, I was already asleep and disappointed that she didn't come home in the afternoon as she said she would. That Monday morning I got myself up early and quietly. I didn't tell her how bad I wanted to see her and the baby. How in such a short period of time so much had surfaced for me. I didn't share my anxiety and insecurities about the things I knew this job was going to make me do.

There are things a man needs to push out of his head in order to remain focused and sharp, especially when trauma is swirling around causing a chaotic whirlwind of emotions that can consume one's energy and ability to perform any action. I felt like I was creating a quality balance of leaving my head at home, and just taking my body to work.

The days were long, and my time with my family was never long enough. Alyson and I tried to stay grounded. We would go on long walks through the back side of Panther mountain, in the Catskills. It was a preserve so there were no trails, just the rugged rocky trail off of a road we drove my Forester up with excitement. Even Alyson would get filled with joy as I would drive over rocks and shift carefully, as the car faced the sky. When we would get to the top, it would be completely silent. We never understood why there were no bird sounds. The first time we went to the top of the mountain we became startled as we felt there was someone, or something watching us. And in the middle of Nowhere, Catskill Mountains, with a baby we didn't take any chances. But we kept going back. It was our spot.

I would always hope that the baby would fall asleep on the ride up there. Alyson and I would leave him in the car and we would go have sex somewhere in the woods like we used to do when we first met. Her and I would hike into the woods to one of my climbing spots. She never rock climbed with me, but she would assist and spot me. She would tell me how crazy I was while I was climbing. I'd smoke a spliff, and then we would let nature consume our appetites. I needed moments like that again. I needed reminders of how good life was at home. I needed to know how special my love was, and how much that love would keep me sane.

But love can only do so much. And like all consuming energies, love needs to be fueled, cared for, nurtured, and appreciated. In those moments I thought we were filling up our tank , refueling our desires for each other, and watering what was to be the growth of our love.

In long term relationships love usually fades like pencil writing on paper. It's still there, but it's not very legible and one finds themself trying to make out the words, squinting, focusing, using one's memory as a guide to correctly reimagine what the words said. That's what happens to love. We know it's there, we know what the words *did* say at one point in time. We will refocus, look a little deeper, try to remember all the good that was probably there, and assume that we remembered correctly. But we do lose meaning. We do forget, and we find it hard to read the messages we wrote to ourselves about love.

What tends to take the place of the memories, are the present realities that love created. Those realities come in the form of bills, rent and mortgages, children's clothes, trips to the doctor's, family visits and play dates, and most of all, loneliness. Two people come together to be one. They spend all their time together loving each other, putting each other first. Then one day, the couple will stop and realize, or so often it's one party that realizes, that their time together is no longer about their time together. But now, together, they give their time to others.

As this pattern of behavior continues, the giving of love to all around and not to each other, couples are left sitting together, quiet, emotionless, alone, with thoughts they no longer share, and wait for the next time they can see someone other than their partner. They long to see the "other" people they give love to, because they no longer give it to their partners.

Although my salary increased we were loaded with debt from months of me not working. It seemed like we weren't making any progress. My hate for that farmhouse apartment grew deeper, resentment started to creep in. *"Is this what I'm sacrificing everything for? To live here and work at the YLA. Imprisoning my own people, my people I swore to free? Is this my life?"* Again I had all of these thoughts.

I was lost in a forest of thoughts and emotions. My mountainous dreams seemed to be overshadowed by the depths of the valleys I was lost in. Then I received a phone call that would change everything.

While my dad was in his last months of life my uncle G came to stay with us. He was my dad's nephew, so technically he was my cousin. The only son of my dad's eldest sister. He and my dad had a bond that I envied. They hustled together, went to war, had each other's back, and both he and my dad were real street vets, as well as military vets. When I was younger my dad told him to have a talk with me, as he lived rather close when I was a teenager. I was making a lot of money as a street dealer. G, as I called him, was fascinated by my ability to earn good money on the streets, alone, with no support, and he recognized my "real" ability.

"I'll take a kid like you, you making your own money and all, and turn you into a fucking beast!"

And he did.

After my dad died we started a real estate investment company. I had plenty of money saved up, he considered himself a financial wizard, and together we set out to claim the midwest as real estate adventure capitalists. We were street guys with money, looking to make our money legit. What better way than to buy and invest in real estate in the areas of Cleveland and Detroit, where New York money can go a long way.

The long and short of that story is money and blood don't mix. As street guys we knew this, and when we started to clash we recognized what was what, and we ended our legit business together. He remained close to me, and I to him. Even when you don't do dirt with the family, you never forget what the family is capable of, and when you'll need those capabilities.

G called me randomly. He asked how things were going, about Alyson, the baby, and how the job was. We always talked real so I gave it to him straight. I told him everything. Above all we were family and he became a father figure to me. He was there for my dad's last days. We cried together and smoked and drank our pain away, together. So I was comfortable telling him my "man fears". He asked what my salary was, and I told him,"$55K".

"Shit bro! How'bout this. You find a house, we put our money together and I got you, but I need you to do something for me." he responded.

That was always his line,"....but, I need you to do something for me."

I felt he could sense my desperation, my internal struggle to do the "right thing", to not die broke and broken like my dad. In classic street predator fashion he preyed on my weaknesses.

"No doubt! What's that" with no hesitation I inquired.

I should have known better.

There was a good reason that after our real estate venture that I didn't think of doing anything concerning money with G for the last ten years. But the devil always finds you at your lowest moments in life, presents to you light in the form of a trusting soul to lead you out of darkness. In the chaos of the mind, the devil seems to provide peace and stability out of all the madness. I didn't have the grace of patience to endure any longer.

My faith was already fleeting and I was grabbing for the reality of life, its harshness, its coldness as reminders of what life really was. That being the constant balance of both negative and positive, or good and bad, whatever you want to call it. That balance of life, and the mismanagement of that balance, can dictate years of unknown repercussions or benefits. One never knows the influences of a decision until after the decision is made. We tend to make permanent decisions based on temporary situations, and the ramifications of our actions are never seen until they slap you in the face.

"You're gonna need to make more money too, right?" He continued. "So here's what I want you to do. Find us a house that is large enough for both of us. Ya' see I can't stay here in the VA, I ain't dying in this bitch. And you made me a promise when your dad was alive. So here it is. Let's get ahead of the legalization of weed in NY that's coming soon and start our own farm. I know you got the skills, I foot the set up cost, let's set up distribution and make it happen. That will supplement your income, allow us to get a large enough house for you, the baby and Alyson, and me too. Then when I die, you get the house, and you'll have a good setup for the future."

It was like he knew what I needed to hear. Even though we were three states away, he could smell it in the air. All hustlers do, they smell opportunity, smell money just yearning to be spent and made. They can see the "want" in a buyer's eyes and can masterfully sell ice to an Eskimo, in the arctic, in a blizzard, and convince them that they not only need the ice, but that they need *more* ice.

I knew G. I watched him outwit unsuspecting sellers to drop to a Cash I never thought they would go to on deals. I watched him call out predatory lending practices, in the middle of a contract phase for a property purchase, and force them to provide a better interest rate. He knew how money talked and he knew how to make it talk for him. He would say,"Yeah, ya' know what, I'll just buy it with cash."

He'd wink at me as they would explain that they would need more time to redraw the contracts. We would then make some moves on the street, which always involved me doing some middle of the night driving and picking up, dropping off, and collecting. We had an ex-con on our team who was a master forger and counterfeiter. He would draw up bank documents, paychecks, transfer documents, anything we needed with exact precision.

We ensured we both had multiple bank accounts in New York and Ohio. We would create a paper trail of transfers and paychecks, usually from fake out of state construction companies, that I "worked' for. We did all this during the weeks they needed to have a large cash purchase capability verified. Once they saw that the money was legitimately there, we would always get a call, with an apology, and how after "refiguring" and "taking into consideration" and blah blah blah, they would magically come up with a much better interest rate.

"They need to know we have money like white people." He would say."And that we know money just like white people do. They can't fuck with you if you know the game." And he was right.

"Go big Ant" He said. "We need a large house. Together we should be able to get a $300k to $350K house, and be set. Whatchya think?"

A hustler knows when the opportunity is ripe. A desperate hustler will find opportunity even if it really isn't there. I knew what I could do with front money for this operation. I knew I had Rick to help with distribution. Not once did I think of any impact of my actions on Alyson and my baby boy.

A man only knows he has to provide. A hustling man will do anything short of a real crime to do so. But a deal with the devil is a deal with the devil, no matter how bright it shines, or the growth potential of the outcome may appear to be, and with that, I agreed.

Chapter 12

A Trip to The Land

I believe it was the French intellectual Voltaire who said, "The more a man knows, the less he speaks." The Enlightenment philosopher and writer, like many great thinkers of the time, rejected the authority of the church. He believed that man defined his own destiny, and that "reason" was to be the great influencer of the time, not "fear of damnation" as taught by the church. This enlightenment was the foundation for what we now hold true as our modern reality. We are no longer forced to pray with our collective thoughts and assets are no longer completely dedicated to the allocation of the church. We have freedom of expression, religion, and speech. We have individualism.

Ironically, Voltaire did not believe in democracy. He believed that the king, in his rational and "reasonable" mind, with the assistance of great philosophers such as himself, would do what was best for the welfare of his subjects. Voltaire believed that the common man did not have the intellectual capacity, nor the self control, needed to govern. He believed that it was not in the common man's DNA to rule, and that they only followed "mob rule". And that is what was precisely preventing the common man from grasping the tangible necessities, whether monetarily, spiritually, mentally, or physically, needed to maintain dominion over themselves, and the masses.

Voltaire was a man who made great wealth scamming a bond lottery system created by the French government to raise money for the wars. He teamed up with other "enlightened" men of his time, and together they bought a vast majority of the bonds. He consolidated his earnings and invested back into the government arms business, investing hundreds of thousands of dollars into the manufacturing of weapons. This he did to ensure his own freedom, after being imprisoned for over a year in the Bastille for exposing the fallacies of the French Monarchy. And of course it worked, and he, and many others are now credited with the ultimate historical change in the thinking, actions, and beliefs of our shared present condition.

It's not like your common man understands the genesis of his thoughts and actions. The men at the YLA, the veterans who were proud to defend democracy and our freedoms at home, don't walk around quoting enlightened philosophers. They rarely make connections to the patterns of control. Yet, they find themselves so eager to defend theory and practice that they have little understanding of. They understand the basics - freedom. Freedom of speech, thought, rights to bear arms, and all that is encompassed in the American constitution. They often fail to understand the benefits the men credited for this change in history were seeking for themselves. All men seek power and influence, some find themselves in a better position to do so more than others.

"Shit, the man just showed that no matter what, a man needs money to have any type of influence or say in society. Period." Rick responded in his usual smooth response.

We were taking the five hour drive to Cleveland to meet G and to set up the groundwork for our operation. We had to discuss distribution, set up costs, projected overhead costs, and how the operation would be handled long term. These sorts of talks didn't happen over the phone. It was code, like Volataire said. We knew we couldn't talk, and therefore we didn't. And hence, the five hour car ride in the middle of the night across the state.

We had left at 11pm, and figured getting there at 430am in the morning gave us time to get some sleep for a little bit, have our meeting over breakfast, and be home by 6pm the next evening. That may sound crazy, but for us, that was just how we handled business. We had made many trips as teenage twentie something year olds, seeking opportunities and angles in every, and on any, corner. But for that five hour trip I was able to release a little of what I had bottled up.

I still was keeping many experiences from the YLA from Alyson, and was becoming an expert at deflecting her inquiries about the job. She was spending more and more time at her mothers house while I worked. The patterns being formed were isolating. My schedule was not consistent, but Alyson's was. She would spend Thursday to Sunday in the valley. Come home late Sunday night, well after I was asleep. She would then be home from Monday to Thursday morning.

"It's not like I care that I don't see her." I explained to Rick."But I don't really get to see my kid. Not sure how I feel about that...I mean it's harder to leave on the days they're home, but then it's a breeze coming home alone....but I don't know." I tried to expand. Lost in weed smoke and balancing my thoughts about our trip and business plan, and the YLA.

"Take your man Voltaire, right." Rick kept it going. "Even he, with his intellect and quote un quote wisdom, look at what he did with the game. He understood it for what it was, figured out how to play the game, when to make his move, got the right people, then Boom! He made his power move, and they couldn't fuck with him after that. He already dismantled their whole shit, with his freedom of expression and thought. Right?"

I felt where he was going with that. I couldn't help my mind from cycling through the depths of my own circumstance. My struggle to gain power. In a system controlled by big men. Just like the streets. Right there, taking that car ride, with my right hand man. Like I always had. Doing what I needed to do to survive.

"No doubt!" I replied like my mind didn't just race through all of those thoughts, and more.

He continued. "It's like from the beginning they were recreating the game to their own benefit. My man didn't want to be king. He wanted to be one of those dudes that gets to influence the king. And since your spot has no king, they're all vying for position. And it sounds like some of those ma'fuckers are trying to recreate their own game."

He was right. And that's why Rick was my man.

There was no "king" at the YLA. Just a temporary director in Sue Conklin, who just wanted to do the mental health side of the agency. The Assistant Director Mike Larson who was, as the story was told, sent straight to the office on his first day on the job after causing a real riot. The kids really tried to kill him, is what was said.

This all came from Vernon Smith. So when I asked him to give more details to fulfill the cliffhanger, all he said was, "Cus, he's a fucking bitch!" And he spit into his facility plastic cup and cleaned out the brown slop of tobacco from his bottom lip. After he told me that story, and the look he gave me with shit remains of tobacco lingering on his lips, it hit me. Every time Larson goes to serve a resident he takes me with him. In fact, he would wait until I got on my shift, and do them right before he left, at 6pm. Usually leaving me and the others to handle the anger and fury of a young male being told he's losing certain privileges coveted by the incarcerated, or even worse, extending or pulling release dates.

At first I thought that I was the muscle for him to handle these situations. There were times where my ability to talk, de-escalate, and reason with the young men, had saved him. He reinforced everything there was to know about running any shift I ran, and by the book. He would commend me on having integrity and that it was seldom seen in "these places." I started to wonder if the other AODs were plotting behind my back and sticking me with him, as his bitch. I felt like I was the bitch to the bitch of the facility. I couldn't take that shot to my manhood.

So one day, when I arrived for my 2-10 shift, Holland and Burch were outside of Unit 1. A resident was pacing back and forth, and they were obviously trying to talk him down from something. I went into my office and strapped up my cuffs and clipped my walkie talkie onto my belt and hustled back down to assist. It took me about four minutes, or less, to get back, and to read Holland and Burch's energy, and to assess the kid - Ross. He was a proud "bug out" kid, meaning he'd just go crazy for no reason. It also meant that at any time he could stop the program, cause disruption, almost always ending in violence, and more paperwork.

He was one of three in a set of triplets, all identical. I couldn't help but wonder how could all 3 boys be locked up? What was going on for all 3 of them, being separated, being all by themselves, and they all still ended up behind bars? As I wondered about him, I also thought about how much I didn't like him. He would always turn off the Playstation in the game room while younger kids played, or simply refuse to leave any room at any given time, and dare you to restrain him.

The majority of the time he would pull his antics on the shift prior to mine. He was the resident who took the 7 inch piece of plastic from the light in his ceiling on my first night. He was still there, after three months. Two full cycles of kids came and went, and only a few residents there knew about that one particular incident, there were no other residents remaining from that night, except Ross. He couldn't have been more than 115 lbs soaking wet, of pure bonafide crack baby with lean muscle and all skin and bone. Sadly, he was now a 15 year old young angry black man. Always,"Ready, to fuck you up!"

So walking over there, I knew Holland and Burch were just waiting to dump this kid on the ground, like they've done a handful of times before.

"What's good Ross?" I asked as I approached them.

"Naw Ace, nothing's good nigga...shit!" He responded, fists clenched as he stared intently at Burch.

Holland tried to explain how After Care, aka probation, had delayed their side of the paperwork, and how they were still lining things up for his release.

"It's not like they're 'pulling' his date. They had to make sure he had a home to go to." Holland tried to explain to me. He looked at Ross and continued," Your aunt is setting things up with them, she's trying to do that right now Ross, but I gotta tell ya' this doesn't help your cause bro."

"*Ok*" I thought to myself, "*I mean that's kinda what it is.....*" But I didn't share my thoughts. I was constantly regulating what I said, how I said it, who, where, and when. Always careful. Instead I looked at Holland. He blew air out his lips and shrugged his shoulders. His eyes looked at me to tell me that he's trying, and that it was out of his control. I looked at Burch. Same look he always had, "Just say the word..." was staring back behind the glaze of his eyes.

"Ross, my man...." but before I could say anything else he took his shirt off.

"Naw fuck that, ya'll sending me home right now!" He demanded and flexed for the audience, which was the side brick wall of Unit 2, some trees, and the grassy hill they all feared because they had heard about the "kid who broke his leg". He turned his back. I knew he was just waiting for us to make a move. I also knew that in our last administrators meeting we discussed that if he was restrained again we were going to transfer him to Brookwood, a maximum secure facility. There, his time would more than likely start all over again.

When you threaten someone who already has nothing, all they can do is laugh in the face of oppression, and dare their oppressors to make their move. That's what Ross did. He waited. I knew he was waiting, whether or not Holland and Burch did, I did. He needed the violence. He needed to get his anger out. The kid needed to go somewhere else. So with his back turned, shirt off, posing no threat, I went for restraint number two. For me, I felt like *I had to do it*. For being Larson's bitch. To show I wasn't afraid to enact violence on a given notice. To show myself that I could make the transition from teacher man to the darkside. Most of all, because I didn't want Holland and Burch to use violence on him. I couldn't allow them to hurt my people. So if it had to go down, I was going to do it.

In a perfect restraint you put your arms straight in front of you, slide them down the shoulders and the side of the arms, as the resident has his back to you. When you get to the elbows, you bring your arms in between their arms and in the midsection, interlocking your elbows onto their arms, and placing your hands flat in between the soft spot of their shoulder blades. A little pressure and their arms go straight back. Pushed forward and they are easily moveable. But that only happens when the resident is standing still, and does not resist.

"What usually happens?" Rick asked and hit the spliff.

I looked deep into the dark highway. As always, just he and I on the road. Making money. Putting it all on the line just to make sure we got ahead.

But, looking at Ross, knowing he had 2 brothers just like him, hoping his aunt could get her shit together. I thought about my son. Ross took a deep breath. Before he could exhale I made my move. I caught Burch off guard because I heard him say, "Oh shit!"

Holland called, "Code White", as if he was just asked what he wanted for lunch.

Ross brought his arms close to his body, and as I struggled to get my arms in between his arms and body, he bent over. I felt him try to go to the ground. If a resident falls to the ground, and is not in a restraint, we can't touch them and we cannot pick them up off the ground. Now, I'm trying to keep him from going to the ground, get my arms into position, and not hurt him, all at the same time.

"Coming in to assist in a Standing Double Sir." stated Burch, and he went for his right arm, and I continued to get a lock on his left.

He head butted Burch and the top of his eye split open. We were close, shoulder to shoulder, and as his blood rushed out, so did the cheap beer and USA Gold cigarettes stench.

"Your bleeding Burch, stand down!" I ordered.

In that split second of a move, I was able to secure both of my arms behind his back, and as he tried to bend over again, squeezing my arms into his side, I pulled him up and his feet came off the ground. I slammed them back down and kept him on his feet.

But that was just the beginning. Now that I had him, we had to move him. We were in the middle of a shift change, so I wasn't going to bring the shit storm on to the unit 10 minutes before they were supposed to go home. Doing that could also excite the other residents creating a heated climate for the next shift to step into. As I thought of that, Holland said,"Let's bring him to Rec Room 2."

Although that was on the other side of the grounds. It was the most strategic room. It had backdoor access to a transport ramp, and we never used it. Holland stepped in to assist in a Standing Double Escort, and he said,"Alright Ross, now don't fuck around! Were gonna fucking move you. Do you understand?" It wasn't a question.

When any law enforcement agent asks you that, it's never a question, only the warning that they are about to exercise the force they are authorized to use. I let Holland take the lead, not only because of our sizes being so polar opposite, but because I knew what was about to happen. I didn't want to be a part of it anymore. I told him to take the Single Escort position, and I radioed to CSU.

Everytime Ross tried to shake loose, Holland would squeeze him, and the kid would yell out and stop, and go limp. But he was just saving his energy. He let Holland and I escort him through the main gate. Enter the main entrance, down the long corridor of classrooms, to the end where there was an old double door entry; it used to be a barracks during the military days. It was in that small corridor, between two doors - the door to the hallway and the door to the Rec Room - where he decided to make his move. While I went to unlock the door into the Rec Room he lifted up, placed his feet on the wall, and pushed off sending Holland into the corner of the small, 8 x 8 space we were sharing. In one motion, I opened the door and grabbed his legs. Without having to communicate we both rushed him into the Rec room. I put his legs down and Holland barked,"Are you gonna fucking chill out or what Ross!?" and he let him go with a toss to the ground.

The shift change commenced and in came Levy Simms, as Op2 for the day. I was glad to see him. I instructed him to do the post restraint paperwork with Ross and follow medical protocol if he insisted, but not to push if he didn't want to go. Often they don't want to go to the medical unit, but a bleeding heart young YDA will convince them to go and then they turn it up in the nurse's office, or worse yet, they really are injured and they report it. I wanted time to talk to Conklin to see if we would be transporting him that day. If so, that meant Simms was no use anywhere else for shift, or at least until the kid was gone.

Smith and Thompson were already in Conklin's office when Holland and I arrived. Holland said,"That piece of shit has to go!" like his word was the last word. Smith sucked his teeth, and Thompson reported in his Marine way, "The transport was already on its way" and he was going to "Brookwood, and to be ready around 6pm."

"Great, just in time for dinner." I said.

No one paid me any attention. But for me, having our evening program and dinner, without an Op2, would put more stress on me to keep the peace in an already increasingly heated environment. But what did that matter to them?

When the transport van arrived it had to drive around the facility and pull up to the back where Ross was being held. He heard the second steel curtain of a gate open up, and when he saw the dark blue van pull up outside the window, he went off.

"Code White" Simms radioed.

I ran to the Rec room as fast as I could. Opened the doors and ran to assist Simms who had his back pinned to the wall inside the bathroom stall. When he saw me, he tried to step back and put himself in a position to get him out of the stall, but Ross slipped out. I was still in mid run and grabbed him in somewhat of a bear hug and we both fell to the ground. I still tried to get my arms in position for a proper seated restraint and envisioned Simms grabbing his legs and us carrying Ross to the van. Instead, I struggled with him and when Simms came out of the stall to help me, Ross kicked him right in the face busting his bottom lip. Simms secured his feet anyway, and that made my adrenaline kick in even more.

"AOD to CSU, ready for transport." I radioed. We weren't ready, but I knew that Conklin and Pearson, who was the counselor for the shift, would come.

During that time Simms and I were able to get him to his feet, extra pressure on his knees by Simms helped out......I faded out.

Maybe because I was tired, or just way too high so early in the trip, or maybe because I didn't want to share anymore.

"Did you get the nigga in the van?" Rick pressed.

"Yeah." I replied slowly, "We did."

I didn't tell him how Ross kicked, bit, and screamed the entire ten yards we had to carry the kid to get him into the van. How he head butted Simms, and spit blood on Pearson. How he told us all he was going to "kill" us and how we couldn't "hold him down." How Simms was shaking after the van left. Conklin asked me if I was OK. I asked Levy if he was OK. His lip was quivering, and you could tell he was just trying to hold it together.

"Damn bro! You let that shit go out." I said, and reached for the spliff and put my lighter to it. I looked up at the sky and it appeared lit up. We were on the Southern Tier of New York, on an empty highway, but there was this glow that I couldn't keep my eyes off of.

"How's the baby and Alyson?" Rick asked.

"Shit bro. My schedule is so fucked up, she just asks me when my pass days are and plans on being home for that." I told him

"Dam bro, shit's like that?"

The schedule really was killing me. McIntyre managed it and now that we had more YDAs he was trying to consolidate his own power. He would give his buddies and long timers of the YLA the shifts that they wanted, usually the 6-2 shift. He was putting the new guys, like my guys Icheman, Cash, and Johnson, on the 2-10 shift. The AODs seemed to balance the 6-2 and 2-10 pretty evenly, and where there was a gap or any overlap, that's where he would schedule me. Certain YDAs got their overtime, certain YDAs were prevented from getting any extra hours, and some would be stuck with scheduled doubles in order to benefit another vets' prime schedule.

A kingdom with no king.

If there were no king, would there have been a Voltaire? If there wasn't some form of oppression would the seeds of enlightenment ever have grown at all? The tree that grew into the Age of Reason has borne the fruit of man's eternal quest and struggle, that being the idea of freedom. Aren't we all men of the state? We all have positions. We all had roles to play for the state. Voltaire was imprisoned when he spoke against the crown. Yet when he got his freedom and was released he invested in the state and found a position within the state to flex his own power and influence. He was completely motivated by his own expanding self-interest. Perhaps, I thought, I need to tap into my own inner Voltaire. Learn the system, play the game better, exercise my power more wisely and with calculation, and gain a better position to be able to flex my own power and influence.

"Ma'fucking Volataire!" I said emphatically.

"Yeah!" Rick responded with a laugh.

"You know they were saying that we could see the northern lights from mad far away this year." I tried to shift. "I'm pretty sure that's what that is. Over there, up in the sky that glow. It's the Northern Lights!"

Rick lit the spliff, looked at me and said, "You know I've seen the Northern Lights before, right? Like...I've really been there?"

Chapter 13

Making it Happen

My dad gave me three pieces of advice that I had held on to and found to be true. The first being, a real man needs to be able to provide for himself. A man needs to be able to cook, clean, iron his own clothes, and maintain his own house. "A man should not need a woman for that" he would say.

Second, you can say anything to anyone; it's all in how you say it. A man needs to know his audience and gauge the manner in which he addresses the audience if he is to be truly heard. Third, he would ask me in question form. He would ask me, "What does a rock do when you throw it into the water?"

I would respond with, "It makes a splash" or "It sinks to the bottom."

Then he would provide the simple answer that made so much sense, and I later saw much of life this way.

He would say, "When a rock is thrown into the water, it makes a ripple."

Every action we make leaves a ripple in our lives. The larger the action, or stone, the bigger the ripple. Sometimes we commit actions that create title waves and it can be destructive and have unintended consequences, or it manifests an entire new world. He would challenge me and ask about the size ripples or waves my moves were making. He would ask me if I was going big enough. I didn't understand what he was trying to tell me when I was young. He wanted me to make moves that mattered. To make moves that made waves, not just ripples. He wanted me to be bigger than what I saw myself as. However, he was never shown how to maximize his own ripple effect and therefore couldn't show me either. Like most men, I was left to make sense of a dead man's words.

Our trip to Cleveland went as scheduled. After the long dark drive that was filled with moments of realization of my own ripples. We arrived in Ohio around 430am. We slept until 9 and met with G for breakfast at 930. The three of us put together a solid plan that we all had separate roles in, and that made it all work. G was going to help me purchase a house. A house that was large enough for me and the family, G, and adequate space for the growing operation.

"We need a large basement or attic, but we should make sure we have space so we are not on top of each other. You know I like to listen to my music loud, at all crazy hours and shit." G was very clear.

Rick already had equipment ready to go and we just needed a few more items which he said he could cover. My role was to find the house, and to run the operation. Rick would handle distribution, as he maintained his street connections and could move the weight we needed in order for the operation to be lucrative.

We needed to produce at least 20 lbs a cycle. We would sell wholesale for $3000 a pound, that was $60,000, every 10 weeks, providing on paper $300,000 a year. That was for our five year plan to build capital for larger and legit investments. It was realistic, we were capable, and we solidified the plan with a handshake, and a monetary tag of $3000 each in the pot. We would hold that for lawyer fees if they were ever needed.

Just as scheduled we were back on the road by 12pm. The ride home was like most rides home from a long trip. Als talk, more sleeping, and the occasional affirmations on the original plan for the trip. We had a difficult time deciding where we would purchase the house. Rick lived in the valley and G wanted to be there for the VA hospital at West Point. I had to take over that part of the conversation. I was to be the primary facilitator of this operation, I was going to be caring for the growing 24 hours a day, that was my role. There was no way I could take on that responsibility and drive 2 hours everyday to work. It had to be upstate.

"Besides," I added, "property is half the cash upstate, and the property taxes, in comparison to the valley, are nothing. We're talking tens of thousands of dollars cheaper." That got them.

G knew his money would go further up there, even if it wasn't ideal. I knew Rick would see it that way as well. They both agreed. But that didn't stop Rick from trying to persuade me to think differently for the next 5 hours. He wanted to be closer so he could help set up and take care of things between my weird work schedule. He had a point.

I was dreading going back to work. I had to work the 10-6, 2-10, 2-10, 10-6, 2-10 shift's, that was my schedule from Friday at 10pm to Tuesday at 10pm. When I described the schedule to Rick he gave me a look of disbelief I hadn't seen before.

"Bro! That's like…working the entire week through, sleep in between shit, what the fuck?" There were no philosophical words left to share. We were too tired, and my body was already preparing for work.

I thought about my work schedule. How I would be reporting to work on Friday night for the overnight, the one late night shift that things most likely have some sort of disruption, go home to sleep for a few four hours, work another eight hour shift and come home late, sleep six hours, work the overnight again, sleep four hours, and work another late night eight hour shift. As bothered as I was about Alyson not being home, when reflected on the work hours, on that long drive back to her, I understood why she was doing what she was doing. But that didn't make anything better. I became even more bitter and felt less supported than before.

Surprisingly, when I got home at 6pm, as scheduled, Alyson and the baby were home. Greeted with a warm hug and kiss, and the greatest words a dad could hear, "We missed you!"

Her greeting moved me. I felt a sense of calm and ease, and a sense that maybe everything was going to be alright after all. Alyson and I stayed up after the baby went to sleep and talked.

"So, how is G?" She asked.

"He's doing ok. He's still stuck in his bed, but his spirits are good." I responded.

I had told her that G had had another bad medical situation, which he was always having, and that Rick was driving out there with me because we needed some time to catch up.

"Is that it?" She asked inquisitively.

"No… it wasn't." I took a deep breath. "G wants to buy us a house. He's sick of being stuck in Cleveland and dealing with the VA out there. He wants to move back here."

"So…he's buying us a house?" She was confused. And I didn't really want to say what was happening. But I did. Sort of.

"Well. He said if he could buy a house large enough for all of us, that would be cool with him."

"Is… that….cool?" She tacked on quickly with a tone of uncertainty.

I knew what she meant. I had shared with her some of our exploits and she never found them as fascinating and thrilling as I did. I could tell that she never wanted my past to have a place in our present life. She would dish out blows about G. Even before she met him she felt he manipulated me, that he only cared about making money, and that he didn't care about who he hurt in the process.

"What do you mean? Yes! It's fucking cool! It's really fucking good, Al!" shocked by her unwillingness to see any positivity.

"Well what does he want you to do for him?" and she looked at me as if she knew the answer.

"Look, the man is like my dad, I owe him, you wouldn't understand that shit." I tried to walk away.

"Do you owe him? Or do we owe him, Anthony?"

"I have to work the overnight shift, and then I'm there all fucking week. I need to go to bed." I turned and went to the bathroom.

"So, I'm going back to the valley tomorrow morning. I wanted to see you because I knew your schedule would be crazy. If you give me a minute I'll put the baby down, and you can come lay with me..."

"I need to sleep. I'm shot. When will you be coming back?" I asked like I didn't care, and part of me really didn't.

"Anthony, you work all week."

"Ok, then I'll see you next week!" I was done. I brushed my teeth and checked out.

I slept on the couch that night so I would be able to actually sleep. My role was as a warm blanket for her while she snored, and the baby while he sweetly cooed a medley in my mind that was soft and beautiful but did nothing to promote sleep. The internal aggravation was festering, and I was infuriated by Alyson's response to G trying to do something for us. Her family wasn't trying to help us at all. They weren't coming up to see us, they just expected her and me to keep coming down to them. G was providing the only assistance, and the only assistance truly needed. We needed a home, a real home. Not a dank apartment in an old farmhouse. We were better than that. I was better than that. I slept hoping I would wake up and the week would be over already.

Of course it wasn't and there was something else brewing in the deep depths of the state, OCFS, and the YLA. State legislation had passed raising the minimum age to 18 for criminal offenses. And they were also offering step-downs for 18 year olds who were sentenced under the previous stature of the age of 16. Many young men were being transferred out of maximum security OCFS facilities, where they had spent years prior to the shift, to medium secure facilities like the YLA.

Some were being shipped out of Rikers Island where the juvenile population was far beyond capacity, safety, and any hope for dignity. Rikers is the hell that people imagine the worst floating island of a fortress prison could be. The youths that come out of there are never the same again, and the level of organized crime, corrupt and gang-affiliated guards, and the racist system that perpetuates the vicious cycle are not, and can not, be replicated anywhere else.

With OCFS changing its policies on restraints and the now mandated use of de-escalation techniques, along with the influx of transfers and the shuffling around of residents all over the state, facilities were under constant changes and inconsistent population numbers. This would affect staffing and facility management. So there was a very intense hiring period. From Industry near Rochester to Brookwood in Claverack, every facility was taking in new YDAs, YCs, and administrators, and with changes coming from above, OCFS was responding accordingly. And so was the YLA.

We had a full facility staff meeting scheduled, and it would be the first that I had attended. Full lunch spread, cake, danishes, coffee and juice. I was rather impressed with the spread. It was then that I realized how many new people the YLA had hired. I also realized what a blur the first few months on the job really were. Even drinking coffee and cracking jokes with Icheman and the other guys, in the back of my mind I felt uneasy.

I was thinking about G, and our deal. How he was willing to put four hundred thousand dollars on the line in a mortgage, and front money, just to start the whole thing. How he looked at me, saying "But you're gonna have to do your part...Rick, you're gonna have to do your part." I couldn't help but wonder what his real reason was. Then I came to the serious conclusion that I had no choice but to tell Alyson what we were doing.

Then Sue Conklin called us to attention.

"All right, everybody. I want to thank you for coming...." she provided the necessary formalities, and then said, "After being long overdue, I will be moving back to my position as Director of Mental Health..." I looked at the guys and they gave me the wide-eyed stare right back. I was praying that it was not going to be Mike Larson, but he was Assistant Director, maybe it was his time. And then she said, "I'd like to introduce you all to Gary Leichtenberger. Mr. Leichtenberger was the Assistant Director at Industry" - meaning he probably has been laying residents down for decades- "and has been with the state for 22 years now." - Exactly! - " Gary, will you stand up?" And then, he did.

Gary Leichtenberger. We had some really big men amongst us. Andrews was 6 '8, Holland 6' 4, Pearson 6 '4, Burnett 6' 3, all probably close to, if not over, 300 lbs. Along with Icheman 6 '2 340 and Ericson at 6'1 360, these were all big country upstate farm boys. Gary Leichtenberger had battled prostate cancer years before. I assumed that in his recovery, to ensure the safety of his facility life at the infamous Trion facility, and then his long days at Industry, he had to have become obsessed with steroids. This man was huge. I'd never witnessed a serious bodybuilder before.

Weightlifters are different. They pick things up and put them down. Bodybuilders do just that, they build their bodies. Leich was

6' 1 and had been building his body for the last 10 years. When he took his hit from cancer for a year and a half, he went berserk from using steroids. Constant muscle and jaw flexing, veins coursing in his forehead under his blond spiky fade haircut. His light blue polo shirt had nowhere to go, it was stuck to every muscle it covered. The captain of our facility from the military days was still present, although he didn't do much. Gregg Perney was a combat veteran Master Chief Sergeant, and stood 6' 4 and had a barrel for a chest. Even Perney looked at Leichtenberger as the beast he was.

All of the YDAs, and faculty and staff members were sitting down in organized rows of chairs. Larson, Conklin, Sharon and Bernard, the pay grade 22 who did paperwork on the overnight shift, sat in the front as the important people. The rest of us, Perney, Holland, Pearson, Thompson, Sparaco, MacIntyre, and I all stood, in the same big man stance, shoulders tight, arms crossed, and rested into the heels, like men do. We watched and listened.

"Listen fellas." His voice was deep, thick but not raspy, with a distinct central New York accent, and you could hear the violence in his voice. He continued, "I know that the YLA has had some issues, a lot of restraints, people getting hurt, staff have been put on 'hold' " - if a YDA is put on "hold" they can not perform a restraint until they have been through proper re-training, this happens if a staff member gets cited for performing a restraint improperly or a non designated restraint as per the guidelines of OCFS - "we can't have people not being able to do their jobs here gentlemen. That just can't happen. 69 restraints last month alone, Guys! What are we doing here? Now I know we are in the land of the lost, this place is like the freakin' land that time forgot here. I mean we have all that equipment just sitting there, get those kids out there, get them doing shit. We need to change the patterns of the YLA. You gotta dump a kid ya gotta dump a kid, but when we look at the numbers we have one kid getting dumped three times a day, what the hell is that?"

We were all a little surprised with how real he was coming, and glad that he saw what we saw. There was a rocking of bodies in agreement, head nods, and "Yups!" being said out loud in response. Was he giving us the green light to get control of the YLA?

"Who runs this place, the kids or the adults here, huh?" he didn't stop. I looked for Vernon Smith, he would have the lowdown on Leich. "*What was his take on this?*" I wondered. It later dawned on me that Smith was AOD at the time and he was running the units with minimal staffing, and that he previously had his meeting with Leichtenberger, and that the green light was already given.

"We have to get this place back gentlemen. What's our recent max here, 15 residents? C'mon fellas, with all the shifts going down in the agency, if we can't hold kids here they'll shut us down. We have to step up. I am telling you now, that I got your backs, but we gotta do things the right way. AODs that means you guys have to step up. It's you guys who run the shift. So, I'm expecting more from you all." We all gave the head nod in recognition and adjusted our bodies.

I knew that at that point in time that my presence at the YLA was rather insignificant. I did what I could by building relationships. I understood how to leverage their privileges and provided extra incentives for doing the "right thing". I met with parents if I was on duty for visits, checked in with them and their school work when I worked the day shift. I still wore my teacher clothes, minus the tie, under my now state-issued black fleece with "Cortes" embroidered on my right chest, the seal of New York on my left chest, and the American flag on my left arm. I was still unaccustomed to the handcuffs on my hip, the badge hanging on my neck. I may have followed the physical displays of an AOD; I stood like one, acted like one, but I wasn't really AOD yet. That had to be earned. I looked around at the men sitting in front of me. I started to formulate my team, and how I was going to silently make my move and how I was going to make it all happen. I looked at the other men in black and in uniform, I wondered what they were thinking.

I analyzed and calculated each of their mental responses to what was happening. Using all of the intelligence I had gathered reading these men, studying them, trying to figure out their motives, to better use them to my own advantage, by out manipulating them. I had them all down, they were all maneuverable and easy to read. And it came down to just one man, Mike Thompson.

Chapter 14

"Pippen And Jordan"

It became clear to me that life on the block, the corporate world, politics, and every single facet of life is dictated and organized around systems. Systems keep the organization and structure of all the functions in our shared reality. I even lost myself breaking them all down.

There are macrosystems that encompass our reality on a large scale. These macrosystems consist of our educational systems, forms of government, systems of laws, and our economic systems. Those systems have a role in what we call the exosystem, or our environment, which has external influence on us. And it is important to recognize that we have little control over that.

These influences are defined by our neighborhoods and communities, places of work, media sources and other tertiary external factors. We also live in our own system called the mesosystem, which includes our family, school, and our religious affiliations and organizations. This one system, the mesosystem, with the other two powers swirling around it, with all of their mass and influence, impacts the individual the most. Yet, all are heavily co-existing and affecting each other, like miniature galaxies, with the direct result of these dynamics being displayed on one singular apparatus, the individual human.

Around the individual, there is a new system created called the microsystem. This is where the impact of communities, schools, peers, family, and the such, have direct influence on the individual. If we were to go even further into the "micro" level, and farther beyond ourselves up into the "macro" level, we would find even larger systems at play which have tremendous influence on our shared reality. If we dive deeper into the micro level, we will come across internal systems: the digestive system, respiratory system, and nervous system.

Yet, if we go smaller we find cellular systems, and atomic systems, that define our natural world. If one were to extend above the human plane of existence, they will discover new planetary systems, solar systems, star systems, and galaxies working together as collective astronomical organisms. Here we find, just as in the depths of the micro world, the basis of our reality and the formation of what we define as real, whether elemental or scientific. The creation of all living and nonliving entities are dependent upon a system. No existence has derived itself from anything other than a functioning system. Everything that we know to be "real" is a by-product of, or an indirect by-product of, the gradual effects of some sort of system. Everything.

"Right! When I was in Iraq, it didn't matter the rank of the officers, or the equipment being moved, our transport system was a system, and they had to take orders from me, because that was the system." Thompson explained trying to connect to the depths of my understanding of our current shared reality.

I was making progress on Mike Thompson. There are several rules of engagement when seeking to influence other men, especially when you desire these men to participate in a shared reality that you envisioned. A shared reality being a product of the "motivating process of experiencing a commonality of inner states, attitudes or judgments, with others about the world". It was forming our commonalities that proved to be difficult. Yet, I found that our shared interest in sports, hating our home lives, and our desire to have full control over the facility was a great common ground. I ran with that, and he willingly followed.

Both of us had interesting childhoods. He shared with me that his dad was an alcoholic and treated his mother badly. His anger towards his dad made him join the Marines. He wanted to kick his father's ass so badly that he decided to be trained how to kill. He prided himself in his military tactical experience and how he had lost part of his hearing due to an explosion near his transport convoy. He shared other experiences that opened my eyes to the war in Iraq and what had happened to the men who were deployed there.

One story he told was about how the Iraqi kids would throw firecrackers on the roofs of the homes the soldiers were housed in. When they would ignite and explode the soldiers would often jump up and grab their weapons. Only to come to the realization that they were duped by local village children. For payback, he and his fellow Marines would give the children Slim Jims and would laugh at them after they ingested the American snack.

"Wait" I asked. "They're all Muslim there." I replied to him in order to gain a response that would inform me of his true character.

"Yeah, I know!" He quickly threw it back. "And we would say, 'Ha Ha see you in hell fuckers!" And he laughed saying "Muslims can't eat pork!"

I knew that. I also knew what he meant as soon as he said he had given them the Slim Jims. He encapsulated the American war experience for me. He was a true die-hard American who believed that America was the greatest because of brave men like himself. This so-called brave man poisoned innocent Iraqi children with American pork products, thought it was humorous, and expected me to feel the same. I pretended I did. I had my own mission and it was to win at all costs.

Mike and I continued to bond as our schedules allowed us to. We would often team up on the 2-10 shift, he would cover one unit and I would cover the other. Holland and he would manage unit 1 and Pearson and I would hold down unit 2. Most of the restraints that were still happening were a product of the 6-2 shift and still during the school program. Thompson and I would often devise plans in our 2-10 shift to motivate the residents to improve their behavior. We would bribe them with extra phone calls, snacks, music time, and whatever else made their eyes loosen up and soften their demeanor.

We had our share of flexing force and enforcement as well. One evening residents decided to "turn it up" right before lockdown for bedtime. Only a code Yellow was called, and we were able to get the residents into their cells with minimal difficulty. One youth decided to cover up his cell door window. This is a severe safety concern as the residents could hurt themselves and we wouldn't know, huge liability. So we couldn't allow him to do that.

"Gentry!" I commanded his attention through the door. "My man, I need you to take the paper off the window."

"Fuck that! I ain't doin' shit!" He responded with a false sense of strength.

"Gentry, I'm gonna have to come in there if you don't" I tried to reason with him.

"Come in here Cortes, and I'ma straight stab you! I fuckin' promise! I'll fuckin' stab you right in the fuckin' face!" Again, with a false sense of strength and ability.

Icheman was next to me. He looked at me with a deep sense of concern. I wasn't sure if it was because he was worried about me, which I did have a sense of, or himself. They all seemed to be protecting me like I was their "little" big brother. Maybe he was nervous because Gentry really did have a shank ready in his hands and was not afraid to use it.

"I gotta a shank, I'll use that shit. Don't fuckin' come in here!" Gentry reminded us as the thoughts raced.

"Gentry, my man." Again I tried to reason with him. "I'm going to give you another shot to do this, bro. Please do the right thing. Take. The. Paper. Off. Of. Your. Window!" I said with a voice that ensured it was about to go down if he did not comply.

"Nigga! Suck my Dick!" the universal response they all gave when they felt that they were ready for us to commence the violence.

Icheman looked at me with a sigh, and in a concerned voice asked, "So what are we going to do Ace?"

I could tell he was counting on me. My insecurity told me that he was worried about me getting stabbed and that he was losing trust in my ability to maintain order. But mostly, he was truly looking to me to do what was right. At that moment I didn't know what to do. I knew, by law, I couldn't leave him in his cell with the window covered. I also knew, by law, that if a resident threatened to use violence with a weapon that I had little discourse in any action I could take. I had to go in, disarm him, and ensure his safety.

I looked into Icheman. Not his eyes, or directly at him. I looked into him, and the huge 340-plus-pound country boy looked at me, as if he were a 12 year old kid expecting to receive the greatest secret of life ever told. As if it were already done, I said, "Nick, here's what we're going to do." And I gave him the plan.

"I'm going to unlock the door. He's going to try to stab me. Don't worry -

he won't. All YOU need to do is hook'em ASAP. That. Is. It. Do you understand?"

"Yes sir!" Icheman assured me.

"On 3" I said.

"Yes sir" Nick responded in sync.

With the key already in the lock, I counted down.

"1 - 2 -3" And I opened the door.

There are moments in life when instincts take over. What you know and do combines into an action that is not premeditated. Men in action, who are capable, do not conspire acts of violence. They can often predetermine motives of others and have a calculated response. They just need the proverbial green light. Only men capable of violence are able to do this. Men incapable of being threatening do not think this way.

The incapable man seeks exit strategies and ways to protect and cover what they deem to be threatened. The capable man sees a threat as a dare to display what he is truly capable of. It is always in the time of high threat, chaos, risk of loss and life that the capable man sees an opportunity to display their true nature as protector, defender, and the importance of their self-control. For if a man does not need to control himself, he is a threat to no one. It is the man who must maintain self-control at all times who is truly to be feared and regarded as a threat. I was in control, and I was the threat incarnate.

With a turn of the key, and a push on the door that left the keys in my hand, and an angry teenager in my sight, it was as if the entire world slowed down. I saw that he had a pen with a long nail sticking out of it, it was in his right hand. He was standing in the center of his room, his bed on his left side, Icheman's side. I took one step into his cell and he lunged at me with the pen shank. Blocking his right hand with my left forearm, I grabbed his wrist with my right hand and swung him towards the door, right into the grasp of Icheman. With all of his country strength he grabbed Gentry and perfectly placed him into a standing single restraint. Icheman squeezed and Gentry winced out loud in pain.

"What? Now you're hurt?! You wanna fuckin' kill me muthafucker!" I looked into his eyes in a manner only familiar to me in a former decade of street life. Gentry saw it. Icheman saw it, and he loved it.

I think Nick ended up sharing this ordeal as the other men who did not witness seemed to give a new level of respect. Thompson even asked, "Did that fucker really try to shank you? You should've broken his fucking wrist" As he laughed.

He and I were able to build through the violence. Leichtenberger was putting pressure on everyone to maintain order. At times we did, and there were other times that he set us up for failure. No matter what was happening Leich's response to any situation was completely unpredictable. If we did something right, he still would give us a hard time because it wasn't done in the "Industry" way, his former facility. If we actually did do something wrong he would have a steroid-induced fit of anger that would provide an easy pass for employees to find a new place of work. Many quit, many were fired. Mike and I were feeling as if we were indispensable. "He can't fire us" we would joke. " We run this whole fucking facility!"

We felt as if we did.

V. Smith was messing up the 6-2 shift, residents still routinely disrupted the school program. The overnight didn't count, and that left us, the 2-10, to show everyone who the YLA was, and where we were taking it.

Sporracco retired, and since Simms had a bachelor's, in English, he applied for the position pending passing his exam. We had no doubt he would ace it so he started gaining more responsibilities with us on the 2-10. We had the staffing to position ourselves in a preventative formation. Leichtenberger hounded all 18's and AODs to be where the kids were. He was right. The more present we were the less they acted out. Which is why the 6-2 shift was having so many issues. Not only were they staffed with all of the known racist employees, but they also didn't care to do much more than sitting down and watching TV. They're crisis prevention and de-escalation techniques consisted of yelling across the unit or posturing to incite an escalation that they never intended to handle in the first place. This never ended well and usually involved multiple residents being restrained.

But not all was perfect on our side either.

Paperwork.

I ended up being terrible at it. And it was my weakness.

One day, I was working the 6-2 on a Saturday, which is consistently a decent and easy shift. It was Skinner, a redneck skinhead. He had a large American bald eagle tattoo across his back, shoulders and right arm. A former county sheriff who was fired for doing cocaine on the job. He may have lost his job as a real cop, but he certainly found more time to do cocaine at the YLA. Thompson and I would laugh watching video of him, on his overnight shift, going to the bathroom, coming back and sitting on the couch, and giving the classic rubbing of the nose and long cocaine jawing, while the TV glowed on his translucent white face. I hated him, and I never saw him put a kid down, only threaten a kid that forced someone else into a position to do so.

So as usual, he was sitting on the couch in the dayroom area of the unit. The common area was furnished with two steel tables with extending chairs mounted to the floor, and the hard, yet soft, plastic completely unbreakable blue chairs that the couch matched, and both were easily movable. He sat between resident Smith and Foster. Those two didn't want to go to the game room for Activity time, so of course Skinner agreed to stay behind with them and watch TV.

As AOD, I was making my rounds ensuring I was present at every location at once, just like I was ordered to do by Leichtenberger. I entered the unit, said, "What's up" to Skinner, Smith and Foster, and made my way around the unit to ensure all of the doors were locked, and the bubble and offices were secure.

"Hey Skinner" I said, "Let me get the log book."

He gave it to me and I went and sat at one of the steel tables thirty feet away. In all prisons, especially medium secure, the common area or dayroom is the largest open space in the unit. The cells create a square around it with double doors on opposite sides, and sandwiched between the bathroom and the counselor's office on the backside, was the bubble. The unit bathroom was located in the far left corner, opposite the back exit door. I gave another visual inspection of the entire unit, marked the time, and entered my log entry, all secure.

Burch walked in.

"Hey Sir!" he said with enthusiasm. Like most drunks his mood was terribly erratic, but that day he seemed in good spirits. He went to use the bathroom. I waited and watched the back of Skinner's bald head, Smith's afro, and Fosters ....."*what the hell is up with Fosters hair*" I thought, "*why didn't he get his haircut with the others the other day?*"

Burch came out of the bathroom.

As hard as these young men claim to be, they always make sure they're are plenty of YDAs and AODs to do something. Not like my first days at YLA when there was a coordinated effort. These kids wanted to be violent, but they also wanted to be controlled and forced physically. For many it's the only time they've been held. They yearn for physical contact, even if it is through violence.

Smith decided that it was his time to pop off on Foster. In the blink of an eye, he jumped up and punched Foster in the face, and Burch hooked him, while Skinner pushed Foster back. Smith was trying to break free, and was breathing heavily. I ordered Burch to put Smith into a single seated position. Smith continued to resist, and to Burch's credit, he began to tire. But his breathing began to become abnormal.

"Smith, you good?" I tried to question him.

"Smith, let's take it easy so we can let you go, Ok."

His head just flopped, and he gave a moan.

"Smith!" I gave more emphasis in my tone. "Yo! You good?"

"Sir, he's gone light on me," Burch said. Indicating that he is no longer resisting and his body is going limp.

"Shit! Fuck!" I didn't really know what to do. "Code Blue Unit 1" I called over the radio, trying to sound calm and in control.

Minutes later the nurse arrived, but none of that was the issue. In fact that was pretty standard everyday happenings. It was the paperwork that sunk me.

I described Smith as being "unresponsive" in my description of events.

"Do you know what un-fucking-responsive means? Do you fucking know what that fucking means!?" Leich laid into me. "That means he's fucking dead! Was he fucking dead? Cortes for the love of God, tell me that this mutherfucker was dead!"

What could I say, but, "Sir, he wasn't dead."

"Then why the fuck would you put 'unresponsive'?" By this time his veins were all bursting, and his steroids had taken over. I was preparing to have to fight him. I was intimidated but couldn't show it. He couldn't see any fear in me because monster men like him feed off of the fear of other men. They will slowly pick you apart until you destroy yourself in the attempts to defend your own manhood. So I stood there, emotionless, all the time thinking - *"Gary you're not perfect. You make mistakes. Shit look what you made us do with Benson."*

Benson was a white kid from Long Island. Freeport to be exact. We were getting a lot of kids from this area and it made me wonder what they were doing down in Nassau county. But Benson was a rare breed of resident. He had the walk, talk and swagger of an inner-city thug, showed no fear, and laughed - literally - in the face of any force or authority. He was a menace to our facility from day one.

He would spit in the face of the YDAs before he attacked them. Had no issue grabbing chairs or tables to use as weapons. He had sent several older staff out on medical leave from blown out knees and concussions, and left Thompson and I with a collective, "What the fuck are we going to do with this kid?" attitude.

For some reason Leich had a soft spot for Benson. I assumed it was because he was one of the few white kids that came through the YLA. Or maybe because he had seen so many kids come in and out that he felt he could help him. As Benson sent our men out on leave, Leichtenberger would commence destroying us. He would place blame on the AODs for not being present in the area of the restraint. He would blame staff for not seeing the premeditated behavior that signaled he was about to turn it up. Staff who would get hurt would often be placed on "hold" and wouldn't be able to engage in any physical contact. Only because the kid forced the men to fight to control him, not hook and restrain him. This only weakened our ability to maintain the already loose order we had over the facility. Leich would tear apart the manhood of any YDA or AOD who was placed on hold, got hurt, or couldn't keep Benson under control. Everyone was a "Fucking pussy!"

Mike and I devised a plan and tried to push Leichtenberger to follow. He needed to go and his mandated time was short. We couldn't keep him and keep order in the facility at the same time. We knew Benson couldn't control himself so we preyed on that. We described how we dealt with Ross. How we had a transfer set up prior to his last restraint and how that set a tone for the other residents. The message that we would send you somewhere else and you could start your time again if you continued to disrupt our program. Leich didn't buy it.

"Then what?" He shot back. "The fucking kid will just come right back. Trust me he'll remember what you guys did to'em. Then you'll have holy fucking hell on your case. And I'm not dealing with that shit. That will be you two's fucking mess."

Mike and I looked at each other. Reading each other's minds we knew that Leich was in a league of his own. He was king and he wasn't going to let anyone handle the throne except him. He dismissed us. And when we left his office and went outside Mike looked at me and said, "Ace it's fucking you and I here. That fucker is too fucking juiced up to think straight."

"I know, but what the fuck can we do?" I asked, knowing he didn't have an answer. And he didn't.

"Let's show that mutherfucker whose boss then." In his classic Marine tone.

Leichtenberger had his own plan for Benson and he put his plan on Thompson and I. He called us into his office to inform us of his decision a few days later.

"Benson was restrained early this morning." He started.

We both gave a look that said, "So why are you telling us?"

He continued. "We gotta get this kid home! I can't keep having this pussy ass staff afraid to dump this kid. Every fucking time Benson starts some shit, Skinner, Klien and even Vernon, don't do shit. But when another kid pops off they want to bring the force like they're doing shit. They're not doing a damn thing!"

Thompson and I stood side by side, in a military at ease, both hands locked behind our backs, straight backs, and side eyed each other. This time, we looked with a sense of relief. Leich was seeing the issues we were seeing. We've been telling him from the very beginning that the 6-2 shift was ruining what we were trying to do. Mike's thoughts were a mystery to me, but I know I was wondering where Leich was going with all of this. No matter how good and positive a topic was, I never left Leichs office feeling like, "Alright boys, let's go make it happen!"

I almost always left wondering how I was going to make his vision of the YLA a reality with the little resources and support I had. Yet, I felt the promise of something big.

"So here's what we're going to do," Leichtenberger continued. "We're going to put him in Rec Room 1 (the room Ross was in for his transport), we're going to keep him on PC (protective custody) until his release. He has 2 weeks and he's gone. I'm not losing my hold over shit because those old fucks on 6-2 are afraid to their job."

"So we're going to need a man on duty with him 24/7 until then." Thompson stated the fact.

"Yes! That's why I am telling you 2. You're going to have to keep that in mind for scheduling

"Will we be adding additional staff for that?" I asked.

"Fuck no! Our OT is through the fucking roof. And MacIntyre will only put his fuck head buddies in there with him. The fucking kid will never get home if we let him do that." Leich barked.

"We need to get MacIntyre off the fucking schedule is what we need to do." Thompson always got credit for stating the obvious.

"We'll handle that after we get this fuck Benson out of here."

"I'm concerned about being short staffed for the next two weeks. That's a long time and we're already short with people out and all these safety holds." I tried to bring some sort of logic into what seemed like a rather illogical decision.

"That just means you 2 are going to have to step up." Leich responded pointing at us with a harsh tone that suggested he misjudged my willingness to impose force.

"Sir, we've been stepping up. But Smith and 6-2 keep fucking up all the progress we make. That mutherfucker is the problem." Thompson responded with confidence.

That also gave me insight as to what Mike was actually planning. He was making his own moves to be king. He was already planting seeds of dissent against his adversary, that being Vernon Smith.

"I'll deal with Vernon. You two handle Benson." and Leichtenberger dismissed us.

"What the fuck bro!" I said to Mike.

"The fucking guy has one mode, that's it." He replied.

"Let's go get Benson." And we both headed towards the unit.

On the way we decided that we would have Cash be with him during our shifts. He was capable of managing Benson by himself, and he was certainly not going to hesitate to dump him on his face.

"Yeah, he's smart enough to do it off camera too," Thompson said as he laughed.

"He is! But we have to make sure MacIntyre doesn't fuck us with the schedule." I threw back.

"I'm getting that fucking schedule from that fucker. Give me a fucking week and I'll have that shit. Then we will be able to really lock this shit down." he encouraged with a shit eating smile.

"Seems like Leich is expecting us to make all of his visions actualize through us." I shared my true thoughts with Dan, one of few times I did.

"Let'em. Fuck it! We got this Ace. We're like Pippen and Jordan. You're Scottie Pippen and I'm Michael Jordan. You like helping kids and I fucking hate'em!" And we both laughed. "But we got this shit!" And we dapped each other up, gave a serious look at each other, and went inside to tell Cash his job details for the next two weeks. Then we had to get Benson to follow us to Rec Room 1.

"Let's play good cop, bad cop," Thompson said jokingly.

"Ok, I'll be the bad cop." I said.

"Good that'll fuck him bad" and Mike continued his joking mood.

I provided the suggestion that we have Cash go ahead of us to get Benson by himself. It wouldn't seem so obvious that he was being corralled. Cash was really good at talking to residents, and keeping them calm. It definitely had to do with his size. Cash was making a name for himself as a YDA that never hesitated to hook a kid, and never deviated from the danger that was presented, and was strong enough to handle any man, let alone a kid.

When we arrived Cash had Benson sitting down in the empty Rec room. Benson's attitude was worn on his face. His carrot top spiked hair and acne made his face pink. He had the look of prenatal alcohol syndrome, with slanting eyes, chest pushed out, always looking at his arms as he crossed them, like the pink acne pock marked arms of his had any potential.

But there he was, waiting for us. Cash already knew the drill. If he turned it up, he would put him down. We made sure he sat him on the left side of the room, closest to where the bathroom stalls were, and the camera angle was out of reach. Cash was perfectly precise in his position, and he gave the nod that informed us that he was ready.

But of course Benson had the first words.

"Yo! What the fuck am doin' here yo?" He asked in his deep, hood, Long Island accent.

"Benson, we're trying to do you a favor." Thompson quickly responded.

"Da'fuck for?" Benson was great with words.

"Because we want you to go the Fuck home Benson, that's why!" I made my point as the "bad cop".

"Ah, ok, yeah, '' Benson said with a tisk sound of his teeth. "But what the fuck am I doin' in here though?" He asked.

"Like we said, Benson, we're doing you a favor." Thompson added.

"Get the fuck out of here, you tryin' to put me in PC Yo, For real, Ima bug the fuck out. You aint leaving me in this fucking room." Benson may have been lacking in some aspects of intelligence but he knew the system, and he knew the ins and outs of OCFS.

"Yeah, Naw, I aint doin that shit, fuck that!" And he stood up.

So did Cash.

"Oh what you wanna fuckin' dance Cash?" And he gave Cash a look that encouraged Cash to make a move. But Cash looked at me. I nodded for him to stand by.

"Look, it doesn't fucking matter what the fuck you want, or don't want at this point. You got 2 weeks left on your time. Spend it here, like this. Or you can start again, but I swear to fucking God Benson, it won't be here." Again, in my bad cop tone.

"You's aint doin shit!" His aggression rose.

"Your right fuckface, we aren't going to do shit." Thompson quickly gave him a different tone. The tone that reminded us all that Thompson was never the "good cop".

"What the fuck yous gonna do then?" He was preparing for us.

We had already decided that we were going to entice him so Cash would fuck him up. We wanted him to know that WE would fuck him up without cause or hesitation. We wanted him to know that if he didn't give a fuck, then we REALLY didn't give a fuck.

"YOO, this is fucking bullshiiiiiit!, Fuck this YO!" Not only did Benson's words indicate his temperature was rising, he positioned himself away from Cash.

I slowly made my way to his back which forced him to move closer to the side of the room we wanted him on. Cash read me, and sidestepped to allow Benson to walk forward a little more. I waited, looked at Mike who was locked onto Benson, Cash was locked onto me, and I was just waiting for him to take a few more steps. When he got to the spot on the floor I made the mental note of, I gave Cash the order.

People never know what violence truly does to someone. When violence has been normalized in the home, on TV, music, it is never seen as something that you shouldn't do. Violence has been proven to be the most effective way to transfer power, gain power, resources, women, money, and whatever else you may want in life. People may even disagree with that statement. But the odds of them being violent are probably close to zero. To tell a real street kid to share his emotions could cost him his life. We had to understand that some of these kids would never leave gang life unless they were dead or went to real prison. The kids who weren't gang affiliated, whose parents came to visit them and called them, those kids, those kids only wanted to talk to their mothers. Real street kids, they only wanted to talk to their "bitches".

Benson had no one to talk to. No one called him. He had no bitches.

He had nothing. And when someone has nothing, they lose all fear. Cash mopped the floor with Benson, and we let him. We ordered Cash to let him go, only to stoke Benson up again and ordered Cash to toss him around some more. He cursed, spit, and did all the Benson antics. But when we were done, all he wanted was some water.

The kid was all shits and giggles for the next two weeks. When he was released none of us gave a shit. We had no words, no final thoughts, we turned the Rec room back to a recreation room. And most of all, we were glad we had our staffing back to normal.

Benson went home on a Monday. The same Wednesday of that week, Mike and I arrived on the grounds at the same time. We dapped each other up and proceeded to our offices together. It was raining so we moved with haste and found Pearson in there as well.

"You guys see the news?" Pearson asked in his melancholy voice.

"No, what's up? We both said in unison.

"Look at this" and Pearson showed us his computer screen.

It was a mugshot of Benson. The Monday he was released, he met up with his boys and robbed a house. The owner awoke, startled from the break in, and went to investigate. He found the same red headed, acne pocked body, shit for brains in his living room. And Benson shot him 3 times. The man died. Benson was tried as an adult and he would never be free again.

At the end of the shift that night, walking back to my office, I saw Thompson waiting outside of the building. It was still pouring rain. He was standing like a Marine, weathering the storm.

"What's good bro?" I asked him.

"I'm getting that fucking schedule. We can't let shit like this happen again." said the Marine.

We shared our thoughts on Leich, his decision about Benson, to protect the white kid who ended up killing somebody, what was happening to the staff, V. Smith, and shared honest moments that for men, were sentimental. His life as a Marine was much like mine on the streets. We both had to outwork, overcompensate for size, fight, win, and that made us who we were, for good or bad, it was who we were. We stood out in the rain under the yellow glow of the office building entrance. It was a two story house that connected to a larger barnhouse structure which connected an archway to the other stable barn and workshop. The place was old, and the "new" buildings from the early 1990's, with their flat-topped square brick design, stuck out against the military housing quarters, mess hall, and recreation rooms with high-pitched wooden thatched roofs.

"They were designed for one thing. That's to house those juvenile fucking delinquents in there. Fucking adapt and overcome man. Adapt and overcome" he said and looked me straight in the eye the way a familiar friend would.

Both of our high collar black state-issued fleeces were soaked by now. Both standing, hands in our pockets, same posture, stance, we both knew that in systems there was no room for individuality, and one cannot disrupt the system. However, one must also maximize their full potential within the confines of the system. The tree has a system and it maximizes its growth everyday. The world itself is a predatory system that preys on the weak, and as we know only the strong survive.

"Get that schedule bro!...and get home safe!" I responded. We dapped each other up, accepting each other's once dry hand.

Chapter 15

Turning Points

Whatever the mind can conceive and believe, it can achieve. This philosophical statement came from a man named Napoleon Hill. He is not as well known as he should be. His book *Think and Grow Rich* is the basis for neuroscience today. He was one of the first men to explore the power of the mind and how to unlock human potential. His understanding of the human experience led him to discover foundational facts presented in the statement about conceiving, believing, and achieving. From his perspective, the human will of the individual is the ultimate driving force in life. It is God's gift to us all.

My life experiences supported this claim. I saw first hand that when an individual's will is broken they will accept what their situation or reality really is. However, they do not accept accountability for the creation of their reality because they could not conceive of anything different than what they have. They don't believe that they should, let alone could, have more out of life. Therefore they achieve very little.

I watched success for some come easy, because their reality was created for them. They didn't need to believe, all they had to do was achieve. Others may conceive it, but they'll lack the belief in themselves to actually manifest anything. For many, their minds are so jaded and tattered from life that they are unable to formulate a world any different from what they experience everyday. They lack belief in a higher power, their own power, and the power of others. What they accomplish may be done on a micro level, but they cannot see past the macro world in which they find themselves trapped in. One must find the will to define oneself based on one's own beliefs and actualize a world that they envision themselves participating in as who they want to be, based on those beliefs. Once that is accomplished all one has to do is go out and achieve it.

That's what I was trying to do.

I had conceived and believed in what would be done at the YLA. I was giving my entire self to make sure that it was achieved. Mike was able to get the schedule from MacIntyre. Although that was a great accomplishment, and he and I were working quite well as a tandem, his Jordan/Pippen comment revolved around my head uncontrollably.

"Was he secretly dissing me? Was he trying to say that he's going to be the greatest, but he can't be great without my assistance? Did he tap into Michael Jordan more than I did? MJ just wanted to win at all costs but knew he needed sound teammates to win a championship. Was that his reference?" All of these thoughts collectively kept me unsure, and untrusting of Thompson. Yet, I followed in his endeavor to clean house at the YLA.

I was also still on the search for my own house. Summer was turning into fall, and G was beginning to become impatient. We had found one particular house fitting for our venture, but when we offered a cash price of $275k, they got scared and backed out. Fear is the only reason I could come up with for a person to turn down $275,000 cash as far as I was concerned. A brown man with an uncle, out of state, willing to put cash down for a home purchase may seem unbelievable to some. Not possible I suppose. Maybe they wondered what we were trying to achieve, and who did we conceive ourselves to be?

Alyson started to push for a house downstate. She wanted to be closer to her mother and the support system there. The fact that I worked an hour and half from where she believed we should live made her vision unrealistic in our shared reality. But no man should discount the force of a woman who has her own vision of life and her willingness to carry it out. For many men have fallen victim to the desired achievements of their women. Samson and Delila, Hellen and

Prince Paris of Troy, Lot's wife as they fled Sodom and Gomorrah. The bible is filled with stories of men being disconnected from their vision due to the vision of their woman. My dad did the same as he tried to meet the expectations of Janet. Only to find himself living in a beautiful house that he couldn't afford leaving his children with nothing more than a last name. I knew I had never shared my vision with Alyson, and maybe that's why we weren't connecting the way I felt we needed to.

So I decided to break it all down for her.

Trying to explain illegal ways to provide for your family to someone who has never even formulated such notions, never had to, and never had any intentions to, is an extreme ordeal. They don't know that to know the ins and outs of the street game, one has to know the ins and outs of the law. Fear takes over. They only know what was presented to them in movies and their Netflix shows. They don't understand that for some of us it's all we know.

Some of us know that there are rules to live by in the same manner that those who blindly follow the rules and constructs of modern law. They often wonder why they didn't get what they wanted out of life. In the streets the reason why something doesn't manifest can be easily identified at times, but it's all corrupt. We're all going against the grain of society and there is enforcement for those of us that do. It's called prison. However, if one follows the grain of society and fails, are there not just as severe ramifications?

If one follows all the correct steps to a legitimate life, and still does not accumulate what they desire, is that not creating a prison? A prison of thought, lack of control, self-doubt, lack of self-worth, and the immense suffocating feeling and pressure of failure. What's worse? A - living knowing that your mistakes created a world in which you now have zero freedom to pursue your personal beliefs and achievements - real prison. Or, B- believing that you do have freedom to pursue your own personal beliefs and achievements, only to come to the realization that no matter what, you can not? - prison of the mind.

Working in a prison, there was no way I could live in one for a home. I tried to make Alyson understand that.

"If we lived in the valley you won't have to worry about making more money because we will have support there." Alyson tried to impress upon me.

"Are you planning on working if we move down there?" I asked her, knowing the answer.

"We already discussed that Anthony." she responded with her usual tone.

"*Exactly!*" I thought, but of course I didn't say. Instead I said, "Look, I can do it here or down there, but either way this is what's happening. Even though I'm making better money we will never, I mean never, ever, get where we want unless I do more. I can dig that, but YOU need to let me do it. Don't tell me that I can't provide for my family, but have no alternative to making it happen.....that shit doesn't make any sense." I released what I had been holding back for quite some time.

"So, G wants a house that we can live in and he can grow weed in." Her attitude and misconceptions of my lifestyle started to infuriate me.

"Is your mother going to buy us a house? Is your dad going to send us money or keep giving us his old cars to sell?" - he had given us an old Range Rover that we sold for five thousand dollars - It helped but the money was gone before we actually cashed the check. I didn't stop there.

"Seriously Alyson, who is going to help us. You know the answer. NO- ONE! It is up to us. This is OUR family. You knew who I was, you knew what I was capable of and willing to do....none of this is new to you. Unless you thought that I was playing with you….did you? Tell me, did you think I was playing with you?"

Her face saddened, bottom lip stuck out, shoulders sank.

"Anthony, I love you. You're my man. I know you." she said lovingly, and I felt that we were going to be alright.

"Just trust me" I said.

"I do," she softly responded.

"So then let's find a house. He wants a house in the 350-400 thousand dollar range. Remember when we were in Miami, and I said 'If we're going to move back to New York we'll have to move to Cooperstown to be able to afford a house', well it's not Cooperstown, but that shit is only 40 minutes away. And here we are." I tried harder to secure her mind. "It will still be OUR home. No matter what!"

There was no way I was letting her ruin what I was trying to do. For her, working at a prison, risking my life for pennies, while she enjoyed what little benefits we reaped from that, was all part of the logical progression of life. I was supposed to do what I was doing, that being; work, provide, and shut up while she raised my son and spent what was made by her provider. That wasn't me. *"Besides, Once that money comes in, then she'll see."*

To maintain peace I did look at houses in the Hudson Valley that fit what we were looking for. The prices were exactly what I had expected, half the house for double the money. I also managed to make G and his health a priority. He was 500 pounds, more or less, and pretty much bed-bound because of that. His knees blew out after his 20-year service in the military and he was a proud Army retired veteran. The man was very capable. He taught me how to box, he showed me how street money and street hustle were the best knowledge to have in the legit business world. He proved to be correct on that part.

We made a lot of money on both sides of the game and he always had checks coming in. Ten thousand dollars here, twenty thousand there, and he had his military retirement with the additional one hundred percent disability payments. To him, he was set. I was his project son. The son he wished he had. When my father was dying he was the only family member who came and stayed. He stayed for 4 months, while a few other family members came in for a day or so, and went on to their original intent for their trip to Florida. Not G. He stayed. He helped. He suffered through it with me as we cried together watching my father lose his manhood, and die. But, G left before he did. Before he left he made me make a promise. A promise to not let him go out like that.

G was a real G. A long-time, old-school, Puerto Rican hustler from the LES, Lower East Side, of Manhattan. My family were proud survivors of the Alfred E. Smith Housing Projects. He made me promise that I would use his .45 that he had to put him down before anything happened to him. Anything like what happened to my dad. As a G myself, I knew that he meant it. I knew it was an honor for him to ask me to do such a thing. I never wondered if I would or would not do it. I never thought, "Shit I might really have to shoot my uncle." No. I just agreed as my DNA informed me to.

That's also subconsciously why I wanted to keep him alive and healthy. I didn't want that. I also couldn't let him be alone in Cleveland. As we searched for a house, time seemed to pass with the wind. Days were like seconds. My schedule normalized as predicted with Mike gaining control over the schedule. I had Wednesday and Thursday pass days, all 2-10 shifts. After having a deep discussion with Alyson we decided that that shift provided enough home time and support for her. My pass days (days off) were what they were due to seniority. I also needed consistency. Working a 2-10, and turning around and working a 6-2 was killing me in sleep and it created even more tension at home. Alyson and I decided that if I couldn't get straight 6-2, then straight 2-10 was best. We also scheduled all of my guys for the 2-10 as well.

I was managing G's expectations, Alyson's, and the 30-plus state employees all at the same time. And it was all happening. As the end of August approached it was all coming together. Alyson and I finally found a house that was perfect for us. 4,500 square feet of house, three car garage, with a two-bedroom, full kitchen and bath inlaw suite above it. The suit had its own private back deck. The two large bedrooms, 2.5 baths, large family room, living room, dining room, eat-in kitchen with a large island and marble countertops, fireplace, wrap around porch, and a back deck that was attached to the pool was far more than I imagined I could ever have. The attic and the basement were both the same size, and we couldn't have found a better place. It even had an electric seat for the staircase for G. The price and taxes were unmatched. We put our bid in and got things rolling.

That covered G and Alyson.

The YLA was a different story as far as managing all the elements in the equation. We had gotten the schedule situated and we were starting to set our own standards for the systems that we were mandated to follow. Mike had given himself three 6-2 shifts to try and help out on that side. That left me as AOD, alone, for those three shifts. Simms was back and training with us, and Pearson and Holland had split several of those shifts as well. With Andrews set as our standard Op2, I felt we would have a good grasp on things. We did, for the most part.

We had our moments of questionable action, but we were often able to chalk it up to learning by fire. We were doing such a good job at being present in every location, all of us, at the same time, that residents didn't really try much. I also kept my cool "teacher man" talk with them. I cared about them, and even if I didn't, I tried to make them feel like I did, and I was succeeding. I would continue to build with the silent leaders. Took care of them with extra snacks and extended phone call times. I made sure they always had fresh towels and laundry first. It was things like that that made them feel like they were being parented. That encouraged them to do what was needed so they could go home to their families.

If I was the father figure, Simms became the crazy uncle. He surprised me with what he came with. We started calling him the "Whisperer", because he would throw his arm around a kid and start whispering in their ear. He would walk with them to another location, usually into another building. He would then often have Op2 have them call him on a landline. I was AOD. I watched everything. Heard everything. And was everywhere even if I wasn't. I could control that, that was me maximizing my own individual output in a system not meant for individuality. - Andrews would then make his way to the landline location Simms radioed to him. As I watched, and started to put things together, I knew what was happening.

So one night I followed him. He went into the back of the AODs offices. He had Andrews and Cash with him. He had brought an older resident we had. His name was Charles. Charles had been in and out of OCFS and had been to all of the secure facilities. He knew that what we were doing was weak compared to Brookwood, Industry, and Goshen. He tried to take advantage of the younger residents by intimidation. He was stronger than everyone else so my silent leaders were of no service. We managed him by keeping him in good contact with his baby's mamma back in Yonkers. But he was giving hell for Mike and the 6-2 shift.

I made sure I gave them enough time to engage in what they were going to do. I entered from the side door as it provided a barrier for the sound, and then made my way through the back part of the building, in the dark, to not blow my cover. I just walked towards the golden glow in the back. When I got close enough to see inside, I saw Andrews sitting on Thompson's desk and Cash in a chair next to him. Their arms were folded and they looked relaxed, with their eyes locked to the ground. As I got closer I confirmed my suspicions. Simms had Charles on the ground and they were wrestling, but they were going at it, for real.

"Whoa! What the fuck is this ?" I said.

And they immediately stopped. I sat down at my desk to state the mandate. "Resident's aren't supposed to be in the AODs office building." I reminded them.

"Yes Sir!" Andrews and Cash replied in unison.

"You good Charles?" I said with a serious but concerned tone. I wanted him to know that I saw it, saw him handling himself, was good with it, but also that it wasn't good.

"Yeah, I'm good." And he put his jacket on.

"Make sure you get him something to drink. Shit, have him go do the snack run with you. The rest will be back in the unit by the time you get back." I added.

Simms wiped the rug burn from his elbow.

"Bro! What the fuck was that?" I asked him.

"Yo, some of the kids need to get that shit out. I figured I'd get to'em before he wild'out. My bad Ace." Simms said.

I felt he dismissed it. I knew he was better than that. We had long talks before about how we related more to the kids than any of the employees there. He was from Brooklyn and the first in his family to get a college degree. A degree in English no less. He wanted to write therapy curriculums for incarcerated youths. He wanted to do right by them.

I reminded him of that. I also reminded him that those kids needed something more than what they were used to. If we continued the same violent communication with them they would never have the skills to produce healthy families. And that the destruction of the family was the first assault our oppressors implemented on us when they enslaved us. We can be here and not become the oppressor, IF we did it right. We can help them heal. I would tell him and he would feel that.

I saw that he felt that. We exchanged some deep sentiments about staff and where we both thought we were going in our careers with the state. He liked Leich and I didn't, which surprised me. He was more prone to hooking a kid, and I wasn't. Where we agreed and disagreed was interesting but we respected each other enough to be comfortable with it. He also agreed we needed to keep our restraint numbers low to keep Leichtenberger at ease.

I also kept messing up the paperwork. Mike saved me from the mess with Smith, and he continued to review my paperwork and made sure I crossed my T's and dotted my I's, sometimes literally. But we were managing nonetheless.

Progress was felt all around. We had gotten a closing date. It was set for the day before Thanksgiving and two weeks prior to that date we had gotten our first big snow of the season. At the YLA we made sure the residents received their winter snow boots. Program never stopped due to weather. We just gave them government issued clothing that was stitched a little differently, thicker material, but it was still shit, and a jacket that couldn't keep a person warm even if they were inside, where they weren't allowed to wear them.

That night was a regular night. The kids had fun sliding in the snow when we went to the gym for rec time. They were catching snow on their tongues as we walked them back to the units. But when we got to the unit, like they so often do, it only took one action to set things off. The set off was a snowball. Charles had made one and put it in his jacket pocket, and no one noticed, not even me. Cash led the residents in and I brought up the rear with Icheman providing commands and reminders. McGhee, another new staff member, was also with us. He was still a little fresh on things, but he was a good brother and was also a veteran.

When Charles threw that snowball, it wasn't the spark that lit the fire, it was the placement of the fire. We handled it well. We laughed at first and took it as just kids joking around because we just had shared a moment in the brisk darkness of the Catskill Mountains with dime sized snowflakes falling. With the bright yellow lights up high you couldn't even see the fence with the thickness of the snow. We were all feeling nostalgic in our own way. We went to our own places of memory, of good times, a feel-good time from another time and place. Yet, as we went inside ourselves separately, that moment, we shared together.

"Yeah Cash, that's right pussy!" Charles laughed.

That was the match.

Worse yet, he stepped to Cash.

There were twelve residents housed in unit 1 that night. There were four of us. There were twenty-five cells in each unit. Cell 25 was always used as a storage unit with extra mattresses, pillows and other basic necessities. They were housed in almost every other cell.

Icheman and McGhee both immediately stepped towards Charles, not aggressively but to de-escalate. All his little cronies got riled up, and *that* was the spark.

There's a particular posture you have to maintain in these situations. A man's response to disrespect depends on the level of respect that a man has for himself. Cash knew what he was capable of, and maybe we unleashed him one too many times, but he didn't feel disrespected, no, not at all. Cash was embracing the challenge, and that is a different type of response. No longer in our trained stance of hands up and open, slightly to the side with a front foot lead, his shoulders squared up and loosened, as he stepped forward.

Charles flexed, just enough, and Icheman hooked him before he had any opportunity to do anything. We were in front of the bubble. The bubble juts out as its own room from the back part of the square-shaped building of the unit. Directly in the center, with its own door on the side. It's the unit's main control center.

I called the code in. "Code White."

That was the flame.

"TURN IT UP!!!" was all I heard in a chorus of anger and rebellious youth.

Things didn't slow down, I didn't gain focus in the turmoil like in the past. There was no muscle memory. No mental reference on how to react. There was no time for my existence to register what was happening. There was nothing but hesitation. Hesitation is the fear of making an incorrect decision. There wasn't time to hesitate, there was no time for fear, only time for action.

Resident Riley grabbed the garbage can and threw it across the unit. Garbage flew through the air like confetti. Resident VanLeuven flipped the couches. Two residents attempted to attack Icheman. I ordered him to move with Charles in his standing single. He moved into the corner of the bubble and the back wall. Charles was kicking his knee and stomping on his feet, while the other two residents were punching him in the back of the head. McGhee and I ran to get them off of him. McGhee hooked one of them and the other ran away.

Two residents were now secure in restraints. Two men and two residents. Two men left, Cash and I, and 10 residents.

Cash was able to wrangle up another resident as he tried to flip the couch, and placed him in a single seated restraint. One more resident down, 9 left, and just me.

Van Lueven ran up and punched Cash in the back of the head. I tried to grab him, not restrain him, but he slipped away. He ran and grabbed the garbage can and threw it across the unit at McGhee while he was still in a seated restraint. The others were running around the unit, yelling, picking up whatever they could and throwing it at whoever they saw. As they would circle the unit they were trying to hit Icheman, McGhee, and Cash while they were stuck in an isolated restraint.

Holland entered the unit from the back. He immediately hooked a resident and went to the floor.

I finally snapped out of it and tried to order the remaining 8 residents to their cells. I had lost control of the unit. The other residents just kept running around popping shots, kicks, punches, and throwing the garbage can. They threw the log book at Holland. He looked at me and yelled, "We need more cuffs!"

There it was. My brain turned back on. I had the only pair of cuffs on.

I radioed to CSU, "AOD CSU channel 2."

We needed backup immediately. But I couldn't radio that. If the other unit heard the announcement it could've put the other staff on that unit in a bad situation. And there would be absolutely no one to respond to them.

"AOD Lockert - he was running CSU, another veteran, but he wasn't trained for the floor so he wasn't able to restrain kids - I need you to bring 4 sets of cuffs."

"Copy"

I knew the timing. I knew how long it would take him if he was hustling like I counted on him doing. Lockert was watching the entire thing unfold, he knew he had to get there as fast as he could.

I looked at the door, the unit seemed to have lessened with noise and chaos. I was hoping to see Lockert coming in with the extra cuffs. Instead I saw Simms in the corridor between the unit and outside. He had 4 of the last 8 residents with him. They were all watching. Eyes wide, not concerned, but watching intently and seeing who was doing what, and who bodied who.

Lockert came in.

"I grabbed ankle shackles too," he said.

"Get cell 4, 9, 12 and 17 open" I ordered.

Those were the cells of the residents who were in restraints. I had to free up my men.

"4 Open!" Lockert yelled.

"Icheman, Put Charles in his cell!" I ordered.

He moved to do so while Charles still continued to struggle against him.

"9 Open!" from Lockert

"McGhee get Jones out of here!"

"12 Open!"

"Holland Go!"

They tried to rush Holland. I flexed to intervene and they diverted away from him. Picked up the garbage can and threw it across the unit at Lockert. He dodged it and ran across to the other side for the last room.

"17 Open!" He yelled.

"Cash that's you!" I shouted out, not even looking.

I was looking at Simms and the other four residents. I signaled to him to get those residents to their cells. I watched him give them orders and they quickly shuffled in and went to their cells and waited as Simms opened them individually.

Icheman was in a struggle with Charles in his cell. Cash ran over to assist inside the cell. Inside they manhandled Charles and left him unable to get up as they left his cell with haste, slamming the door behind them.

McGhee and Holland grabbed 2 of the last 4 who by this time had become tired. And seeing that things were getting under control they became less threatening. Another ran by me, who I grabbed by the shirt.

"Go to your fucking cell, Now! Open 6 NOW!" I ordered.

Lockert responded. I marched him over and threw him inside the cell, Lockert slammed it behind him all in one action.

One left. I had the mental count in my head, but he had already witnessed the end. And by the time I located him visually, he was being escorted to his cell by Holland. And just like that they were all in their cells. There was nothing left but the silence in the air. The heavy sound of our breathing was like a pulse rate in the heart of the entire facility.

"What the fuck!" Holland said out loud.

"Let's pick this shit up." I ordered trying to keep my command of the men I felt I lost.

They followed the orders and we organized the unit and picked up all of the trash on the floor.

"Lockert, we need 7 packets. Get those back here asap." I commanded.

"Yes sir" and he ran out.

I looked around at the men. They all looked scattered and lost from the mayhem. The rest of the shift was lost in a blur. We did the paperwork that took 3 hours to complete and ensured we covered all of our bases. I handled the pre-shift meeting for the overnight staff. And eventually made my way to the parking lot. Icheman had just walked away from Cash's car and was standing by his truck when I called out,"Yo Nick, wait up!"

He did. I hustled over to him with a quick step. I was still his leader and wanted to make some attempt at displaying that in any way I could.

"Yo, you good bro?" I asked.

"Ace that was fucking crazy!" he responded without hesitation.

"I know, but are you OK?" I wanted to know.

His eyes widened, his body softened, and the large young country man was holding his emotions together as best as he could.

"That was nothing like the Academy, was it?" I asked, trying to make light of the serious emotions we were both holding.

"They can't train you for that," he admitted.

"Fuck no the can't!" I fired back.

"Ace they really were trying to…." he paused. His eyes watered.

"I know man…they were." and I looked at him to console him. "It's late bro, and our asses gotta be here again in a few hours - it was already close to 1am - get some rest. You know we're gonna have to clean this shit up tomorrow."

"You got it Sir." and he took a deep breath.

I walked to my car, opened the door, turned the car on, and while it idled and warmed up, I cried. My mind was gone. I couldn't conceive of any other alternative to the evenings events. I didn't know what to believe in, and definitely had no idea what I was actually trying to achieve at that place, but to stay alive.

Chapter 16

Aftermath & Thanks

They say hindsight is 20/20. I'm not so sure about that. Our hindsight is a point of reflection. As we reflect, especially on events and or actions, we often fall victim to our own minds. What was said, the body language, our personal responses all may be skewed or not as clear to the mind, as emotions and "what ifs" tend to fill in the gaps. However, for the state, hindsight is called the security cameras. They capture every moment as it is. No sound prevents any distortion of words or misrepresentation, as actions are clearly observed and, in no way, can it be contested.

The cameras capture the moment as it is.

I didn't sleep that previous night, severely stressed about what I was going to return to in just under 8 hours. *What was Leichtenberger going to say? Would he actually give me respect because ultimately I was able to secure the situation? I was pretty sure the paperwork was all good, but was it? What are Mike and Smith going to say? What is Holland saying? Why didn't Simms come in and help me? Did he do the right thing? How was that the right thing to do? What if they do it again? What if they......*I had to stop as the avalanche of thoughts cascaded through my mind like an uncharted wilderness being completely engulfed by a white cloud of cold. I felt cold, and buried. I was searching for light and some way to regain my footing on solid ground.

Alyson wasn't home, again. And my thoughts kept me company for the evening like a pack of hungry wolves just waiting for me to get tired and collapse, so they could consume every ounce of my flesh.

There was no calling in sick for a shift without insults and disrespectful comments with very simple intentions, emasculation.

I felt sick from my nerves, it was crippling. For the first time, after five months of working there, I felt like *I* was the one going to prison. I decided to head in early. I didn't know what to anticipate, so I figured I should just go and face the music.

The day was cold, the snow had stiffened and there now was a thick crust blanketing the ground. The barbed wire fence was unscathed by the wind and there were still thick patches of snow that collected on the top where it met the tall steel beams, whose light was now at rest. The gate opens differently when the weather changes. The button will freeze and won't unlock, forcing you to give it a kick, it wasn't that cold yet. But the frosty sheen on the steel foreshadowed a harsh winter.

I did the usual, went to my office strapped on my cuffs and badge, and grabbed my radio. I made my way back to the main gate. As AOD, I am automatically buzzed in, once seen on the camera. CSU door unlocks as I reach for it.

"Hello, Sir." Bruce is running CSU with his square head and upstate country monotone voice.

"What's up Bruce?" As I enter the control room of CSU.

I checked the log book, and noted that the day was very calm, not one code. I checked the cameras and noted the location of the residents and watched their interactions. They were all calm, relaxed, playing cards and scrabble. The rec room had a few residents playing video games and working out casually. The facility was as calm and quiet as it was outside.

"They're all in Leichtenberger's office." Bruce told me

It was a Saturday. Smith was AOD, and Thompson was already there. The shift didn't start until 2, and it was 1:15. Which means Mike got there a lot earlier than I did. A lot earlier. I felt it. I could almost hear the burning heat. Not knowing what or where my senses were taking me, I made my way to Leich's office on edge thinking that the residents were gearing up for another round. I walked into the main office, greeted Lori, secretary to the Director, and went to Leich's door, which was half open, his sign for "come in" if needed.

There Leichtenberger, Thompson, Smith, and Holland were all watching the video of the previous evening's events. The paperwork was all on his desk in seven separate piles.

"Alright gentleman," Leich said abruptly.

All three of them got up and left, they gave me silent eyes and a head nod for a greeting. I understood the rank and file system and seniority of the state. Holland was going on year two, Thompson had been there about a year and a half, both had "permanent" status, which is tenure and protection. As in all tenured positions so solidified one would have to do something extremely egregious to earn termination. And Smith. Smith had been there fourteen years, and just recently earned state pay grade 16. Which is the highest pay grade a veteran can earn without a bachelor's degree. Nonetheless he was, and remained AOD supreme at the YLA. Leich trusted him because he was so old school and had worked everywhere, just like him. I trusted Smith for the same reasons. Also because as a black man he saw the angles I saw. But he never gave two shits about anything that I said, so we remained distant.

"Close the door Cortes"

I close the door, and he takes a deep breath. He looks at the paper stacks in front of him, and touches them lightly as if they were going to blow away in the stiff air of his office.

"I don't know where to start."

But he knew where to start.

"You have here on your file" he looks for that particular stack of papers and finds it.

"You have here, the box marked riot, and then proceeded to document last night's events as a riot." he stopped and looked at me. His jaw tweaked making his bottom lip go down and to the side. He flexed.

"Cortes, have you ever been in a riot?" He asked me.

"No, I haven't Leich" he hated being called Sir.

"Then why the fuck would you put that in the paperwork? Do you want IS - Investigative Services - up in here? What the fuck! If it were a riot you were supposed to call me. Did you know that?"

"No I didn't"

"Did anyone get seriously fucking wounded?"

"No"

"Were there any weapons?"

"No"

"You fuck! Do you see what I mean? You put a goddam riot down Cortes! That was no fucking riot!"

My eyes got tense, I looked at him hard, at that point I didn't care how big he was, I wanted to grab a pen and pop the steroid vein bulging out of the side of his forehead. I wasn't going to let him emasculate me.

"What do you call it then Gary?" I said, in a tone seldom used, and only to let someone know that I just dug in for a fight.

He looked at me. "This is a fucking large group disturbance. That's what the fuck this is!"

"A...large...group...disturbance?" I asked back and looked at him with eyes that said the words I wanted to say.

"Yes" I felt him start to settle. "And the rest of this paperwork is a mess. Kids never went to medical, they didn't sign the paper, your missing fucking initials on here and here. I mean golly Cortes. You're lucky Mike came in early to clean this shit up."

And there it was.

Mike had come in early "to clean it up."

Leich adjusted his tone more, and walked me through the paperwork, and described the wording and what it reflected. That each category of offense had a different registry, and that once IS gets into a facility they never leave you alone. He told stories of being in a "real riot" and getting stabbed in his chest with a pen.

"Yup, that's why I would've stabbed you right in your temple with that huge vein of yours" I thought to myself. He did give words of encouragement and acknowledgment. That "we are never trained for these things" and that you learn from "trial by fire". My attitude shifted towards him that day. I started to understand his madness a little bit. I wasn't impressed by his physical stature anymore. I saw it as him taking what he did seriously. But, he never did watch the video with me.

He let me go for the pre-shift briefing. Same men as the night before. They all looked tired from drinking the night away, security belts around their shoulders, large coffees and red bulls in hand, and they were still talking about the girls from the bar when I walked in.

I gave them the day's agenda, made a brief comment about our previous shift, and noted, "Let's leave it where it was, last night, we have a new day gentlemen. Let's work on rebuilding relationships."

They all agreed. They went to their posts, and I went to the camera room. I watched the video. I understood why no one talked to me. The cameras don't lie. Your hindsight fills in the blanks with personal emotion, and personal opinion. The cameras don't lie.

I watched the snowball lob across the unit from the door and hit Cash, right after I walked into the unit. The snow got under the collar of his jacket, and you can see our faces make the expression of "Oh shit" and laugh. Cash and his posture was clearly remembered. I walked over and put myself in a good position. When Icheman hooked Charles, instantly everyone scattered in different directions. I paused it to see where each one went. All of the residents were in their red sweatsuits for the gym and their blue jackets and black hats. No one went directly at the staff, they all just ran around.

I understood why it wasn't categorized as a "riot", right there. Even when the other two residents went for Icheman in the corner, they weren't really assaulting him. Plus McGhee and I were there so quickly they couldn't do anything. But McGhee hooked the one, I just pushed the other one away. In my mind, at the time, I thought I couldn't be in a restraint, I'm AOD. But something was telling me I should've done more than just push the kid.

When the resident flipped the couch, he actually posed no threat. Yet, Cash hooked him and put him in a seated restraint. *Shit!* He should've just escorted him to his cell right then. I was now standing still and just watching them run around in circles. They weren't even trying to attack me. They were just running around. One did try to punch Cash. My attempted restraint was comical to say the least. I bear-hugged the kid, and tried to stop him from running. He slipped out of my grasp. It looked like a very bad defensive football play, where the defender had the running back at the goal line, and he couldn't stop him from scoring a touchdown. I couldn't believe it. It was VanLueven, the one string bean normal-sized white boy, who tended to get restrained a lot, but was never seen as a threat, and very manageable. But I couldn't take him down.

I watched the rest in disgust. Simms hiding out. I realized that he had grabbed the four kids who weren't involved and they were standing by the door. He just slipped in, grabbed them, and stayed with them there. *I guess that's a good move* - I thought. But really, he just watched, he didn't radio for assistance, and he let Lockert go inside of the unit, instead of him with the extra cuffs.

Holland went to a seated restraint. He didn't think to escort the kid to his cell. He just sat there too, yelling things out and looking around. The garbage can that was thrown at him, it was just picked up and tossed indiscriminately, there was no malicious intent by the resident. I pressed pause.

I rewound back to where I tried to restrain Van Lueven, and then watched in slow motion. I didn't want to hurt him and it showed. The camera showed me that *I* was not a threat to anyone there. Maybe that's why the kids didn't try to go after me. Or maybe it was something else. Maybe my relationship with them was stronger than I thought. But I couldn't bank on that. There was too much at stake to rely on the loyalty, and actual feelings, of any of those kids. I felt my mind and body harden

I tried to get to Smith's office before he left. I felt I needed to finally talk to him and gain his perspective, at least on what happened the night before. I called his landline.

"Yo Smiff, it's Ace, you gotta minute, I need to holla at you?"

"Yeah man, I'm still here." he said back, and I rushed over to his office on the other side of the grounds.

I knocked on the door.

"Yo" I said softly and sharply.

"Hey what's up Ace?" and he swung around in his chair, spit cup in hand resting slightly between his soft grip and lap.

"I take it, you saw the video from last night?" I figured I would be as direct as possible with him.

"Yup." and he spit in his cup.

"Leich bugged out on me, but seriously none of us knew what to do." I said with a serious tone.

"Yeah, but you didn't do shit." and he looked at me.

"What was I supposed to do Vernon? That's kinda what I'm trying to get at here." Another attempt at being extremely direct.

"You know what AOD stands for Ace?" he asked.

"Administrator on Duty…..?" now unsure of where he was going with that question.

"No Ace!" and he looked me dead in the eye. "Asshole on Duty!…..Because no matter what happens, no matter what shit goes down, you're the asshole who gets the blame for everything. Ya see? You're the one who has to maintain control."

"I thought I did! They said that the AOD isn't supposed to be the one who engages. They have to monitor the entire process, we have to make sure we are able to move and keep all things above board….. No?"

"Man get the fuck out of here with that Academy shit." And he started to get his things together to leave. "Let me tell you something, it takes a lot to do this job, and it takes a lot out of you. Shit….." he spit in his cup again, "I'm AOD of my house." and looked at me with a deep look to see if I understood him.

Vern wasn't going to willingly tell me what to do. He wasn't going to assist me in my development as his co-worker. He didn't care about my questions and concerns. He had been doing the job so long that he had become numb to anything other than OCFS, and even that, his only job since the Navy 14 years ago, he had no emotions for.

I knew he would be no help to me and had no interest in my quest for self empowerment in a chaotic environment.

So, fuck it. I carried on with the day. Face steel and eyes sharp, all shift.

As instructed, Icheman and the other guys did a great job at rebuilding relationships with the residents they engaged physically with just less than 24 hours ago. It was watching them having fun with the residents playing Uno, chess, and Monopoly, cracking jokes on each other, that I realized that they were *all* kids. The YDA's and the residents were all so young, and naive.

I caught up with Mike towards the end of the shift. He was correcting all the paperwork that I had jacked up, so I left him alone during the hours. But Mike was stewing on something else.

"Fucking Smith" he said when I came to his office.

Those words certainly caught my attention, and intrigued me because I was thinking the exact same thing since I left his office earlier that day.

"What's up with Smith?" I asked, but in a nonchalant way.

"I'm going to get that fucker fired."

"Whoa! For real? What did he do? Or….should I ask what did he not do?"

Mike proceeded to tell me that he was going to get him for sexual harassment of another employee who he had been trying to solicit sex from. She was a young YDA named Stephanie Mercel. Mercel was not the typical young YDA I thought Smith would try to get to have as his side piece. She wasn't very attractive, short and round, and brushed her teeth inconsistently. The residents always said she had terrible breath.

"Yeah, cus she's suckin' Smith's dick!" Thompson said with extreme emphasis.

"Shut the fuck up! No way!"

"Yup! And she's going to sing like a fucking bird!"

"But if she did it….. then….. why would she admit that?"

"I'm going to have her say that she didn't… and that he was forcing her to. I drew up the docs already. We just have to get her to give a statement and sign that shit, and that fucker is done….fucking period."

When Mike was saying how he was going to "clean house" I had no idea that this is what he meant.

"But that bitch is scared, so we're going to have to convince her that this is the right thing to do." Mike continued. He tried to get me to conceive of what *he* was trying to achieve. And that became clear. He wanted Smith. All this time I thought he was trying to take me out first. I knew that I was trying to dominate my realm of "iguanas", he was going for the bigger one first. And he was seeking the assistance from another smaller iguana like me.

"Wow! That shit is crazy." And I really meant that response.

I was shocked that it was happening. I was completely put back by Thompson's willingness to spearhead this, and on top of that, asked me to help him. And that's when I saw a play. I remembered who I was, and what I set out to do. I was meant to walk on water.

Days away from the closing on the house and taking tabs on equipment with Rick, I was gearing up for the next real venture in my life. I felt like I had to put everything I knew, everything I learned on the streets, academia, mental health, everything, would have to be put into action all at once in order for this all to work. It had to, or else I would lose everything.

You find out who you truly have bonds with in time of needs outside your occupational interactions. I had not only continued to make strong connections with my men, others had come in too, who were friends, or friends of friends, of friends of some sort. Lamont and McGhee proved to be effective. They weren't big bodies, but McGhee was a veteran so when push came to shove, he shoved. And Lamont was a local stoner and former maintenance guy for the facility. He was a younger brother to a long-time vet of the place, Richie, so he knew a lot of the older guys there. But he was loyal to us and was always there when we needed him. And Grudene filled the last spot. He was tall and built like a tight end, and had ambitions of following his family tradition of raising buffalo, and being a state trooper. He was built like that, a blonde upstate buffalo herding state trooper. So all together, with Icheman, Cash, Johnson, and with Andrews as Op2, we were solid. Plus we had Simms, even though his antics had me keeping a close eye on him. I had Pearson and or Holland, and *their* big bodies were always ready, and we usually moved as one. So I was confident in my handling of those men, mixed with a veteran here and there, that we could get any job done.

But Ericson and Kevin Smith from the overnight proved to be my largest assets. They would come in early and talk to me about their years at the YLA, and the people they saw come and go. They would always pick up "fill in" shifts when others were out, and would often take a 2-10 shift because they were both friends with my men.

Kevin Smith though was a different kind of man. And he and I connected on a different level. He handled private security on the side and kept that part of his life to himself. But he was Op2 for the overnight shift and he was always up on the latest gear, state mandates, and would be able to expound on so many topics in a manner unmatched by most college academics that I had come across. And of course, he loved 'Merca!

The day before Thanksgiving it snowed heavily. If I wasn't so excited I would've probably waited to move. But our closing was at 9:30am. I had the truck scheduled for 11. And none other than Kevin Smith was able to help me on that cold wintery Wednesday morning.

We expected the weather to be what it was. It was predicted to be close to twelve inches of snow. But it wasn't supposed to start until late afternoon. So Alyson and I went to the lawyers office for the closing in separate cars. She would leave with the baby, and I would meet K. Smith to pick up the truck and to finally move our life out of the shit house that time had forgotten.

I had POA on the house as G was not able to be physically present for the signing. I played the game for the realtor and the lawyer, and told them that G was my uncle and he was giving me a marriage and new baby "gift". The lawyer was a military historical fanatic and his office was filled with old maps framed in dark hardwood and other collectibles that showed his luxury interests. I told them that G was disabled, a combat veteran, and had retired from the Army, to which the lawyer ensured everything met the unique criteria and services we requested. We left him a $5,000 retainer just in case we needed him for any future dealings.

I signed the documents. Alyson looked excited. I was feeling proud. And we left the office in high spirits, and a sense of connection we hadn't felt in a long time. I hugged and kissed her, and buckled my son into his car seat, kissed his forehead, and told him that I loved him. I looked at the keys in my hand and put them on the key ring of my car keys.

"The only three keys I'll ever need."

I got into my car and drove back into the mountain to get the truck, meet up with Smith, and move the few things we had. All of our furniture was still at her mother's house, and we had boxed up everything we had and prepared well for the day. I knew it wouldn't take long. I would then head to her mother's house where we would spend the night and go to my mother's house for Thanksgiving. I was excited to see my family and to share the news of our new home. My son would experience the extension of his father for the first time.

Kevin was all business, and that's why I asked *him* to help me. When I picked him up he was ready and hopped in and sat shotgun.

He asked where we were moving to, and did his habitual calculating time, weather, and the other calculations that men like us always consider when we embark on a mission. We made light of the first part of the move and quickly loaded the truck with little issue. I knew he had an idea of how much money I made as AOD. He had been there long enough to have known the state grade pay scale. I knew I had it memorized, as motivation. Yet, for Kevin, as smart as he was, would never be able to be in my position due to his lack of "education". He knew he was a perpetual cog in the system.

"But, I'll tell you this. Those mutherfuckers aren't pimpin' me. Shit why do you think I work overnights? I have time to do my security shit, and when I do the overtime it only makes things better. As long as that shit doesn't take time from my family, and I try not to let it, but you know the YLA ... .but for real. I don't let that shit fuck with my life. It's that simple." He told me. And I appreciated his point of view on our shared reality.

I told him that I always envisioned myself living in an earthen home, like a Hobbit. And we shared environmental ways to homestead and completely live off the grid and self-sufficiently. It was that fundamental desire for independence that drew us close.

But when we pulled into my new three hundred yard long driveway, which had a McMansion on the top of a hill, nestled in the middle of ten acres, with a picturesque fast moving brook running through the tree line, he couldn't help himself.

"Damn Ace! So much for the Hobbit house." and he laughed. "You're going to need to get some furniture bud." and he continued laughing.

I admitted that it wasn't what I had imagined, but given the "gift" how could I say "No."

"You don't." and he looked at me with understanding.

We knew we didn't need long to unpack the truck. I was naturally hesitant to show him the house. The big blue house on the white hill, with the long driveway making its way through the country brush, the complete white landscape, and the snow started to fall. It was immediate, thick, and fast.

"Yeah…we'll have time. C'mon I'll show you around."

"Alright." he said in an unamused manner.

It was the first time I had opened the door to the house, as the owner. I crossed the threshold of my home, and I was accompanied by my co-worker. The notion hit me there. Maybe it was a sign. Maybe I was starting a journey with new accomplices. It didn't matter. I had bigger plans than just this place anyway.

We made our way around the house, and I was trying to not sound impressed myself while I showed him the master bedroom and bathroom with white marble floors, double sink with long full mirrors fully lit, full jacuzzi tub, separate shower stall, and large linen closet. It also had a large walk-in closet that we were going to use for the baby's room. Our king size bed, which was the only heavy thing we had to carry, looked small in the large hardwood floored room.

Then I showed him the attic. Fully framed out, one side the full length of the three car garage, and the other half split up into two rooms, full electricity and lighting.

Kevin whistled in a high pitch.

"You can grow a looooot of weed in here boy!" and he laughed seriously.

I looked at him with a smile, but serious. He sharpened his smile and nodded.

"Yeah, I want to turn this into more bedrooms, drywall it up and insulate it real good." I tried to pivot.

"Yeah, but there's a lot of opportunity here….." he stayed on it.

I watched him as he inspected the framing and wiring, looking out the window, and gazing at the moon like snowy scenery.

"Yeah, let's roll before it gets too bad. I still have to head down state."

I couldn't believe I said "down state", like I was from "up state" or something. I had never said that before and only mocked the upstaters who used those terms. But there I said it, like I too was a member of this "upstate area", working an "area state job", but would always be asked if I was originally from the "downstate area", exclusive man club. I could feel a shift in me. I started to feel the burn and depths of Mike Thompson's plot, and mission to be king. His hate for the residents, and fake appeasement he provided at his own amusement.

"Nice to have that Thursday pass day, you know you'll get Thanksgiving." Smith said like he knew I was thinking about the YLA.

"Yeah, I guess." I said as we got back into the truck.

The ground was covered with a thick layer of snow by now, and the roads in the distance were waiting for the non existent plow trucks. We made our way home slowly and talked about simpler things. We went back to talking about self sufficiency, our families, healthy lifestyles, and guns. When we got back to the truck rental shop, we didn't say, "See you at work."

We said,"Have a good Thanksgiving, and enjoy the family." Shook hands and made a solid fist.

I took my time through the mountainous backroads down state. I made it to Alyson's mother's house just before dark, and was able to enjoy the evening with them. And we did enjoy ourselves.

The next day, Thanksgiving, we went to my mother's house. It was the first time she hosted, and although her house was small, the cozy atmosphere was warming. Everyone was so surprised I was able to get a home for my family so quickly. As if they were shocked I did something good, legit, and family like. They knew me, at least they thought they did anyway

My cousin and brothers were there and were asking me what it was like working in a "prison". They looked up to me, as I was over ten years their senior. Their entire lives I had been traveling all over the country, stopping in for holidays, wrestling them with body slams, and then disappearing until the next family gathering. But, I was more present than ever for them now, and they were eager to know what was up. I didn't share with them though. Instead I just kept talking about the house and how they need to come up and just hang out. I tried to impress upon them that they now had a place to come to and just chill.

We stepped outside to smoke a joint. We started talking our usual trash to each other and one thing led to another and the oldest of my two brothers, Zeek, and I started slapboxing and wrestling. He was my big younger brother. He was the starting defensive nose tackle for his varsity football team, a senior, looking to play Division One football, and he was a beast of an 18 year old. He was an all honor's class kid, who Ace'd all of his AP state exams. He was my pride as a brother, and he was tough as nails, because I took so much pride in making him that tough. His dad being an old school brother himself, didn't play when it came to discipline, so the kid had a lot of tough love.

So when we started to get into it, and I felt how strong he had gotten, he forced me to level up from playful big brother strength, to *"hold up, let me show you who your big brother is"* strength. By that time some of the little kids from their dad's side were outside. They saw us "play" fighting and started pumping us up. We were both still holding back, but I decided to take it to the next level and I rushed him and brought him to the ground.

"Aw shit" he said, in a playful, but much more serious tone.

We exchanged grunts and attempts to wrist lock, leg lock, and arm bar each other. I tried to really apply some pressure on him, but the little ones were distracting me. But they didn't distract my brother, and he was able to get his arm around my neck. I protected myself from a choke, by pinning my chin tightly to my chest. He wasn't going to get me, and I knew I could outlast his young adrenaline filled muscles, as I've done before in "real" fights. But I glanced to the side, and there was a small black boy looking at me. While all the others were running around, shouting and laughing, he just stood there. His eyes pierced mine, his face had concern on it, his brow slightly furled.

"I gotcha now!" Zeek said.

"Naw kid, never!" I gave back.

But my eyes were still on the kid watching us, watching me. I never knew who the kid was. I didn't know his name or his relationship with anyone there. The family was a long time "hood" rooted family. So, there were always random black and brown kids at their house, and actually, it was the only thing I liked about their marriage.

That innocent beautiful black boy, in that moment, represented all of the black and brown boys who were locked up, who watched their brothers and cousins fight, do street shit, go to jail, have broken families, get trapped in addiction, abuse, crime, hate, and anger. I also felt the physical pressure of my brother trying to move up a notch in his own right.

I was supposed to break cycles. I was supposed to be setting examples. I went back to school to show my brothers what a good man does, because they needed to know another side of life than what their father could, or could not show them. It was all for the kids. It was all for the future.

My brother was in his own right to fight, struggling for his position. When a younger brother challenges his older brother, and they tussle, it's the will of the younger against the arrogance of the older. The arrogance keeps the older blind and susceptible to exposing their weakness. The will of the younger makes sure that they take every opportunity to find that weakness, and attack it. That day, my younger brother found my weakness. It was my heart. I didn't really want to hurt anyone, I really didn't. It was fun to play with my brother, but I wasn't going to hurt him just to prove a point. None of that was really inside of me.

My eyes still locked on the boy. I tapped Zeeks shoulder, and said "You got it bro."

"Yeah!" He shouted in self victory.

I rolled over and patted the nameless little boy on the top of the head, and smiled.

Brothers bond through violence, like all men. It is the one thing most women will never understand about male bonding. That somehow, it is embedded in our DNA. I loved my brother and I would do anything for him to feel, think, and do great things for himself. Letting him get the best of me empowered him, made him feel like he could accomplish anything. And I was proud to see that in him, and proud that I had the heart to make myself present for him to gain that self actualization.

I made my way home early that next morning. Alyson stayed behind with the baby for her family's gathering. My thoughts were of my brothers. How when my younger brother in Florida was messing up after my dad died. He came home to me, beating him up and forcing him to defend himself, yelling,"Man up!" and "Dad's dead, so now what!" forcing him to face it, and to find strength he thought he didn't have. And he did. I had been doing it to Zeek since he was a baby, and look at how he responded. There was truth to this violence.

I made my way to my new home. I was then going to make my way to my new family of brothers. And I knew that to win this battle for position and power, I needed to make myself the indispensable leader that I knew myself to be. By empowering others to recognize something in themselves that they didn't know existed.

Chapter 16

Chapter 17

Wrecking Crew

My own beliefs were the catalyst for the work I was trying to accomplish. I believed that there were only two forces in the world. One force that oppressed and controlled power. The other force was coming from those being oppressed. And ultimately their willingness to push back on that power. I was a liberator. And spoke, thought, and moved, in acts of liberation. I taught my students to analyze, identify, and harshly criticize the power structure. I wanted them to use their knowledge and power against their oppressor. I was armed in oppositional rhetoric that questioned the very fabric of existence for an oppressor, and anyone who took that form.

When you question the very meaning of an oppressors' existence they are forced to come to an understanding that many oppressed people, and oppressors, do not understand. That the first act of oppression, the first steps towards the dehumanization of man, is the dehumanization of the agents chosen to implement the oppressors ideology. A man cannot oppress and dehumanize another man unless he too has already been so deeply oppressed that his own view of humanity has been distorted. The slave master had already been dehumanized before he captured and enslaved any other man or woman. That reigns true no matter the continent.

This mastery over other human beings gave the slave master the false notion of what it is to be human. Because they failed, and to this day still fail, to recognize the loss of their own humanity which "normalized" oppression and subjugation. They in return believed they were doing good with their actions. That these "wild" and "savage animals" needed to be controlled because they could not control themselves.

I wove this knowledge into history lessons for my students so they could overcome their oppressed mind states and actualize themselves in their own vision. I was pushing my men to do the same. I wanted them to see themselves as men, not men of the state. Not men who were assigned one job, and one job only; the job of using state mandates as an oppressive weapon. But, the mandates are only designed for that one purpose, and that one purpose only.

My own paradigm shift was set upon these notions.

I was, liberation. I was, freedom. How do I teach my men to be that as well? How can we? When we are now appointed agents of the state, and the state is the oppressive organization?

I didn't know how to live that duality. So I stopped trying. I made my men agents of liberation, and I embodied the state. The decisions were mine, the actions were my call, and the results would be mine to bear. But if I could walk on water, I could do this too.

I became obsessed with the state mandates and all of the requirements outlined by OCFS. I wanted to know the "ins" and "outs" of the politics at hand, and how those hands created policy. I wanted to know how policy translated into action and how that affected my role within the state. One has to know the reality in which they live if they are to be successful. Understanding this aspect forces a shift inside us to change, and accept what is true. Data will support the shift through experience and observation. But if the data falls out of line, from whatever an individual's baseline is, we may find ourselves struggling to accept any new reality. When this happens we will often fall short of any true accomplishments because we need these shifts to happen in order to evolve. I know I did.

Failure wasn't an option. Success was the only goal. Yet, I was going to define success for my men and I. We had a job to do. For me, it was to get everyone home safely. To get home, the residents had to follow the program. The YDAs job was to ensure that the program was followed and residents were kept in order. My role as AOD was to ensure that all of that happened during my shift. As an agent of the state, I could use any means necessary (as outlined by the state mandates) to ensure that all of this became reality.

There are rules and they must be followed. Residents were to walk in a straight line when leaving the unit. A resident would be asked to form a line. If they complied, excellent. We would give them respect and props for doing so. If they failed to comply we called a code Yellow. If they still didn't comply by the time they got inside, I would be waiting for them.

"Can you walk in line with the rest of the residents?" In my firm AOD voice I would provide clear and answerable questions. Their answer always determined the outcome.

A,"Yes" would lead to a response like,"That's what I thought, I didn't think you wanted to get in trouble just for not doing something simple like walking to the gym."

A, "No", would be easier. "My man! Do I need to ask you again?" Knowing that this question put them in a position to challenge authority, and I would always prepare for the response. And it would lead to this -

"Fuck no- I was walkin' in line and this ma'fucker kept fucking with me." a usual resident response.

"Whoa! No need for the language. You're making me feel a little uncomfortable."

"I don't give a fuck"

"You dn't give a fuck right now you mean?"

"Man I don't give a fuck! Man - suck my dick!"

A "Code White" would be called in the calmest manner and sharpest look to my men.

Any man I had on shift, in that interaction, would be just waiting for the word. They knew they had the green light at the instant the words, "Code White", came out of my mouth.

And we would dump them.

The resident would get mad and say there was no reason for us to restrain them. But if they weren't following the program, that was reason enough.

I was making it a point for all to see. That I was the one man responsible for their lives. That the YDAs and the residents were at my mercy. I felt that I could balance the duality faced in my own mind. My men only needed to do their job. If they followed my directives when it came to discipline it would allow them to find their true selves through more positive engagements. Or so I believed.

If a resident refused to leave any area, that was fine. The men were directed to give one extra directive to the resident, attempt a de-escalation, and call a code Yellow. I would show up with Andrews and try one last time to convince the resident to do the right thing.

"I don't really give a fuck if you leave or not. If you go home or not, but your mother does. Tell me who do I call next? Your mother and tell her you were restrained again? or am I calling CSU and telling them to let your chic on the phone at 7: 30? Your call….."

The ability to show no difference on any decision they made, strengthened my position. Usually Andrews, or one of the men, would talk to the resident and try to make them do the right thing. This was part of the psychological play I was handling. I wanted my men to be the agents of positivity. I wanted the residents to rely on them, to lean on them, and to trust my men that they, and they alone, if followed, would lead them to their freedom.

I wasn't necessarily trying to vilify myself, but by empowering the men, they began to see the state for what it was. An oppressive organization. And they knew that I was not about that. So, in return, they trusted my authority. And knew that I gave it to them to exercise in a just fashion, and that I was to be called to do anything "unjust".

Is there really an actual way to speak, think, and be "freedom", and an oppressor, at the same time? Is there a way to teach others to be agents of liberation and agents of oppression? It takes a special breed of man. I believed that we were that breed.

It didn't take long for the residents to pick up on the pattern. They stopped asking me directly for any extra perks. During the shift they worked through Icheman or Cash, the floor leaders by mutual acceptance of the men. They would then come to me with any requests. I was establishing a hierarchy that suited me and what I was trying to do. The old vets of the YLA would call me for any little thing. They would release their authority as soon as they could, because they didn't want accountability. Not my men. They wanted accountability. They wanted authority. They wanted to help these kids and wanted the power to do so. Why would I not let them attempt to set these kids minds free, and in addition, their own minds.

They were strong, capable, good men.

The table was being set.

I didn't give my power to anyone because I was afraid to use it, or that I didn't want to. It was quite the opposite. At home I invested in a complete home gym for my basement. I started to lift weights everyday before my shift. Protein shakes flowed through me as I worked out seven days a week, 2 to 3 hours a day, and visions of bouncing fake thugs danced in my head. Literally. I was forcing my body to fit the image of strength that I would be willing to use. An image already created in my mind from a long time ago.

I was their leader.

By empowering them to be the agents of power, for me, I knew that they had to see the errors in the ways of the state for themselves. I wanted them to follow me to be agents of change and freedom. One cannot act upon their oppressors, they cannot evoke and change anything, unless they know for themselves the injustices in which they seek to dismantle. One may think they have a notion of what change and freedom may look like. That is, until they keep those very ideals from someone else. They had to see what their job was.

That this was not some fraternity of grown men who lived off the state and its mass incarceration of the youth. The pipeline that moved juvenile delinquents from down state to reside upstate in areas that have no industry but state employment. They were not that. But they had to bear witness to the force necessary to do the job. And what was the job?

1. To keep the residents safe and secure.

2. Maintain order throughout the program.

3. Follow the program schedule.

4. And protect ourselves.

What was done in between those standards was up to us. They had to build the relationships and trust from the residents in order for those four simple orders to manifest. And manifest consistently, is what we wanted. So we applied the pressure where and when we could. The residents started to pick up on how heavy we were coming and fell in line. They also saw that they weren't up against old men, who didn't want to hurt their knees, backs or shoulders. We were young, healthy, and relatively fit. We weren't the ones getting hurt in the restraints. They were. The worst they could do is pinch or bite us, and they did that a lot. But I had no issue plugging their noses for them to let go, grabbing a finger to rip their grip from one of the guys' skin on the back thigh or his side. The men would look at me for the magic words -

"Squeeze that motherfucker."

Oppression through violence was the way to maintain order. If we maintained order they would be free. And so would we.

As the residents caught on they would wait until the evening and not lock in for bed. That's when we became the "Wrecking Crew".

It started with having to train Simms as AOD. I would give him a shift or two when he was with me. Again, he continued to surprise me. He would revoke residents' phone calls, he would have staff do write ups for everything, even if a code wasn't called. But he also asked the staff to write more positive conduct reports as well. I could tell he was having his own internal battle over how to maintain order. Only his idea was clear. He was going to be the enforcer of the rules.

I continued to catch him in the residents' cells, tossing them around, picking them up and throwing them on their beds, with the lights off so the cameras couldn't detect anything. When kids started walking around with rug burns on their faces, that's when people started to ask questions.

I had to talk to him on the side. But this time I was more direct. He was young, he had the opportunity to do something good, and with longevity. But he had to understand that what he was doing was making bigger waves than he thought, and that I wasn't one to get caught up in that type of energy. I wanted him to know that he and I could show these kids how to move in a world that seeks to destroy them, and make it. We both had gone to college, both had street credibility, both wanted to help our people, and both were trapped in a system we sought to escape when we were young men ourselves. But we didn't have to be. He didn't need to be that. I wanted him to know that we would always have the opportunity to bounce a kid, but it's when we decide to do it that matters most.

He seemed to have understood that, but he continued his straight and narrow vision. When he would revoke a resident's phone call they would wait until it was time to lock in. And then they would stick it up.

"Code Yellow unit 2"

As per my orders, when a code was called, I would show up with Op2. But, I ordered Icheman or Cash to come if they were in the other unit. That way there would already be staff present for the "show", but three more bodies were coming to handle the situation and end it.

After a code Yellow was called, and we all showed up, the usual response was,

"Damn, *ALL* y'all gotta come?" from the insubordinate resident.

Simms would be barking in the background, while I tried to de-escalate and prevent a code White being called. All too often though, the resident wouldn't go to his cell without putting up a fight. And we had no issue obliging that request. It became a simple act that I no longer hesitated to implement. If they weren't listening it became easier.

Take one step back. Ask them "one last time", and if they refuse, "Code White."

And we would scoop them up, they would usually be scratching, clawing, kicking, and any other attempt to do bodily harm to us, and we would toss them into the farthest part of their cell. Turn around, slam the door, and lock it.

There were times when the residents tried to outwit us. One time a resident covered his door window with paper and soap. We couldn't see inside the cell, again, posing a threat or danger to themselves. I knocked on the door and told the resident that he needed to remove the paper from his window.

He responded,"Fuck you bitch! I'm in here butt ass naked and I'm trained to go!"

"Where are you training to go?" I asked mockingly.

"Bitch Ass! I'm trained to go and I'm naked, what the fuck you gone do?" he responded with anger.

I couldn't help but laugh. I let it go for a minute and secured the other residents and ensured all was clear, and in good energy. I made sure that there was really only one issue at hand. And then I returned to the resident's cell door.

"Hallooooo, you need pillow fluff?" I asked him in a terrible Chinese accent.

"Fuck you!" he responded, and you could sense his frustration mounting.

"You need pillow fluff, Yes?" I asked again in the same voice.

"Fuck you bitch!", this time in a teenaged cracked voice of fury.

I walked away again laughing. Gave him another minute, and then went back.

This time I slipped a piece of paper under his door with a note that said;

Are you ok? Circle one - Yes or No

I heard the resident trying not to laugh behind the door.

"For real, my man. You good?" I asked one more time.

This was tricky because I couldn't allow him to keep his window covered, but I also would not be allowed to restrain him if he was naked. Him saying that he was "trained to go" is gang vocabulary for "let's fight." But he was no threat, and allowing him time to calm down, kept the order, and allowed for a non-violent solution. A big win.

I wasn't always so lucky.

One resident refused to leave the game room near the gymnasium. There was a foosball and a pool table in there. The pool sticks and balls always made me nervous because they're great weapons and easily accessible. So when I responded to the code in that room I was already on edge.

I immediately ordered staff to remove all the residents and return them to the units. I ordered Andrews, Op2, to stay back. Icheman and Cash both asked if they were needed. I dismissed them and looked at Andrews. He was standing by the game room door to make sure the resident didn't leave. After they all cleared out, I stepped into the doorway.

"Yo what's good? Whatchu tryna do?" I asked calmly with a blank stare into his eyes.

"Fuck that! Nothing's good" - what a surprise- "This is a stick up, I aint fuckin' leavin" he told me, in his fake tough guy voice.

I looked at Andrews, he looked at me with eyes asking "What's the plan?"

I looked back at the resident, rolling the pool balls on the table, bouncing them off of the sides and making them crack into each other. I knew what he was thinking. He wanted to use one of those balls. He was trying to distract us with his movements and the loud sound of *CRACK* as he slammed the balls into each other.

I nodded to Andrews to step forward. We stepped just inside the door, and I got his attention. I slowly closed the door behind me, locked it, and said, "Yo…Well, now you can't leave…….So what's it gonna be…?"

His facial expression changed. Andrews gave a grin, and we automatically split up to take our separate sides on the resident. He saw our intentions. He now saw that he had nowhere to go, no one to put a "show" on for. It was just him.

"You wanna leave with us….?" I asked one more time. Still serious, but a gentler tone.

"Naw Fuck Tha…" was all I let him get out.

"Code White" I called.

And Andrews hooked him and lifted him up off of the ground.

"Squeeze that mutherfucker!" I said with intensity.

And he did as commanded.

"Awwww Owwwww" the kid screamed.

"Oooooh, that hurts? I thought you were fucking hard? …..I guess not." calm and collected with a chuckle.

"Fuck you - aaaaaaah ooooowwww!" he responded in pain.

He tried to kick me. I ordered Andrews to put his body, face first, into the wall.

"Can't kick now, can you?"

Andrews tried not to laugh.

"Push'em Andrews." and he did. Right into the wall.

This time the kid tried to take the pain. That's when you know you have them. When they don't want you to know that they are hurting, that's when they comply. They just need to meet their threshold of pain. For some, pain is freedom. It's a release. When they no longer believe that they can defeat their situation through violence, they are forced to communicate. Communication is one of the first steps towards liberation.

This proved to be true as the men started to communicate with me, and honestly.

"Yo, Ace, you've been letting us handle things, for real." Cash said at the end of shift one night.

Icheman looked at me with a smile, and the other men were there too, eager for confirmation of their collaborated inference.

"I am." I said smoothly. "I trust you guys, and you need to maintain order regardless of who's AOD, know what I'm sayin'." and looked all of them in the eye.

"Yeah, Simms be doin' some crazy shit sometimes." Lamont said in his goofy stoned voice.

"Yeah, I never really trust what he's going to do." Gruden added.

"I feel like he sets me up to do a restraint after he does a kid dirty. Then I look like a dick. Then I'm always targeted after his shit." Icheman opened up too.

They were trusting me, not only with the job and commanding them, but they trusted me with their personal insight on the job, and points of concern they felt I could assist them with. My strategy was working.

Then Cash asked,"Yo, you should let us see the video from the 'large group disturbance' ". - he air quoted "I want to see that shit."

"You all wanna see that shit?" I asked all the men.

"Hell yeah." A chorus of excited men called out.

"Aight, follow me."

I took them to my office, all of them. They were cutting loose with each other cracking jokes, pushing each other, and being their younger selves. I led them with a smile on my face. *I was a proud big brother of some very good men.*

I knew what the video looked like. I knew the grief I received from Leich. Smith telling me I didn't do shit. Everything about that night haunted me still. But to actually get over it was to expose the truth, and to let them see the truth too.

I pulled up the video on my desktop.

They all eyed where they were during the mayhem.

Cash called out Simms."Why the fuck did he hide in the door way?"

"Why didn't Holland escort that kid to his room?" Icheman questioned.

"What the fuck is happening in the corner with you Icheman?" Gruden asked.

"That fucker was trying to kick my knee out!" Nick responded

Then they all watched me try to restrain Van Lueven, and fail miserably.

"What the fuck was that Ace?" Cash asked with a chuckle.

"Yeah, I know. Honestly, I didn't want to hurt him……." I let that sink into all of them. "But, like I said, my job is to make sure you all get home to your families at the end of the night." I looked them all dead in the eye. "And I *WON'T* fail at that."

They all nodded in silence and gave me an intense look back of deep understanding.

We were in a new reality that we shared. We were all experiencing a paradigm shift. Theirs was more concrete because of their level of ignorance to the grand scheme of things. Yet, mine was not complete. I was not going to fully accept the shift I was entering. I wasn't ready to let go of being a liberator, even as a man of the state. Their choice was an unconscious one. They were happy to have a job with benefits and longevity. Longevity for me had nothing to do with the state, the job, or the benefits. Freedom for my people remained the goal. Perhaps it was just freedom for myself. Whatever it was, freedom was going to be achieved by any means necessary.

Chapter 18

Winning On Both Fronts

As a lover of history I would often wonder what people thought when it was discovered that the world wasn't flat, or that the sun, moon, and planets were actually revolving around the sun, and not the earth. This complete paradigm shift created a new reality for people living in those historical times. Imagine, that for your entire life you believed that the earth was the center of the universe, and that it was flat. You would've believed that life can only be formed on this flat plane of existence, and that this flat plane had an ending point that one will fall off of if they went too far. These ideas sound ridiculous to many living in the present because we now have proof, factual evidence, to support this shift in reality. That evidence came from Ferdinand Megelin who was said to have navigated the complete circumference of the world.

It took a man, brave enough to face the false claims of reality, to push out the doubts of his own beliefs, to challenge the status-quo, and to no longer accept the dogma of others, to prove that everyone was living under a false pretense of life. This paradigm shift, or acceptance of a new way of "doing" and "believing" is based on an accumulation of evidence. Once this evidence is seen as truth and reality, it becomes hard to declare it false. My reality was undeniable. I had to face it that I had to stand up against the status-quo. I had pushed out my old beliefs and prepared myself to live under this new paradigm shift and new reality, but I would do it differently. With this new lens of reality I would lead the young incarcerated men to a better understanding of life and how to be successful at it.

"Bro! It just sounds like you're bodying kids. Is that any different than what was happening before? Ma'fuckers still believe the earth is flat even with the evidence…because today you can just fucking make evidence up….so everything can be questioned, right…..but Yo…. you bodying kids like that, even with the evidence that supports that that shit don't work, just sounds like you perpetuating the same lie to me…."

Rick and I had been putting in work into the operation and he was spending a lot of his free, and not so free, time up at the house making sure we got everything going. G was putting pressure on us. He shifted his thoughts, which was another constant recurrence for him, and he wanted the funds from the operation to cover not just the electric bill, but the mortgage as well. This was of course after he made the first payment and he realized that he didn't want to come out of pocket if he didn't have to. The way he saw it, with this operation that was the scenario. It was a good thing Rick and I could handle business the way we did.

But with all that, Rick didn't understand what I was dealing with on the other front of my life.

"And maybe I don't understand…..but I do know, out of all of our friends who went through the same system that you hold down now…..those dudes are dead, or still in prison. So what help did juvie do?"

It was as if he could see the contradiction I was trying to hide. I tried to hide it more.

"Bro! I would have had to body Frankie too!" I referenced an old friend who experienced exactly the same outcome Rick described. His life ended in early death. Franky didn't reach 30.

"True" and Rick laughed with sincerity.

"Trust me I never thought I'd even have this type of job, but Yo……if it's gonna be anybody, it might as well be me…." and I paused to break up some weed to roll up.

"That's one way to look at it." Rick adjusted a light before he sat down with me.

The attic was looking professional. The lighting and air system were perfect. The cold temperature outside kept the heat from the lights at the ideal sixty eight degrees. We were still in the vegetation phase. The plants were still little and could be mistaken for any vegetable, but the room was something to be proud of. Knowing that we were pulling this off increased my confidence in all areas of my life. Alyson was staying home more. And although her attempts to make our home, an actual home, was minimal, the fact that she stayed alleviated the frustration with her.

We had hosted our son's first birthday, both of our families were present, and both displayed sincere pride in our home and our family. We had invested in some quality furniture and bedroom sets, and the baby boy had more than I had at 10 by his first birthday. Alyson's dad provided us with every kitchen item needed from his restaurant in Manhattan. He also filled us with restaurant quality cut meats, and the quantity that came with it. We were painting and decorating. We were homeowners. And I got her to understand that we were homeowners with a secret and to how to maneuver with that. We kept it to just family visits, and the attic was off limits because it was cold and filled with dead flies. Which it was, until Rick and I cleaned it out. There was a two week stretch where a local construction company drywalled and insulated the entire attic. But no one knew that, and we kept it that way. The attic was just never mentioned.

"You still hitting those weights down there aren't you…?" Rick asked

"You know it."

"Yeah you can see that shit. I know when I was working out I was like….'yeah let's get it!' - too…..You getting big bro."

I flexed, feeling my own strength. I was going hard. The more testosterone that flows through a man's body the more aggressive he becomes. Hence steroid users are known for their erratic moods. They want to destroy one minute, then they realize that they're not normal. That they really are dangerous. When a man feels like he's dangerous, as much as he wants to fight it, deep down, he thrives off of that feeling. Men gauging themselves against their willingness to wage war against humanity is rooted in their genetic response to testosterone, and their knowledge of their capacity and physical strength. From sports to war, it's that simple.

But when testosterone isn't enough, men will scheme to destroy another man. Just like Thompson was trying to do to V. Smith. Mercel was still hesitant to sign any documents against Vern and was starting to become scared. Mike was really pushing her to "not let him do this to anyone else." And Mike, with all his military experience, could not see that Stephanie did not want to ruin this man's life.

One day after he was pushing the papers in front of her face and she refused to sign, Mike stormed out cursing leaving her and I in the office alone.

"Steph." I turned and looked at her. "Do you want to do this?"

"No," she said. "But Thompson is making this sound serious and I don't want to hurt anyone."

I looked out the window and Smith was walking with a teacher, Mary Salerno, and they went to his office. I looked at the clock and noticed that it was 2:45. School had been out for over thirty minutes. *Why was Mary still on grounds? And why was she going to Smith's office, WITH Smith?*

I went back to Mercel.

"Look." I continued. "It is serious, but we can't make you do it. But if you're not going to sign those docs, I suggest you keep away from Vernon. For real Steph, leave him alone."

"Thank you." she said with emotion and she looked at me.

The look was weird, and somewhat engaging. I locked eyes with her, but gave my AOD furled brow and said, "You're welcome. Now go home....get the hell out of here." And smiled.

"So she never signed?" Rick needed to know.

"Naw Bro, and I couldn't really let her take down another brother too, shit was fucking crazy. But I tell you, she was definitely fucking around with him. But for real - I have a sense she's not the only one he's fucking at that place."

We looked around at our operation. There were eighty one marajuan plants in my attic. Nine lights, two air conditioners, two air filters, completely enclosed in thick plastic. The smoke from the spliff surrounded us, the heat from the lights made us sweat, even as we sat still.

"Bro....I don't know how you work at that place? I see why you keep tossing those plates around though. But you need to make sure that you take care of yourself there.....shit bro, take care of yourself here. How's the baby boy?"

"He's good." I responded with a different tone. "They've been staying home a lot more which is nice."

"Shit you got this big ass house...I hope she's staying in." And he continued.

"I wouldn't be a part of that sexual harassment deal though. It's one thing to put the hurt on the kids.....it's another to put the hurt on a grown man and his family." and Rick hit the spliff. "Especially if the chic doesn't even want to pursue the shit....you guys are forcing her to do that.....I don't know bro? I think we need to get this shit right here to pop off so you can devise a new plan."

I always relied on Rick to provide me with positive insight. But this time, he didn't know. I was embarking on my own journey around the world. I was the brave soul who chartered the new territories in search of new ways. He was accepting the old ways of perceiving the world. Truth can only be realized by those who seek it within the confines of their lives. Rick couldn't see my reality because it was mine to see, not his. All too often individuals expect another individual to have the same perspective or vision as them. However, this rarely happens. Even when they experience the same event, their perception of the event will differ.

No. Rick didn't know what I saw. He didn't know what I needed to do to maintain order within the chaos. The only other people who saw the truth as I did, were my men.

Chapter 19

The Big Run

Winter finished itself. Spring had come and gone, and so did the summer. As fall set in, it was clear that everything was falling into place. At home, we had produced three cycles by this time, and the cash shut Alyson up. G was satisfied, but I had become so busy that we weren't communicating very much. He would text me while I was at work, and my phone would be locked up, and even if it wasn't there was no service anywhere on facility grounds anyway. I would text him back on my way home and we would exchange necessary information, but even that had silenced. At the time I wasn't too concerned. But when I wasn't able to get in touch with him on the last cycle, at the end of summer to wire his end of the profits, I began to worry.

Meanwhile, Amazon boxes constantly were piled up on the front door of the house as Alyson began to understand the benefits of my hustle. From mom clothes to every kind of all natural "Pampers" replacement diapers from all around the world, to toddler clothing and "the best American made" tupperware there is. She was happy. We went camping with "parent friends" of ours, Tom and Jessica. Tom was a jeweler, and his wife Jessica was dedicated to making their local jewelry business thrive, and it was. They were doing well for themselves and took no issue with sharing about their special invitation to Antwerp and how it radically changed his business.

Jessica and Alyson both were pregnant at the same time and were in a New Paltz mother's class together. So they could ensure their "crunchy granola" roots would be passed down to their children. Sarah was from Long Island, which was more of an oxymoron to me, and Tom was from the Albany area. His dad was head of the entire marketing division for a large grocery store chain in Mid and Upstate New York. They both came from the complete opposite of crunchy granola. Tom would retell how he almost died when his parents tried to harvest wild mushrooms, and he really did almost die. And Jessica would always reference Long Island and her mother's house and how gorgeous it was and how she wanted the large bay windows like that.

For us, Alyson's and I attire never matched and we regularly did not dress to match on any occasion. She would wear baggy hippie pants and an accessible shirt for our now one and half year old to breastfeed from. I would just try to match her so she wouldn't look too bad. Ripped up wholly jeans and a hoodie would usually suffice. But when one regularly has a large amount of cash on hand, appearances mean nothing. We ate wherever we wanted and however much we wanted. Shopped at Wholefoods for a full home groceries restocking twice a month, eighty dollar bottles of vitamins to keep Alyson's "natural" hormonal balance in order, and to make sure her teeth and hair didn't fall out. I didn't know what half the stuff was, but often wondered if *I* should take some of them. What did I know, it was all top of the line and great for your body. I was ultimately too afraid that it would put estrogen into my system. And that was all I needed to know. I was still hitting the weights hard, and was becoming quite the specimen myself. There was no way I was going to take a risk like that. I just kept drinking my high end protein shakes and eating a balanced healthy diet. Life was good.

The progress was matched at the YLA as well.

The men were doing a great job communicating with the residents. They were starting to talk to them as I would do. Personally, to the side, promoting the positives, and reassuring their progress, all the while holding them accountable. That never prevented them from doing stupid shit though.

One day, when I was responding to a Code White, as I approached the unit I could hear the chaos inside. By now I was always first to be on the scene, and Andrews or whoever Op2 was, would follow shortly behind. I no longer felt anxious when responding to a Code White. I started to respond slower to Code Yellows to allow my men to de-escalate the situation themselves, empowering them with authority and trusting their commitment to our goal. To get them home, and to get home safe after every shift. That made it so when they did have to call a Code White, and I arrived on the scene, it was felt.

So when responding to this in code. I displayed the difference. I walked through the first set of doors, I could see blurs of red from the residents' shirts running around the unit. They were, as if it were the natural order of things, throwing the garbage can and flipping the furniture. But systems quell all natural order, and what was once the natural order of things, however chaotic or barbaric they were, systems are a force, and are therefore created to destroy the barbarism that plants the seeds of anarchy. I was the force. I was the system to follow.

So when I entered the unit, and resident Ortiz ran by me just as I opened the door, I closedlined him to the floor, picked him up by the back of his shirt and dragged him to his cell. He didn't even try to resist.

"AAAAY YO!" I yelled in my most authoritative voice. "If you don't want the trouble…. line up at your doors!" and those that weren't involved did as they were instructed to do.

Of the two remaining, one was hooked by a 6-2 staffer, Brodent. I was always glad when he took a shift with us. He was young, and never backed away from putting it on a kid. So with him having the other resident secure, and the other staff putting residents in their cells. The last one left, just like in all ends of a natural order, he followed suit with the system and locked in. He had no choice but to.

I was feeling like I was becoming a big iguana. Only I was rallying the other big iguanas and even some of the smaller ones to take over the whole lake. I was walking on water. We were taking control and putting order where there was chaos. Yes we were agents of the state. Sure we monopolized the violence. But by monopolizing the violence we took it from them to use on each other. The protocols for after a restraint were taken with care. We always looked to rebuild the relationship after we had to restrain a resident. We would process the shifts events afterwards, like I learned as a therapist. I taught them angles and ways to talk to residents as individuals during pre-shift briefings. I assigned them to work with certain residents in order to ensure relationships were being built. And if the kid faked caring to get home, that was acceptable. Sometimes we all have to fake like we care to make it, and that was a lesson learned as well.

Home office had sent the message out that overtime needed to be cut drastically. Schfraffenberger was not having any of it. All AODs were no longer allowed to get hours for arriving early and meeting and planning, like we did daily, five to six hours over time and a half. And we had to end our shift on time. No more overtime for writing the shift report at night, three to four hours of time and a half. But losing money from the state didn't bother me. I had other means. But what did bother me was the money the state saved from OT, was used to hire new staff. New staff meant that we had to train the staff, and when you have to train new staff, the system becomes vulnerable.

I helped Johnson get his credentials together to teach the Technology class for the education program. Gruden decided to follow his family tradition and join the New York State Troopers. McGhee got a job back in Queens and moved home. And countless of nameless souls had already been hired, only to have quit before we could even send them to the Academy. Pearson left and took a job as a court officer. It was the same pay grade and all he had to do was say, "All rise." and collect a check.

But this created another situation. We needed another pay grade 18.

Leichtenberger called me into his office one day. He gave me a lot of credit for the way things had been going at the facility. Restraints were down, and although we did what we had to do, in the grand scheme of things, it was working. The residents were getting in line.

"Literally and figuratively" he noted. "I mean…I look outside and I see them walking in straight lines, all together, not like some motley crue meandering all over the place. We're in single digit numbers for restraints. A few months ago I thought this place would get shut down." and he laughed.

"But listen Ace." he continued and shifted his focus. "We need a new counselor now that Pearson left. We're going to have to hire a few more 18's, probably a few more staff too. You're doing great as AOD. You wanna keep that, or do you want to take the counselor's position?" He looked at me with sincere intent. "Think about it…..and you let me know."

"Yeah….I understand. Thank you." I responded unsurely.

And I was very unsure. I knew his other option was Simms. I knew that when Simms was AOD the men were more uneasy, and the shift always seemed like it was teetering on the edge of dysfunction. I knew this because the men shared it with me. I witnessed what he would do if he had full control. I also knew that he really wanted to help those kids. So I asked the men what they thought.

"Naw Ace! Let that mutherfucker be the counselor. Everyone here needs consistency." Cash, as usual, the first to speak up.

"Bro. He doesn't like me at all. He takes my authority away from me right in front of the kids every chance he gets." Icheman followed.

"I mean I don't really give a fuck, man." Andrews spoke in an unusual seriousness. "I mean I don't mind the shit he does." and laughed.

"Yeah, because he always brings you to fuck some kid up!" Lamonte cracked on him and laughed back

"That's what I mean!" Andrews continued to joke. "I don't give a fuck!"

"For real gentlemen. We're getting the job done. And the way we want to. If I take Pearson's spot. Will you follow Simms, or will you follow what we do now…..?"

"Bro…" Andrews didn't hesitate. "We're going to follow whoever's in charge."

"Not like that!" Cash snapped back.

"Yeah. No Sir. It won't be the same." Icheman stated like the good right hand man he was.

"Yeah. Fuck that! Y'all know I hate paperwork anyway" I said, and we all shared a laugh. And that was all that I needed to say.

I told Leich the next day that I recommended Simms for Pearson's position.

"I think that this will be a good fit for him. Plus, honestly Leich, I don't want to have to deal with Aftercare and all that paperwork."

"I don't blame you. Those cocksuckers are always backed up. And, Yeah, fuck all that paperwork, and I think those guys really trust you. That's good."

"*What the fuck is happening*" I thought. I left his office before he could switch up his tone. I still never left his office on a positive note, and I took the opportunity to do just that.

With Simms now solidly out of interference, and with Thompson on a solo project to ruin Vernon, I was left with me and my crew. The new staff we scheduled to train on my shift. We got more military veterans, a few of them female, a few other female workers for CSU, and my man Jenkins. Jenkins was the former heavyweight boxer, and still built like one. He was very hesitant to hook a kid and relied on having good relationships with the residents.

He said to me one time, "You know Ace" in his deep somewhat punchy former boxer voice, "I feel like I'll just let a kid have it. You know man ... .I've been fighting my whole life, that's my real training man."

"I got you Jenkins. But you're gonna have to hook a kid sooner or later." I said in the voice of his ranking officer and gave him a hard slap on the shoulder.

"I know Sir, I know. I just don't want to hurt a kid, you know…"

"I do." I said. "But you know what….I fucking do!" and I looked at him with all the seriousness I had. Eyes wide and hard.

Jenkins didn't yet understand that our daily shift co-depended on one of seventeen variables. Those being the choices of 17 individual juvenile delinquents during the course of an 8 hour shift. It didn't take long for Jenkins to get his wakeup call.

"Code White - Unit 2" I heard Jenkins call on the radio one day.

No Code Yellow, or any hint that anything was going down. I was coming from my office which brought me from the back side of unit 2. When I jogged around the corner of the front of the building I saw Jenkins with his fists in the air, hopping on his toes, ready to box.

"What the fuck is he doing?"

Then I saw what was happening. He had taken a few residents outside for some fresh air. Maintenance had left out a few fence posts. The long, 6 foot, green ones, with a spayed point at the end. The resident was swinging it at Jenkins and was legitimately trying to knock him out. It was clear that something else had happened prior to that because the kid was very emotional and crying.

"Get the fuck back I'll fucking kill you." the kid cried out.

He thrusted the post at me, in a jabbing motion. I didn't try to de-escalate. I didn't try to talk him out of it. There was no talking. Only action. I stepped to the side and grabbed him with both hands and threw him to the ground. I looked at Jenkins and ordered him to restrain the resident. I got up, looked at the other 3 residents and said, "Go back to the unit." and took a deep breath.

And they did, as if nothing happened. I called Lamonte and he escorted them back in. Jenkins and I stayed back with the kid and handled the situation. We punked him out a bit during the paperwork protocol. Telling him how he had the right tool but he was to dumb to use it. But I showed Jenkins the energy needed to fight the fight he now faced.

The kid pressed chargers on me. But since I was the union representative and had already established myself in the Professional Employees Federation (PEF), I was starting to feel untouchable. I had already reviewed the tape. I knew the questions they were going to ask, and I already memorized my statement in preparation. However, choices always played a role. And the resident decided to call his ombudsmen, or juvenile law representative "a fucking faggot" and to "go kill himself". I never heard about that case again.

We were doing it. Fuck what Rick thought. That was my man, but he didn't know. He damn sure didn't know what we had to do. If he did, he would know that we were doing things differently. We did find a new way. I believed in what we were doing, and we were doing good. But the grips of winter would return. Although we had a comfortable feeling of control, we knew when winter came, we were all at the mercy of the elements, the variables, and the exponential powers that be. And despite all the new faces coming and going. One thing was constant. The YLA was ours.

Chapter 20

The Beginning Of the End

"I wonder what would happen if you never cut them down....
and like, just let them grow?" my brother Zeek asked Rick and I.

He, and my other younger brother Darien, along with their
cousin and much loved adopted little brother of mine, Brian, had come
over to help trim up the newly dried and ready for sale crop we had just
harvested. A large blue tarp covered the living room floor of the inlaw
suite of our home. A huge mound of leafy buds still attached to their
long stalks lay in the middle of it.

"It would eventually flower, literally, and start to dry up, die."
Rick gave Zeek the answer he was looking for. "That's why we gotta
make it look pretty fellas. Make sure you get all those big sun leaves off.
Then pass it on to me and Zeek, we'll do the final touch."

We had a system that we used to get this part of the job done. He
and the boys would come up on a Friday night. Alyson would go to her
mother's. When I got home, usually after 11 pm, they would already be
set up with the guidance of Rick. We would cut and trim all night. I'd
leave for work at 1230 pm the next day, and come back and continue
until it was all done. It would take us all weekend. We later discovered
that there were machines for this job, but we were too cheap for that
investment. And as much as it pained us to hand trim 20 pounds of
cannabis, we actually enjoyed the time together.

I was able to catch up with my brothers and Brian, listen to what
they were going through and provide fatherly/big brother advice. All
while smoking and beautifying our favorite plant. But Zeek' question

made me think. If cannabis would eventually die if it were never picked, was it subjected to the system created by man? A system strictly for man's own benefit. Or is that just the cycle of cannabis?

If man didn't utilize the plant for its medicinal purposes, what would it be? Would it be just another dead plant blowing in the wind of a wild field? It wasn't like the tree that would keep growing and maximizing its own output, only to meet its fate through the choice of another living entity, like man. That made me look at the plant differently. We had a system that maximized its output. We had a predetermined date that we were going to pull the plants all out. We worked tirelessly for it to be ready on that specific date.I fed it daily with high end nutrients and created a stable environment that even Alyson said, "Was the best room in the house." All the while, it was c0-dependent, and only living because of the care taken by me. It would be just a wild plant, producing low THC count, and no one would even care about it, without man's diligence.

The tree will grow and grow. Whether it's pruned or not. Water or not. Trees will communicate with each other, lend nutrients and assist each other in their growth in countless and amazing ways. They stand tall, face the elements, until they face a system, and become a victim. The system is ours, and so is the choice for humans to cut the tree down for their benefit. We justify the death of the tree with what it materializes into, a house, a deck, barn or whatever. Yet we'll chastise the lumberjack for providing us with the raw goods to build what we desire. We don't ask the trees if they approve of what we are doing because we have a system. And the system is relying on wood for our own reward and growth, it's that simple. And we don't argue that point.

What we argue is the ethical application of our choices. If you are in disagreement about chopping down trees for homes, what materials do you use? If you don't like drug use, like cannabis, but accept pharmaceutical prescriptions, what choice are you really making? Ultimately we rely on the choices of others to predetermine our own choice. We sadly rely on the so-called good decisions of others when it comes to housing, medical care, and access to our luxuries and necessities. All the while, other powers and forces have told us that "this is the good choice" and we blindly accept it. We may not admit it, but we do.

We are all somewhat co-dependent on other people's choices.

Rick was depending on my choices as the grower to produce a product that he could move. G was depending on us both to do our jobs adequately in order for him to make the move he wanted. Alyson was depending on me to produce and care for her. And I was left depending on juvenile delinquents and other men with violent tendencies to get home safe every night. We were all hoping the "system" we were a part of would function at optimum capacity.

The production side of the business was doing well and we had little concern. Yet, one night when I got home a piece of mail gave me a reason to be.

I still hadn't heard back from G in quite some time. About a month had passed by and I received no text backs or phone calls. I was calling multiple times a day, texting randomly and was even talking shit to him via text to get a response. Nothing. Then I read that piece of mail, with big black bold letters on the envelope that read, "Foreclosure Notice Open Immediately." It was December, and the letter stated that the mortgage had not been paid for the months of October and November, and that the house faced foreclosure if payments were not received.

"What, the, Fuck!"

How could this have happened? Where was G? What happened to him? How could I remedy this? All of these thoughts created a vortex in my mind of worst case scenarios of "what ifs". This last crop was even more important now. It became a necessity, a word it was never meant to be. There were other necessities on hand as well. I still had to go to work, and do my job.

Simms took Pearson's spot as the new counselor, and he was doing a rather good job at it. You could tell he enjoyed the power he now wielded. With my approval and the stroke of his pen, we could send, or not send, a lot of kids home. We started to collaborate more on how to better implement state mandates into the facility and improve our work and the lives of the residents.

The biggest challenge was all of the new faces. We had hired one of Thompson's Marine buddies, Sandowsky, as a YDA. Because of his veterans status, and a bachelor's degree, he was able to apply for the pay grade 18 position. And with help from Mike, he was a sure thing. Ericson, also put in for the other 18 position, and was hired. That was a relief because I needed a non-military guy to understand how we moved on the 2-10.

Because of Ericsons long time at the YLA he understood what we were doing and was totally on board. Sandowsky wanted to be like Mike, and only wanted to use force to gain his position and so-called respect. He got his position, but he never earned mine or any of my men's respect. The residents hated him, and even as a YDA he was not very effective at de-escalation or prevention. Watching his episodes on the camera infuriated me. He would often allow the violence to erupt before responding. Only after it was initiated would he then jump into action. It was as if he wanted them to violate so he could call a code and have a reason to put his hands on someone. I shared these same concerns with Leich who never saw anything I said as a true concern, and as usual, they were dismissed.

With Ericson and Sandowsky on the 2-10 as 18's, Mike only had one day that he was on the shift with me, and even then, I was the AOD for the shift. It had become clear to all that Friday to Tuesday, the 2-10 shift was mine. The men were mine and they started to move like a well oiled machine. Even on Wednesdays and Thursdays in my absence, the shift was waveless.

However, training the both of them at the same time posed a unique challenge. We would have four 18's on the shift at times. Ensuring they were all delegated correctly, and that the men and residents all knew who held the real authority was difficult. Simms and Holland alternated and were never on at the same time. So that helped. One night unit 1 had their counselor, and the next night unit 2 had theirs. When Sandowsky and Ericson were both on, I assigned them both to a unit as well. This provided them the opportunity to work with the men who had put in work and created the culture we were seeking to maintain.

I figured if they saw how the men handle critical situations, communicated with each other , and me, that they would see that the men did their jobs. And all they had to do, as 18's, was to support them. Ericson knew the guys well. He went out with them in his free time and he was a part of "the crew". Sandowsky was Thompson's guy. He was treated as such. As a YDA, Icheman would constantly complain about how he talked shit to the residents and other staff. Apparently Sandowsky was in a real underground Fight Club in Binghamton. He regularly would talk about fucking up Andrews, Cash and Icheman. Cash would crack jokes in the parking lot about knocking him out.

"Bro, the guy watches live fire fights on Youtube from Iraq. And he just talks about how he wishes he was there." Icheman blew our minds.

"How do you know?" I asked.

"The mutherfucker told me!"

"Bro...fuck that. I don't do anything to remind me of that place." said Andrews.

"Yeah we know that Andrews, you big stoned baby...." Ericson said, pointing to Andrewss knee brace and laughing.

"Bro, My shit hurts, Alright!" Andrews tried to be serious.

"Yeah, you just can't do stairs right.....?" I stated jokingly giving him a dumb look.

"Yea! They fuck me up!" Andrews said. And all we could do was laugh.

"You know Simms is still doing shady shit in the office, right?" Icheman turned with a serious tone.

I looked at him. We locked eyes to communicate in ways only men can with their eyes. Especially when you have a shared reality, a shared truth, a shared vision. Cash looked at me. Then to the ground, and locked my eyes.

"Bro, I don't see what the big deal is…" Andrews said.

"No, that fucker could get us all in trouble….but, I mean he is rather good at doing it behind closed doors." added Ericson.

"Yeah, not when he asks you to go with him…" Cash pointed out.

They were all right in their own perspectives. Simms was a wild card. He did risk chaos to our order. He did put my men in dicey situations. But, he did do it off camera and behind closed doors. And as long as at the end of the day he did his job, which he did, like Andrews said, maybe it was no big deal.

I remember the first time I came home to Rick and my brothers after work, fully dressed in my state issued black all OCFS attire…….

"Yooooo, straight up you look like a cop B!" Brian said. He was a big teddy bear that always had the first joke ready.

"You really do that shit huh?" Zeek asked. As if seeing me in my uniform made it more absolute for him.

By now, they were used to it and Rick would have them working with chicken wings and pizza boxes everywhere. My brothers never lost their sense of wonder and amazement in the job. They were 18 and 17 years old, and never seen that much and that high of quality of bud all at one time in their lives. But by the time 2 hours of scissoring sets in, the magical impression wears off. And it's work. Which lead to deep conversations like Zeek lead us to.

"The original strand of cannabis wasn't like this though. Like the original corn or maize is not the corn we eat today." Rick was making a point. "It was cross breeding and pollination that allowed for certain plants to thrive and others not to."

"Like tomatoes." Brian said with a joke. "I love tomatoes...with just salt, Yoooo..."

"No for real though, they even have hydroponic tomatoes." Darien added.

"Right! So now there is no way to get to what an original tomato would really taste or look like." Rick tried to hit another point.

The conversations would somehow all tie together and make sense to us in those late nights, smoking, listening to random music, going back and forth from whipping our hands with paper towels from the pizza and chicken wings, or rubbing alcohol to clean the resin off of our fingers. We always tried to bring it back around to the beginning.

"So what you saying is 'Man' being doing shit that benefits him, all the while he fucking shit up for everything else." Zeek capped this one off.

"Riiight...!" we all said out of sync.

"Choices." Rick said with conviction and intent.

And it did go full circle.

"Yo, it gets cold up here B!" Brian said as he and Darien stepped outside to smoke a cigarette.

And it did get cold quickly that year. There was a polar vortex over the area. At work we laughed about it only because it was so damn cold. Trying to explain it to Brian wasn't worth it, but Rick didn't hesitate, "Yeah, it's different up here huh?" and he looked at me.

It had been a dry summer and fall. So when that polar vortex hovered over the area for that month of December the ground instantly hardened. There was already a good 6 to 7 inches of snow on the ground. Winter had put its hands down and its frozen touch put all that was alive to rest. But the YLA kept going.

The stress of not knowing what happened to G was getting to me. I couldn't get in touch with his apartment manager. I didn't have any other family members in Cleveland that I could contact to check on him, or to give me any information. Alyson hadn't seen the letter, so she had no clue about what was going on, again. All there was to do was the job. It didn't matter what was happening to the house, my product, my family, my own health, the YLA was going to run rain, snow, sleet or hail, and we were the men of the state to do it.

The stress mounted and one shift I went in with severe migraine. I met up with Ericson before pre-shift and told him what I was going to do. I wanted Sandowsky to be AOD for the shift. It was time to start letting others take the reins. I wanted Sandowsky to rely on Ericson and the others, and not just me.

"And trust me, I ain't savin' shit tonight!" I added.

Ericson never seemed to be really bothered by anything. He had a happy go lucky stoner nature and a bachelors in aquatic sciences. He was certainly out of place, careerwise, and once I got to really know him he became a close friend.

On que Sandowsky started walking towards the office.

"I mean look at him Ace." Ericson said as we watched him march up to the building. Sandowsky was a big guy, not country big like Icheman, or fat big like Ericson. Not even tall like Andrews, or athletically muscular like Cash. No Sandowsky, standing at 6 '2, about 225 lbs., did three tours of duty in Iraq and still walked like he had his pack on his back.

"He looks like he just pulled himself out of the hamper." I said to Ericson, and we laughed because his khakis were really that wrinkled.

It was negative nine degrees outside at 1:45pm. It would only get colder.

When it came time for the pre-shift briefing, I gave my orders.

"Ok gentlemen, we've been on a good run, and I'm very proud of you guys. Tonight, we have to switch it up and allow for some room for growth. With that, Sandowsky, you're AOD tonight. We're also short staffed tonight. With OT being cut we don't have coverage. So Ericson, I need you on the floor in unit 1 with Lamont and Cash. Icheman, Mercell, and Jenkins you guys are on unit 2. Simms will be there with you guys. Andrews, stay away from the fucking ice Ok - they all laughed - I'm fuckin' dying right now, I have a really bad migrain, like for for real. So I'm gonna be 'big brother' in the sky from the camera room. Sandowsky - You have anything to say?"

Sandowsky had a stupid look on his face like he just ate a lemon and was holding it in the side of his mouth.

"No ... .just, uh, have a good shift guys." he said.

I told Sandowsky to make sure that both units move together. No stragglers. Since we were short staffed it was important to *not* spread out the men in case of a disruption. I told him that he can count on Ericson to hold down unit 1, and for him to move with Simms and unit 2. I was attempting to give Ericson a chance holding things down, which I knew could. He had Cash and Lamont, who had that unit on lock. They had fewer residents and there was no potential trouble expected from that unit.

Unit 2, Simms' unit, was the wild card. And Mercell and Jenkins, put a little more pressure on Icheman to be the single authority. They had Simms, but Simms had to do other work that his position required him to do. I did order him to escort and supervise his unit for dinner and through the evening program. Once they returned to the unit he could handle his counseling sessions and whatever he had to do. That was a directive. Unit 2 had almost double the residents, and they were all potential "stick it up" kids.

"Aren't I AOD?" he asked.

"Yes, Sandowsky, you are but, you gotta move with the unit, I would too. That's what we do." I looked at him this time like he was stupid and was still sucking on a lemon.

He scoffed, made a smug sourface, and said,"Ok, Sir."

"*Fucking Sandowsky!*"

I made my way to the camera room for the shift.

The cold was making the residents resistant to move for the program. They wanted to stay inside instead of going to the main building for the Activity Rooms and the gym.

"Yo its mad cold bro! Can't we stay in the unit?" many of the residents were asking.

I was watching the entire shift on four screens split into four boxed screens each. As I watched body language and positioning, all was going well. It was getting so cold that the cameras that were stationed high on the fence, which would rotate, were frozen and wouldn't turn with the controls. This was leaving some blind spots that couldn't be picked up.

"*When the residents leave the gym, this could pose some trouble.*"

Program commenced.

I sat in the camera room, alone, with sunglasses on. The fluorescent lights were throbbing in my eyes. I got comfortable with the chair, adjusted the lumbar, tilted it back a little bit, and kicked my feet up, one hand on the mouse, the other holding my head.

At 2:15 it was very calm. Not like a calm before the storm. No, the men were all very lax, and chill. They were playing board games with the residents, and I could tell they were showing them movies that they had brought to watch after rec time. Ericson walked around the unit to do security checks, and logged them, and continued to keep a positive attitude with all on the unit. The facial expressions of everyone was a good indicator of the climate, and that all were rather peaceful and still.

Unit 2 was a different story. While Icheman and Mercell conversed with some residents, Jenkins was watching TV with another few, Simms had 2 residents in his office, and Sandowsky was walking around posturing. After he walked around with his chest out, no security checks, no log book check, he stood directly in the middle of the unit. Arms folded, in a strong stance. He just stood there. I watched Icheman look at him and then he looked up at a nearby camera, knowing I was watching, then he looked at Sandowsky again.

I noticed his concern. Icheman was very good at gauging the climate of the unit and reporting back to me. His insight was trusted and he knew that at times I needed to rely on his intuition. Sandowsky was making me a bit uneasy, but he eventually struck up a conversation with a resident and changed his posture. Although I never took my eyes off of the screen there was some rest to be had knowing that, as of that moment in time, all was good.

3:30 pm.

Unit 1 transitioned to Rec Room 1 to play video games. Their movement was good, lined up straight, moved together in order. They carried on as they should.

4:15 pm.

Unit 1 transitioned back to the unit with ease. Unit 2 was to move to Rec Room 1. Icheman was trying to round them up and get ready for movement. Mercell was coxing kids to put their jackets on. Jenkins stood by the door waiting for the line to form. Simms walked out of his office with 1 resident and pointed him towards the line. Sandowsky stood by the bubble and watched.

"It's been a month now as an 18, he still doesn't know what to do? Why is just standing there?"

A resident, named Saab, came over and said something to Sandowsky. You could tell by Saab's body language that he was talking trash to Sandowsky. Saab always did, and was always a mouth that needed to be shut.

"Fucking Sandowsky…lemon sucking fuck!"

Watching the program orchestrate, I had time to think and understand power.

History has proven time and time again that power is not about the might of the force, but the man who holds the force and his willingness to use that strength. And the only thing a man has is his mind to imagine and his hands to create. So all power is derived from what a man is capable and willing to do with such vigor, physically, to gain it. Meaning, true power, is in the choice of action.

Hitler had power. Yet he was plagued with poor decisions, and we are certainly glad he was. Even though he was surrounded by some rather wise and humanistic appointees, he ended up being the destruction of his own vision. The modern United States has all the technological and monetary power the world has ever seen. And yet, the decisions our leaders make leave a wake of disaster everywhere they send our fellow countrymen. Whether it's oil spills, wars, or climate change the genesis is man and what he chooses to do with his hands and the imaginative ingenuity he employs. It's not the state's systems that kept the YLA under control, it was the men behind the system that made the system work, or not.

I kept watching the screens. By now I had adjusted the seat back and forth, and up and down, several times. I found myself in between long moments of lull putting my head down and resting my eyes. I never took off my sunglasses. I watched my men.

Even Thompson getting the schedule wasn't helping me. He loaded the 6-2 shift with four YDAs a unit, an Op2, plus four to five 18's on a shift. Yes, the school program was under better control, but the stress was put on us, the 2-10, as we had less staff and less of a structured program. We had little choice but to stay engaged with them to win every shift. We had to be in every place at once and ensure that all safety and precautionary measures were taken. Mike had the power he wanted in his hands, but he chose to spread the staff out like that. Leichtenberger approved it. Within my scope of control, I had to do my best with what little resources they provided me.

It was just like the streets. Power plays for advantage, maneuvers to slowly erode profits and influence, persuade clients to seek better services, and undermine through weak associates. It was a classic case of how to take over someone else's organization. Thompson learned from the best though, not the streets, but the United States Marines. The U.S is the absolute apex predator to organized, and unorganized, governments. They do all of the above and are able to take over entire countries. I always knew "gangsterism" came from politics. That politicians are the first to run organized crime syndicates to exploit and ransack the globe for resources. They don't care who's back yard it is, you have what we want, so we take it.

Thompson was power grabbing in the exact same manner. Mercell, the schedule, being "Michael Jordan '', and most of all Leichtenberger. To Leich, Mike could do no wrong, and as Vern put it one day, "Ya can't fuck with his golden boy." I mentally spit in my own cup after that thought, in disgust. Was Mike doing this to me? Was he slowly plotting on me? Was Sandowsky his "dummy" sent to disrupt the good work my men and I were doing?

My head throbbed a little more as my brow furled in internal anger. A fire started to build inside of me and I could feel it starting to burn my body. As the ground started to crystalize and sparkle with the setting of the sun, I watched the units prepare for dinner. The units would move separately, but they all eat at the same time. Depending on the evening and how the program is running, at times, we would all go to the gym together instead of breaking them into two, and taking turns between the gym and the Activity Room.

The dining hall was two doors down from the camera room. As the AOD I had a directive to be present. So after both units had arrived, I took the ten step walk to the dinning hall.

"Oh shit, dis nigga Ace been here the whole time! Yo what's good Ace?" a resident said.

And I made my way around fist pumping and checking in with all of them. I would sit down with them while they ate. The other men would stand in their designated positions and maintain proximity to the exits and tables. At times I would even tell the cook to serve me a plate of food and actually eat with them. But not tonight.

"Where you been Ace." resident Jackson asked me.

"I'm the eye in the sky tonight baby." I responded.

"Oh word?" he replied with a head nod.

"That nigga watching everything." another said with a laugh.

"Yo, dat nigga Sandowsky AOD?" resident Stevens asked in hopes of clearing the implied bad news.

"I mean, tonight he's 'AOD' - and I gave air quotes - but you know what it is....dude's gotta learn to hold it down." I said in a low voice so only they could hear me.

I tried to be real with them, this particular set of kids were our best behaved residents, they knew the game, they were playing it well, and they knew that. I always chose to build relationships with the residents before I displayed the power I actually had. So when it was flexed they knew that it was for real. But that's just me.

"Yo, Y'all hold it down." I said, and I checked the log book, signed it, looked at Icheman, Ericson, and Cash for them to give me a signal that all was good, and I went back to the camera room.

Two minutes later Sandowsky came in.

"Hey Sir, can we all move to the gym together tonight?" he asked.

"Sandowsky, it's your show." and I looked at him surprised, and put my sunglasses back on.

"Ok." and he closed the door and I watched him return to the dining hall.

"Sans ... .AOD to CSU moving both units to the gym," he said over the radio.

"That's a Copy. All clear." CSU radioed back.

When they moved to the gym the steam from their breaths made it look like they were walking in a cloud on camera. Huddled together, hands in their pockets, and shoulders and necks tight to keep warm. The men didn't look any happier.

I called CSU on the phone.

"Lockert, the camera's are still not activating. Make sure you watch on your end. You have them all up. I need you to manually do it on your end. Are you able to?"

"Looks like F9 - the camera that views the main entrance of the gym is still frozen. And it ...looks... like F1 and 3 are frozen too."

"Yeah those ones are on the back part of the fence where the lights are dimmer. They're probably not getting warm enough. Ok... once they're in the gym I'm on. Alright?"

"Alright Sir." Lockert replied and we hung up.

I knew it had to be close to negative twenties degrees outside. My body was going back and forth. There was the fire that was still raging inside of me thinking about Thompson. And the freezing as the intensity of the polar vortex seemed to have put its frozen hold on everything. I shivered a bit, huddled up and tried to focus on the activity in the gym as the units arrived.

Everything was still calm. It was as if it were too cold for them to "turn it up."

6:45 pm.

This part of the shift was like the third lap of the mile. If they managed to keep positive energy during this stretch, the final lap, lock-ins for the night, would usually end in the same fashion. It was imperative that Sandowsky kept the momentum of the shift productive and moving in a good direction.

6:52 pm.

They all settle in the gym and Activity room. All still look relaxed. Simms takes resident Jones to the unit. He has a counseling session, so that makes sense. Andrews came to do medical runs. This is when residents who get medication make their way to medical to receive their prescriptions. That's like clockwork 7:30 am and 7:30 pm, that's where the street term "730" comes from. "Those niggas are 730," meaning crazy and they need their meds. Andrews takes Procket to medical. Andrews led him with his long stepped 6'8 body. The residents always looked funny walking alongside him. I saw Simms land back at the unit and go into his office. That's done.

I turn my focus back to Andrews arriving at medical. Then back to the gym and Activity Room. All good.

Andrews returns Prockett back to the gym, and then escorts resident Donovan to medical. Simms still behind closed doors. Sandowsky walking around the Activity Room. Ericson, Icheman and Cash were in the gym. Mercell and Jenkins were sitting down.

7:10 pm.

Andrews returns resident Donovan to the gym and escorts resident Bernard to medical. Simms still behind closed doors. Saab starts playing pool with resident Shabazz. Jenkins was sitting in the chair next to them. I could tell they were talking trash to each other about the game. Sandowsky was talking to Mercell, who was still sitting in the chair by the entrance way. Sandowsky, hands in his pockets looking like a stuffed chested devil dog. I could tell he was trying to do some sort of work/flirt type conversation with her. I never talked to any of the female employees in front of anybody for more than thirty seconds, unless there were other staff around. That way no resident would get any wrong ideas.

7:15 pm.

Sandowsky was still talking to Mercell. Simms was still behind closed doors. Saab is clearly losing in the pool game to Shabazz. Jenkins was laughing along with Shabazz. That doesn't help. Andrews starts to make his way back to the gym. They start to move back to the unit at 7:20. I see Ericson start to move around and give Icheman a motion to start rounding the residents up. Cash gets Sandowsky's attention. I see him nod in acknowledgment. Mercell gets up. Sandowsky watches her. Jenkins stands up. Shabazz misses the eight ball. Saab goes next and makes his shot. He's walking around with the pool stick running his mouth. Jenkins gives him a hand signal to come on. It was plain to see that Saab wanted to keep the game going. Jenkins gives a shoulder shrug and gives a gesture to go ahead. He shoots again and makes it.

7:20 pm.

"Ericson to CSU, moving unit 1 back to unit 1."

"That's a Copy. All clear."

"Copy."

Ericson led the residents out, Lamont held the door and Cash brought up the rear. Mercell and Icheman were lining up the other residents in the corridor between the gym and Activity room, waiting for Jenkins, Sandowsky, Shabazz, Saab, and Perez. Perez was Shabazz's boy. He started talking to Saab too. He wasn't ramping things up though. Saab still didn't take his shot. He was posturing with whatever words he was saying, pool stick in hand. Sandowsky waved them to come on. Jenkins supported him and tried to guide Perez and Shabazz towards the door. They make their way but they move slowly. Saab was still standing at the pool table. Mercell waves Shabbaz and Perez to line up from the doorway. Jenkins was standing closer to Saab now. Sandowsky was trying to coax him along with his shoulders hunched and giving soft body language.

"Op2 to CSU moving one resident from medical back to Unit 2." Andrews radioed.

"That's a Copy, clear to move." Lockert responds.

"Copy."

They finally get all three residents out of the activity room.

7:25 pm.

"Icheman CSU, moving unit 2 back to unit 2."

"Copy, all clear."

Mercell opened the door to lead them out. Icheman held the door for the residents. Simms was still behind closed doors in his office on unit 2. Saab stepped back away from the line. Jenkins took the rear and looked back. Icheman looked at Sandowsky too, who was now talking to Saab in a closer stance, but still looking soft. Saab appeared to be trying to negotiate something with Sandowsky.

7:27 pm.

Sandowsky tells Icheman and Jenkins to leave. Sandowsky was now alone with Saab in the corridor. The residents filed their way through the cold back to the unit where Simms was still in his office, and unseen and unheard from. They landed back on the unit, Simms stayed in the office with the resident.

What the hell are they doing?

Both units were settling into the evening routine of showering and getting ready for snacks and lock-ins.

7:30 pm.

"Op 2 CSU moving one resident to medical from unit 2."

"Copy, all clear."

There were still three more residents from unit 2 that needed to go to medical. Simms finally came out of his office with Jones, only to take another resident in and close the door again.

What the fuck Sandowsky!

He was still talking with Saab. I tried to get a closer look at Saabs face to try to better understand what was happening. I phoned Lockert.

"You see this?"

"Yes Sir."

"What the fuck is going on?"

"Saab just looks like he's being Saab, he doesn't look upset Sir."

"What the fuck! I'm coming over there." And we hung up.

I made my way to, and through, the dining hall, out the main entrance into the main corridor of the facility and walked into the CSU door. Lockert buzzed me in.

"They still there?"

"Yes Sir."

"Jesus Fuck!"

"What do you think he's doing?"

"I don't know but Sandowsky needs to get him the fuck out of there."

7:33 pm.

"Code Yellow in the Gym."

"Copy that. Code Yellow in the gym."

There was no threat, Saab wasn't doing anything provocative and Sandowsky, the AOD, called a Code Yellow.

"What the fuck! Who the fuck does he think is supposed to come....this mutha...fuck!" and I took my sunglasses out of my pocket and placed them on top of the key locker, pushed the door open and made a light jog to the gym.

I felt my eye sockets pulsated with every step, my feet trying to be light on the slick sparkled ground, avoiding the collections of black ice. I made it to the gym before 7:35 could strike my watch.

"Phewwww." I had to take a deep breath before I entered. Whenever I showed up on a scene I always made sure I caught my breath, settled myself, and then went in, even if it were just for literally a half of a second. I took about 5 seconds outside of the gym. It was so cold that as my lungs filled with negative fifteen degree air my head throbbed with every heartbeat. Pounding in my eyes. I took another deep breath and opened the door.

Fighting the blindness of the yellow fluorescent lights, my face hardened, so the manner in which this was going to be handled was on full display upon entry.

"Yo, this nigga Ace." Saab said in surprising delight.

"What the fuck are doing Saab?" I asked commandingly.

"Sir…." Sandowsky tried.

"Dis nigga fuckin' shit up….all I asked was for my last shot. I even said I'd put the shit away…" Saab cut him off.

I looked at Sandowsky with a "give it to me straight" face.

"Sir, I gave him time to take a shot, he was wasting time and the unit was ready to move. I ordered Icheman to take the rest of the residents so he couldn't put on a show." is what he told me.

I looked at Saab, eyes squinted, mouth slightly open in disgust.

"Da fuck? Last shot in pool and …c'mon now?" and I looked back at Sandowsky. "I don't understand." I said.

"Yeah, cus dis nigga always be fucking with me……" Saab was now starting to get excited.

"No I don't." Sandowsky replied dismissively and gave him his patented smug look.

"My nigga!" Saab said more seriously.

"Look, I'm not your nigger ok." Sandowsky replied in the same tone, expression, and delivery.

There are moments when you actually can hear time stop. Just for a snap the full impact of energy is the only thing that can be heard and felt. The low humming stopped. I didn't feel the cold on the tips of my fingers. My headache stopped. My eyes opened and were miraculously fine. I thought about Sandowsky. How when he first came on as an 18 he called me "Spaniard". When he first said it I laughed half heartedly. and When he explained to me that he thought I looked like Maximus (Russel Crow) from the movie *Gladiator* I believed he was trying to give me a compliment. Maximus wasn't a large man, but he was a great leader, and his men loved him. So at first I took it like that. But as he continued, every single time he saw me, "What's up Spaniard?".

I finally had to say to him, "Yo, for real, don't call me that."

"Oh, I thought…." he tried.

"Yeah, no. Like, for real." and I looked at him to inform him of the level of my "forealness".

So when Sandowsky replied to Saab with "I'm not your nigger.", I couldn't help but feel that there was a purposeful target for those words. All of that went through my mind in that quiet stillness.

Reality always comes back with a clap.

"See, I told you!" Saab reacted in outrage."Fuck you bitch ass Sandowsky!"

"Sandowsky, why don't you go back to the unit. I'll bring Saab down. Make sure the snack run was made." I said calmly, my eyes and focus stayed on Saab.

"Yes Sir" and he left.

I gave him some time to get ahead of us by letting Saab take a piss before we left.

As I stood there all of the sounds began to become more intense. The gym lights, the fluorescent lights, Saab pissing. Then my eyes felt it all again reinforced with the toilet flushing, which made me wince. *He didn't even wash his hands.* He opened the bathroom door.

"You ready?" I asked him unamused.

"Yeah." Saab said, but his tone didn't assure me.

"AOD CSU, moving one from the gym back to unit 2."

"Copy, all clear." "Copy."

I opened the door and gave him the head nod to come on. He followed, and I opened the second door and led him into the cold yellow glow. It wasn't snowing but the air was crystalizing in the wind, and you could hear, feel, and see it in the tall lights that lit the passage to the front gate.

"Cold as shit out here aint it?" I said, just to break the silence, my head was still aching.

"Hell yeah!" he replied. "But Yo, fuck Sandowsky!"

And how could I not agree, but I couldn't to Saab.

"It's not about Sandowsky." I tried to tell him. "At some point you're going to have to take some accountability for your own actions. It's real simple shit." My voice quickened with partial air as it froze in my chest.

By this time we were coming up to the main gait. The last part of the building would end and open up into the main entrance of the facility and CSU would be right there. Enclosed in the deep steel fence, it was the most well lit area on the entire campus, and had clear visual and video capability. Twenty five more yards, through the gate, and into the unit, to his cell, and it was done.

But he slowed down.

"Naw see that's why ya'll niggas be fuckin with me." he said walking at an even slower pace, and he put a swagger to his shoulders.

"What the fuck are you talking about?" I asked him disingenuously.

"Sandowsky, this nigga Icheman....fuck all ya'll niggas."

This is exactly what I didn't want. I slowly closed my eyes. Shook my head and looked down as I came to a stop.

"What the fuck are you talking about!" this time it wasn't a question. "Look, YOU fucked up and YOU got YOU here, now YOU gotta do this shit here, that's fucking it! You keep making shit difficult. You're right 'Fuck Sandowsky', but that mutherfucker isn't keeping ME here. Is he gonna keep YOU here?"

"Naw see…" and he picked up a few pebbles that were unfrozen.

The building was lined with mixed pebbles as a barrier from the black top pavement access road and walking path, and the grass. He started throwing them at the CSU window.

"You see that's what the fuck I'm talking about. Stupid ass decisions." now fully expressing my dislike for the young man and my lack of ability to take him seriously.

"Why…? What you gone do….?" and he threw a handful more.

"You're just making my shit easier now." I still wasn't taking him seriously.

"Tssk" he sucked his teeth and walked over to where the food delivery was dropped off. The exterior freezers and HVAC systems all sit in one spot and create a little industrial square on the facility grounds there.

"Man fuck YLA!" he yelled.

I watched him make his way over to the ladder cart on wheels. To me he's still posing no threat. I can simply add the "throwing rocks at CSU" to his paperwork later. He then started to climb the ladder.

There were large plastic bread bins that the loafs of bread came in on, and then returned on the next delivery. He grabbed one.

"No threat right" he looked at me calm, but threatening. "Fucking pussy!"

"Yeah, Okay." I said in a manner and look that wasn't bothered and said "that's enough get the fuck down" at the same time.

He didn't.

"See all ya'll faggot ass niggas can suck my dick!" he shouted and looked at me with intent, and threw the bread basket down to the ground. When it hit it bounced in a twist and slid across the pavement.

I took a deep breath.

"Yeah, get the fuck down! Right! Now!" I said in my most calm, loud, serious voice, that came from the pain and anguish I had bottled up in tormented pulses of fury.

My migraine was talking. My lack of connection and intimacy was yelling.

My anger from my dad's death was shouting. All of my fears and anxieties about my own life stared at this young man as a representation. All of the work to overcome all of that trauma could be wiped away because of some stupid juvenile delinquent. Some kid who wasn't raised right. Fucking fake ass "wanna be" gangsters. And it's always the fake ones who pose the biggest threat. They're the ones who always have something to prove. The ones looking to make a come up and a name for themselves because they lack any real sense of identity. So all they can be is a "nigga".

But I was done with the "nigga shit." I hated him for all the times I was called a nigger. All those times, they thought that I was like that piece of shit. I hated his Troy, New York accent, and in the blink of an eye I had already justified the means.

He came down the 8 steps from the rolling ladder. I met him at the bottom.

"Yeah, what's up pussy?" he said with his own venomous hate and rage.

"Yeah mutherfucker? Come'er!" and I pushed him and guided his body towards the industrial square, ensuring my hands were still in my pockets where they had remained the entire time.

"Yeah....what's up?" he said, his voice in nervous excitement.

I made it as if we were going to take a walk around the paved walking path that went along the fence. I walked behind him slightly and said,"Let's go this way."

I led him three steps into the dark, between the huge standing freezer, the maintenance shed that housed some other unit, the large ventilation and air systems, and furnace exhaust. It was dark and all you could hear was steam, machines, and exhaust blowing.

"Yeah...now what's up bitch?" and I pushed him into the wall of the freezer.

"Oh word?" and he swung.

Men of action see the action before it happens. Their anticipation is what makes them so threatening. Other men know that mental chess is always played between men and their minds, and other men's minds. Yet, the anticipation of another man's move, his actions, and words allows the capable individual to be more deliberate and intentional with their actions. Saab was a punk Troy kid. He was never taught anything, let alone how to defend himself. What could he do, but throw a punch.

I ducked, and rushed him, wrapping my arms around his waist, tightening my grip by grabbing my opposite forearm. I squeezed him. In my mind it was already done. He was going face first into the frozen ground at my feet. I then would punch him in the neck so hard he wished the air was negative 70 degrees so it would wake him up.

But instead, I hesitated. One's degree of empathy is developed by the degree in which they see themselves in other people. The only reason I was any good at what I did was because I saw little pieces of myself, in everyone I encountered. Single mom's, absent dad's, low income housing, drug abuse and addiction, domestic violence, disenfranchisement, mentally enslaved, poor, hopeless souls, all searching for redemption. All searching for love. And I felt that.

But when men need love, they don't ask for it. Men ensure that they show that they don't need it. That's being a man. A real man doesn't need anything, or anyone. No, men climb mountains, search for meaning in adrenaline rushes, or the numbness they prescribe to. We destroy ourselves internally for the sake of "manhood". Maybe that's why men die at higher rates of heart disease and high blood pressure. We never tell anyone how much we rely on the intimacy of our partners. We just display the results from the lack of it in our addiction to porn.

No, men don't "need", we take. And only those willing to take more than the other man will get what they want out of life. Unfortunately, women have accepted this as well. The gauge of a man's worth is by what he has, what he may have, or be willing to offer. If his sexual aggression matches theirs, he wins. But, he first has to be willing to take, even if it's just "taking" a chance. Men can only make decisions, and they need to save their feelings for the true celebrations and funerals. Isn't that what we are taught?

"Fuck Saab"

And in that second he was off of me. I heard his body hit the ground with a thud and the air came out of him. It was Ericson.

I immediately put my knee to his face and pushed down. I could hear the rocks squeeze against his skin.

"Now what pussy!" I said, and spit on the ground.

"Code White." I softly and calmly radioed.

"Code White, Copy." and the radio went silent from there.

I punched him in the back side of his head, by his ear.

"Fucking bitch!" and I reached for my cuffs, and expertly in one move went from my back to his wrists in one motion. Once they were on, I tightened them to the max.

That's when he yelled.

"Hey, Y'all alright" a voice said.

It was Jenkins doing the snack run.

"Yeah Jenkins, go to the Training Unit now!" Ericson ordered Jenkins and then he turned to me. "Take him there for processing, you can hold him over night there, right?"

And that's why those long term YLA guys were my best assets.

"Word" I said and picked up Saab by the cuffs, finally releasing the pressure from my knee in his back.

Ericson led the way, and I held Saab's cuffs and pushed him right behind him, through the main gate, down the low, coldly lit piss colored lighting, to the Training Unit, where Jenkins was waiting.

"I'll go make sure snack runs get done, and keep things cool. You good Ace?" Ericson said to me.

"Good man!" and I nodded back.

That's when Saab started talking reckless again.

"Yeah, take these cuffs off and see what's up nigga, take the cuffs off nigga! You want it, let's fucking go!" as if he had somehow gained some super natural strength.

I looked at Jenkins.

"16" I ordered.

That was one of the holding cells we reserved in the Training Unit for situations like this. This change went into plan after the Benson ordeal. Saab knew I couldn't put him in the cell alone and that I would have to eventually take the cuffs off. I could feel his body anticipating that moment. I felt him waiting for that last cuff to be unsecured. I turned the small key and put my forearm straight into his back. He flung loosely, still tired from the cold and roughing up I did to him outside. Now we were inside, in a jail cell. Just him and I.

Before he could throw another lame blow, I punched him in the mouth and split his lip. I then slapped his face and shoved him down, with one hand, onto the bed. He got back up.

"C'mon pussy!" I taunted him in rage.

He swung and missed, like a little brother mad about a broken toy.

I dodged and punched him in the ribs, and he fell back to the bed holding his stomach. He didn't need any more. I left him there.

I slammed the cell door shut, locked it, and wiped the blood off of my knuckles. I knew it wasn't mine, but I felt the intense throbbing from my heart pulsating directly into my palms.

"I want to call my mom!", he cried out in a gurgle from the blood in his mouth. "Shut up! You had your chance, you're done!" I responded with every ounce of fury I could muster. The adrenaline was still coursing through my veins and the emotional lump in my throat prevented any internal emotion from being verbalized.

"Come back in here, and I'ma kill you!" his voice bellowed with his increased anger, and most likely the deep fear of his realization.

I held his freedom in the palm of my hand. And if that wasn't enough, I went back in.

. He swung, but before he could make a formidable blow, a powerful shove with both hands directly into his solar plexus leveled him into the corner of the cell. I seethed over him. My face tight, eyes red, heart pounding, and a deep desire to continue the brutality. I stopped, looked directly into his eyes, as if to say, "Do you see me? Do you see what I will do? Do you see that I want to do it? Please don't get up." He didn't, and my mouth said, as if God himself said it, "You're done."

Three steps backwards, not daring to take my eyes off him, and I was out of the cell. I locked it again. And looked at Jenkins.

He looked at me with a concerned, almost sympathetic look, and softly said, "You good Ace?" I ignored him. *"Shut up Jenkins! Do your damn job!"* and marched to the bubble and made the call to CSU.

"Get a packet ready, I'm not staying late for this shit tonight.", I ordered Zimmerman over the phone. Zimmerman was training in CSU the entire night. She took the call because Lockert was keeping his eye on the units during lock-ins.

"Sir, are you ok?" she responded through the walkie talkie.

What the hell was she thinking? No one knew anything was going on until that moment.

"AOD to CSU, that's not appropriate radio talk!" with the harsh tone of a drill sergeant.

"CSU to AOD, copy that."

It doesn't matter anyway.

Either way this was all on me. No witnesses. No one else needed to sign off or provide statements for the mandated documentation required. I checked the necessary boxes. Wrote my statements, "refused" medical attention, "refused" a phone call, and "refused" to sign documentation. No care was given to him. No concerns were left for him. I was done.

I submitted the paperwork for the director to review the next morning. I placed my walkie talkie on its charger, took off my cuffs and placed them in my secure locker. Grabbed my car keys and proceeded to my car. It was still negative fifteen degrees outside. The ground was solid. It wasn't just frozen. It was as if everything had turned into rock ice. Hard, sharp, and dangerous, like ice and rock. Deadly.

I tried to keep my composure as I explained the evening events to the next shift and Bernard, the pay grade 22 who was the overnight AOD that shift. I made it sound as if Saab was being "Saab" again, only this time we made it count. No one seemed bothered or concerned, and Bernard just asked, "So, who's gonna sit with him tonight?"

I checked out with a slight solute. For the shift log, it was difficult to outline the shift's events. So again, I made it out to be Saab being Saab, and that we were doing what needed to be done to keep order in the chaos.

The men and I laughed about the black ice on the road all winter. Exchanging disses on driving ability and attacking each other's manhood for using their brakes. Encouraging each other to not care, bragging about the rear end of a front-wheel drive car swinging out and how overcorrecting one way and to the next to straighten the car out, all while maintaining the consistent speed not designated by the road sign, was a badge of honor. It displayed our control, our willingness to live on the edge, our willingness to knowingly participate in an act that could ultimately take our lives, and our unsaid agreement that these things made us men.

Like every other night, we exchanged highlights from the shift in the parking lot. I didn't have anything to say that night. The men all seemed determined to talk about anything else but what I had done.

"Ace, grab a beer bro!" Cash said with enthusiasm.

"Not tonight my man. I need to get home, see my kid and kiss my wife."

"No doubt!" he replied, and in unison they all said "Get home safe."

I was still an emotional wreck inside, but the exterior bravado would not allow me to show it. I started my car and tried to think of something else.

Where the fuck is G? What am I going to do if I lose the house? This would all be for nothing. The YLA is killing me. What's Leichtenberger going to say about tonight? Did I do the paperwork correctly? I still have to get this last bit packaged up for Rick when I get home. I really need this money now!

There was no thought that released me from my own personal hell created within the very depths of my own mind. My mind was my cell. I couldn't even think straight. *How could I expect to act correctly? I didn't respect myself. How could I respect the mother of my kid? I couldn't free myself from the shackles of mental slavery, who was I to think I could free anyone else's.*

I was now driving on autopilot. The road was always solitary in the night. I never passed a car. It was too mountainous for deer to hop out at you. But I wound through those mountains as I always did, half asleep and half processing the events from the shift. Up hills and down. Around the sharp horseshoe turns that reminded the driver of the road's age, I drove.

They say when you are close to death you will know. I always promised myself that if I looked death in the eye, they would know it's me, because I will smile back at the darkness. The rear end of my car lifted, I felt it float off the ground. I counter steered confidently, overcorrecting and back, in the same manner described as a "professional" to my men. But I wasn't a professional race car driver, or an expert on anything closely related. I was a man of the state. And when I knew control was lost, I held on to the steering wheel as tight as I could, and smiled.

And everything changed.

Acknowledgements

Thank you to LastGen Publishing for the guidance and support.

Theri A. Pickens, my editor, for her great insight.

My sister, for unwavering support and love

My brother, for always being a true friend.

My wife, for enduring the process. I love you.

And to all of the men and women whose work goes unseen and recognized. I see you.

About the Author

B. A, a devoted educator with more than 15 years of experience, brings a wealth of knowledge to his debut book. Holding a Master's Degree in Educational Leadership and Curriculum Design, along with certifications in Social Studies, English, and Special Education, B. A draws upon his extensive background in the classroom and life itself to craft authentic narratives that capture the essence of the human journey.

Through his work, B. A delves into the themes of enduring dysfunction and transforming pain into empowerment. His passion lies in addressing the unique challenges confronted by individuals who have weathered broken homes, divorce, and the intricate dynamics of positive masculine and feminine roles and relationships. With a keen insight into the complexities of these experiences, B. A's debut book offers readers a powerful exploration of the human spirit's resilience and capacity for growth.